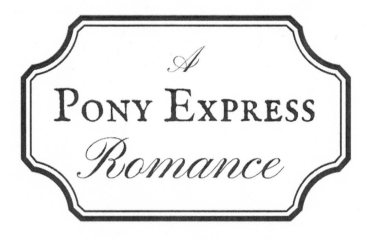

A
PONY EXPRESS
Romance

Sweetwater River Tales

BOOK 1

MISTY M. BELLER

This book is a work of fiction and any resemblance to persons, living or dead, or places, events or locales is purely coincidental. The characters are the product of the author's imagination and used fictitiously.

ISBN-10: 0998208701
ISBN-13: 978-0998208701

Dedication

To my inspiration for this story.
May God give you the desires of your heart.

Delight thyself also in the Lord;
And he shall give thee the desires of thine heart.
Commit thy way unto the Lord;
Trust also in him; and he shall bring it to pass.

Psalm 37:5-6 (KJV)

Chapter One

"Don't move, or I'll shoot ya right through the ticker." Josiah English froze as the hard metal of a rifle barrel pressed into his back. His horse danced beneath him, complaining against his stranglehold on the reins. He didn't dare release the pressure, though. Not until he had a better grasp on the situation. He tilted his chin ever so slowly, scanning the perimeter to get a look at his captor.

The click of a rifle's set trigger rang loud in his ears, and the air stilled around him.

"I said *freeze*."

The sharp bark drew him up. His blood galloped, pounding in his ears as anger started to build. He wasn't a coward to be so easily taken by this highway bandit. But was there more than one? He forced air in through his nose and out through his mouth as he strained to decipher the noises behind him.

A whizzing sound flew by his ears, and within the same heartbeat, a rope settled around his shoulders. He jerked to pull it off, but the line yanked tight, strapping his arms to his sides. With a violent lurch, he was snatched sideways from his horse. For a second, his right foot caught in the stirrup, stretching him between opposite forces like a deer hide ready for tanning. Pain shot through his midsection. Would they rip his leg off?

His foot finally slipped from the stirrup, and for a moment he was airborne. Then he landed hard on the ground, the thud ricocheting through his back as the rope clenched tight around his midsection. The air exploded from his lungs. His chest seized, fighting a weight that threatened to smother him as he struggled to breathe.

At last, a precious breath seeped in, and awareness filtered into Josiah's oxygen-starved brain. He lay on the grass, staring into the blue November sky. A shadow moved across his vision—the dark outline of a man.

Josiah squinted to make out features. A dirty face loomed over him, with bushy black brows and a cigar protruding from thin lips.

He fought against the binding around his arms and chest, but the press of cold, round steel in his right temple froze his struggle.

"Take off his boots," Bushy Brows growled around his cigar.

Another man moved to Josiah's feet, this one tall and skinny with a blond, handle-bar moustache and droopy eyes.

2

He grasped the heel of Josiah's left boot and pulled, setting off alarm bells in Josiah's head. *Not the boots.*

He jerked his foot hard, then kicked out toward the man, but the robber's long fingers clung to the heel like a barnacle on a ship's hull. The gun barrel pressed harder against his temple, pushing his head sideways into the grass.

"Get his boot off."

Josiah paused his fighting, sucking in breaths to steady himself so he could put together a plan. He may not be stronger than the force of that rifle, but maybe he could catch them in a blunder and overpower them.

The skinny man gripped Josiah's shoe and pulled. He couldn't stop himself from flexing his foot to make it harder for the brute to remove the leather.

The man struggled for a moment, then grunted and landed a hard kick in Josiah's shin. Pain ripped through his leg, loosening the muscles in his foot. The scrawny man jerked again, pulling the black leather free.

Papers slipped out as he turned the boot upside down—an image of a rider on a running horse flashing across the top. Josiah released a breath. Only his dispatch papers for the Pony Express, not the more precious documents.

Then Mustache reached for his other boot. The muscles in Josiah's shoulders tightened again. But he was in no position to win a fight yet. He could push through the pain in his left shin, but the rope around his chest bound his arms to his sides, and the cold steel pressed against his head kept him immobile.

The other boot slid off and a stack of money fluttered to the ground. He could picture the bills without looking— tens and fifties issued by the Southern Bank of Georgia. Black and red print forming letters, numbers, and pictures.

Half of his life savings. Maybe they'd be happy with their loot and stop searching.

Mustache jumped on the bills as they landed in the grass, clutching them in his grubby paws. Then he turned the boot upside down and dumped the remaining papers.

"Woo-wee, Charlie. We got us a good'n this time." The man's mustache lifted to reveal teeth of varying shades of brown.

"Keep lookin'," Charlie barked.

The gun barrel dug harder into Josiah's skull. He hoped in spades the man's trigger finger wasn't eager for exercise.

Mustache moved his search upward to Josiah's belly, a sneer taking over his face when he felt the money pouch Josiah had tucked under his shirt. When the man jerked the tail out of his trousers, cold air blasted Josiah's abdomen, raising goose flesh across his skin. The wiry man pounced on the pockets sewn into the cloth band.

Right pocket first. A handful of one dollar bills and a paper listing the Express stops he was to follow. The man kept the cash and tossed the document aside.

Left pocket. Another thick roll of bills. Josiah's stomach roiled, bile churning with his breakfast. They were taking everything he had. Everything he'd worked day and night to save for the last twelve years. The money to start his own ranch. His future.

The man's ugly face wobbled in Josiah's vision. The edges of his sight grew blurry as anger pulsed through him.

Josiah strained to focus on their actions. They rolled him onto his stomach and sweat pasted his shirt to his skin. The rifle barrel moved to his back.

After finding nothing when they padded him down a final time, Mustache seemed to be done with the search. The men exchanged words, their voices coming through Josiah's foggy brain like the buzzing of a bee. He struggled to make his mind focus again.

The gun came away from his back, and the ground thudded with the sound of boots tromping away from him. He twisted around—pulling against the rope biting into his arms—just in time to see the two men tearing down the road on horseback. They were headed west, the same direction he'd been traveling. Were those the kind of men he could expect to encounter in this new territory? He'd have to strengthen his defenses. The pistol tucked in his saddle pack had done little to help him with this fiasco.

He struggled to sit, then exhaled a long breath. With his hands, he loosened the lasso enough to slip it off over his head. At least they hadn't tied his hands and feet. Speaking of his feet, he glanced down at them, his wool socks left exposed without his boots. He reached into his left sock and pulled the small wad of ten dollar bills out from under the arch of his foot.

Fifty dollars. All that was left of his hard work and scrimping. It would get him to his destination at the Rocky Ridge Pony Express station, but wouldn't be enough to buy land, build a house and barn, and purchase good Arabian breeding stock. He wrapped his arms around his knees, dropped his head to his wrists, and took deep breaths.

Inhale. Exhale.

At least he had a job. A good one at that. He'd earn a hundred dollars a month riding for the Express—and improve his horse skills in the process. Now he'd have to stay on longer than the six months he'd planned. But he would still get his ranch, even if he had to scrape and save another few years. He wouldn't be stopped this easily.

Josiah raised his head and looked around. They hadn't even left his boots. The only things still lying in the grass were his papers from the Express.

He took another long breath, then exhaled. His horse had disappeared, and he was shoeless. At least he was alive with nothing broken. He pushed up to his feet, then strode to the road and considered both ways. If he went left, it was about two miles back to Ellwood. In the other direction, roughly seven miles on to Troy. It'd be quicker to go back the way he came and get a fresh horse. Start over.

Josiah sighed, then headed left. One painful step in front of the other on the rocky lane.

Around the first bend in the road, his bay gelding munched a patch of clover. The lean, muscled animal ate as if it hadn't seen green grass in a month of Tuesdays. At least someone was pleased with this situation.

Josiah eased forward, and the horse's ears flicked, but it never stopped ripping at the clover stems. He released a sigh as his hand closed around one of the reins. Stroking the gelding, he checked his saddle bags. Good. His Colt revolver and the few personal possessions were still secure. He lifted a stockinged foot into the stirrup and swung up.

The sun arced a couple hours short of high noon, and he'd been ordered to report at the Rocky Ridge stop on the Sweetwater River by December sixth, just six days from now. He didn't have time to stop for lunch, much less go back to Ellwood to report the bandits. He'd do it at the next town.

Lord, please let them have boots for sale there.

SWEETWATER RIVER VALLEY, WYOMING TERRITORY

Only a few more miles.

Josiah pushed his horse to a canter. This animal's rocking-horse rhythm was much smoother than the last two mounts he'd had. Changing horses every day had been interesting. Even though he wasn't on an official mail ride, the man at the Pony Express office in St. Joseph said he should ride Express-owned horses and stay at the regular stations—

anything to get him to Rocky Ridge faster. He'd be taking over the mail line from a man who'd been injured, so the riders on the neighboring lines were pulling double duty until he could get there.

And after six days on the road, the boulder-strewn hills and buttes he'd been maneuvering now leveled into a rocky grassland. Should only have a couple miles left to the station he would call home.

Already, he felt like an Express rider. That is, now that every move didn't make his body scream. Riding horses woke up parts of his insides he hadn't known existed. But after living in the saddle this last week, his muscles were getting used to the new life.

He'd passed a couple of other Express riders along the way, mostly at the stations. It made his blood pump to see one of them tear out with the mail bag on a fresh horse, as if a pack of Indians was on his tail.

Indians... Josiah scanned the tree line on his left again. No visible movement. At the last few stations where he'd slept, the men shared quite a few stories about Paiute braves attacking Express riders, or burning down stations and stealing the horses. Josiah touched the wooden grip protruding from his waistband. His Colt revolver waited ready, should the need arise.

He turned his attention back to the horizon in front of him where the gray-blue sky merged into pinks and purples. In the fading light, a cluster of buildings stood in the middle of the flat, grassy stretch. A niggle of anxiety tugged in

Josiah's chest. This would be his home station for a while. Would he like the people here? It didn't matter. He'd learned to live with whatever necessary to accomplish what he'd set out for. Life wasn't an easy walk down a country lane. Not for a single moment.

He pulled his horse back to a jog, then reined her to a walk for the last few minutes. The bay mare was lathered, but her breathing returned to normal by the time they rode into the little courtyard between the four buildings. The structure on his left stood the largest by far, and looked to be the barn.

Josiah kicked his feet from the stirrups and rotated his ankles. Sharp needles pierced all the way up his calves, so he let his feet dangle for a moment until the pain lessened.

The door opened in the cabin to his right. On the threshold, a woman paused, then strode down the step and toward him. Her blue dress swished around her feet as she walked, determination marking her stride. She was a willowy thing, and wore her brown hair tied back in a way that revealed the strong curve of her jaw and the slope of her neck. Pretty, but younger than he'd expect for the stationmaster's wife. And she didn't look hardened enough to have lived long in this uncivilized country. Maybe she was passing through on one of the stagecoaches that followed this route.

She neared, close enough to rest a hand on the bay's neck, then brought up the other to shield her eyes from the sun as she looked at him. Those eyes. Even with the shadow of her hand, their shiny brown was wide enough for him to see clear through to her soul. The other features on her face were strong and balanced, maybe even refined, but those eyes pulled his focus so he had to fight to look away.

Pull yourself together, English. Josiah reined in his thoughts and removed his hat.

"Hello." Her voice was sweet and soft. "You're the new Express rider?" He strained to catch her words.

He nodded. And several seconds passed before he realized she waited for him to speak. "Yes, ma'am." He cleared his throat to steady the pitch of his voice. He was ogling like one of the simple-minded wharf-workers where he'd grown up in Savannah.

She didn't seem to notice his clumsiness—or at least, had the grace to ignore it. Instead, she reached for the mare's reins and pulled the loop over the horse's head. "Go on and get settled in the bunkhouse." She nodded toward the shed-like building next to the barn. "I'll get this girl taken care of, then finish dinner. When I ring the bell, come to the main house to eat." She pointed a thumb toward the structure behind her.

He swallowed to work some moisture into his mouth. She must belong to the place. "Is your...uh...husband around?"

Her lips pinched, and one corner quirked up. Her big brown gaze met his, light dancing there. "No husband. But my brothers are in the barn haying the horses."

The tension in his chest eased, but he tried not to look too deep into the reason. It sounded like she had men here to protect her. But not a husband.

Sliding from the horse, Josiah caught himself so he landed softly on his sore ankles. "I'll get my saddle bags before you take her." His fingers fumbled with the leather straps. Finally, he had both the front and back bags off, and she led the horse away without another word.

Even the weariness in his bones didn't stop him from watching her go, her long skirt feathering across the tops of the grass as she stepped with a self-assured grace.

His mouth pressed in a frown. Why hadn't he asked her name?

Chapter Two

ara Reid sliced a knife through the potato, splitting it in half like a cracked egg, then cutting long slices to go in the frying pan. This new Express rider was not what she'd expected. He was tall for a hired rider, and certainly not a kid like the last few they'd hosted. Maybe in his late twenties. And those clear blue eyes… He might be lean, but there was no way he was under the one hundred twenty-five pounds the Pony Express allowed. They must be getting desperate for capable riders willing to brave the dangers.

The surprise of his appearance had flustered her so, she'd forgotten to ask his name.

She tossed the potato chunks into the pan where they landed with a sizzle among the buffalo meat. Giving it a good stir, she centered the pan over the heat, then turned to add grounds to the coffee pot.

The front door swung open, and Ezra—her brother younger by a couple years—stepped in with a bundle of cloth in his hands. "Where do you want these wraps from Roman's leg?"

"In the corner. I'll put them to soak in a bit." Mara nodded toward the wall farthest away from the kitchen. No sense adding the odor from the horse's wound to the aroma of dinner.

Ezra deposited the items and stomped back out the door, letting it thud shut behind him. The silence that settled in his wake was relieved only by the crackle from the frying pan.

She scanned the room, eyeing the piles of blankets, discarded boots, and jackets her brothers had left scattered. Zechariah, the oldest in their clan, was usually somewhat organized. But Ezra didn't seem to notice his clutter.

Of course, their little home didn't leave many options for space. This tiny cooking section comprised one end, with the cook stove, work counter, and a wet sink. A table and chairs dominated the center of the room—large enough to accommodate stage passengers and other guests, along with their little family of three. The fireplace took up the wall opposite the kitchen, with Pa's old arm chair and Ma's rocker standing guard. Even though neither Pa nor Ma were still here to use them.

The aroma of meat tickled her senses, mingling with the stinging in her eyes that still pricked when she looked at the worn chairs. The rocker not as much—memories of Ma had softened to sweet treasures over the ten years she'd been gone. But Pa. He'd sat in that very chair just six months ago.

With her big wooden spoon, she stirred the contents of the cast iron fryer. Chunks from the bottom of the pan had turned dark brown. Time to ring the dinner bell. She cleared the emotion from her throat and made quick work of the job. By the time she had the potatoes on the table and the coffee poured in mugs, the sound of boots thumped on the outside step and the door opened. Ezra strode in first. Then the new man. Zechariah was the last one through the door, and pulled it hard against the wind that whistled outside the cabin.

She raised a brow at her older brother. "Sounds like the weather's picking up. You think it'll snow?" Zechariah was older than her by three years, and the expert when it came to the land, weather, and anything else to do with this wild country.

"Looks like it. Still have a couple hours before it hits, though."

The new man scanned the room. Taking the measure of the place?

Her brothers settled into their usual chairs around the table, and Mara looked at the tall stranger as she motioned toward the empty chair next to Zeche. "I put your place where Henry used to sit. And I guess I didn't catch your name."

As he turned to her, his eyes captured her gaze with an intensity that cleared every last thought from her brain. Those orbs were more green than the blue she remembered from earlier. But the dark shadows underneath added a hint of rogue to his look. Not to mention the shadow of growth

14

coating his jaw. "Thank you, ma'am. Josiah English. Call me Josiah." He moved to the chair, but didn't sit.

She nodded. She did usually call the Express riders by their first names, but they weren't usually so tall and attractive. Not like this blue-eyed stranger whose presence seemed to soak in all the air from the room. Maybe if she treated him like the others, she could begin to think of him that way. "Please call me Mara, then."

She focused on her work, but as she placed the biscuits on the table, the strength of his nearness loomed at the edge of her vision. Why didn't he settle in and relax himself? Surely he was exhausted from his long journey. She couldn't bring herself to look at him again yet, so she sank into her own chair.

At last, he did the same.

While Zeche said the blessing, Mara chanced another look at the new man. His brown hair curled in loose circles as he bowed in prayer, but she couldn't see his face. The few words he'd spoken had been laced with a southern drawl. Where was he from?

Her brother's words to the Almighty pressed through her thoughts, pricking her conscience as she closed her eyes again. *Sorry, Lord.*

When the prayer ended and their plates were piled high, Ezra settled both arms on the table, fork poised in one hand, and eyed the new Express rider. "So your name's English. You hail from the old country?"

Oh, Ezra. Even though they were an Overland Stage stop as well as a Pony Express station, they didn't get many guests in this deserted part of the Territory. He usually jumped at the chance to visit with those from the civilized world.

Josiah nodded, not lifting his gaze as he speared a potato with his fork. "My grandparents."

Ezra swallowed a bite and scooped up another. "Really? Which part?"

"Kent, near Birchington."

Ezra leaned forward. "Birchington-on-Sea?"

Josiah glanced up, then went back to his food. "You know it?"

"We came from Margate, just down the road. Had a farm there where we raised horses and produce."

Now Josiah straightened, curiosity flicking in his gaze. "You don't sound like you were born in England."

Ezra's grin flashed. "You mean you don't detect me brogue?" He dipped into such a strong accent with the words, emotion stung the back of Mara's throat. He sounded just like Pa. Even though they'd come over from England more than fifteen years ago, Pa had never lost his thick, working-class accent.

Silence took over their group while Ezra's stomach gained priority over his eagerness to hear news from their new resident. Then as he speared another slab of meat from the pan, he resumed his line of questioning. "So where is it you hail from, if not from England?"

"Savannah."

"You're a seaman then?"

"No." There was something about the way he said the word. Flat. As though the very thought of what Ezra had asked drained him. What was so wrong with the sea?

She could understand preferring this mountain country over the briny air of the coast, but something in his tone said it might be more than that. Although it had only been one word. Maybe she was imagining his reaction.

Josiah forked more food, but didn't take a bite. The way he stabbed those poor potatoes, something was definitely bothering him. Even Ezra seemed to realize the change in mood, and silence lapsed again as he went back to eating.

At last, Ezra rested his fork on his empty plate and looked at Zeche first, then Josiah. "We're glad to have you with us, English."

Josiah raised the chiseled lines of his face and met Ezra's gaze. A shadow passed across the man's face, turning his eyes a grayish blue. It was fascinating how they could change so completely.

His mouth tipped in the slightest of smiles, but it didn't reach his eyes. "Me, too."

Josiah shoved his left foot into the boot, pushing hard to get his heel past the stiff leather of this new pair. Daylight sifted through the cracks around the bunkhouse door. Maybe it was the long days of riding and his body being bone-tired, or maybe it was the way it seemed he was finally home—even in this shack of a bunkhouse. Whatever the reason, he'd slept like a man with a clean conscience.

In these new surroundings, it was easier to imagine the weight of his past was behind him. He could start fresh. Make a new life for himself. A good life.

After buttoning his coat, he settled his hat on his head. The fire in the little warming stove had gone out sometime in the night, but not even the biting cold had awakened him as he snuggled under three quilts.

When he pulled open the door, a world of white greeted him. No wonder the air had teeth to it. He raised a hand to shield his eyes from the blinding glitter of sun on snow. The white stuff piled higher in front of him where it had built up against the door, so he stepped forward to kick it aside. Once he'd slogged through the drift, only a few inches covered the open ground.

When he made it to the main house and stepped inside, a muted assortment of smells wove through the air. He picked out a yeasty scent that was probably biscuits, and an underlying hint of burned food. Or maybe that was the coffee. One thing he'd come to dread at the Express stops was the fare. Most of the stations he'd eaten at were run by a handful of grubby men, and breakfast had ranged from a hunk of dried buffalo meat, to cakes made of flour, grease, molasses and dirt—probably in equal parts.

But he shouldn't care about the food anymore. That was part of his old life, and he had another focus now. He had to keep that focus in the forefront of his mind.

"You hungry?" Ezra sat at the table, brows raised and mouth tipped in an easy smile. A stack of papers and a book lay in front of him. "The rest of us ate, but coffee's still hot and Mara left a plate of biscuits and gravy for you."

His mind summoned an image of a savory breakfast that tugged at the hole in his belly. "Sounds good."

He moved to the work counter Ezra indicated and lifted the cloth draped over a plate. Underneath lay a flat, blackish object that might've passed for a biscuit—or unleavened bread, depending on which country you were in. It was covered with a gelatinous gray blob. Maybe he wasn't so hungry.

But he had a hard ride ahead of him today, with not much time for a sit down meal as he changed horses midstride. He'd need to build up his strength. At least this stuff would stick to his ribs—probably better than molasses on honeycomb.

He poured a mug of muddy coffee—most likely the cause of the burning odor—and settled across the table from Ezra.

The man focused on what he wrote in the book—a ledger or something like it. He had the awkward motions of an overgrown boy on the verge of manhood. Maybe eighteen or nineteen. His hair was a wavy dark brown, cut short to frame his oval face.

Ezra looked enough like Miss Reid—or Mara, as she'd said to call her—they could have been twins, except for the eyes. Where Ezra and Zechariah's eyes were small and dark, almost black, her eyes were a lighter, luminous brown. Like coffee with just the right amount of milk, or warm caramel mixed into a chocolate cake batter.

Soon Ezra looked up and flipped the cover closed, releasing a long breath. "That's done. I'm the only one who likes numbers in the family, so I get to keep the books up."

Josiah nodded and tried to break through the biscuit with the side of his fork. "The Express give you a lot to keep up with?"

"Between the Express and the stage and the horses we raise, there's plenty. Plus the trading we do with the Indians."

Josiah honed in on one piece of Ezra's comment. "You raise horses? What kind?" He'd seen a few dark dots scattered across the snowy pastures that morning, but assumed they were horses the Express owned. It hadn't occurred to him the Reids may have a full operation of their own. This could be his chance to see a ranch in action before he branched out on his own.

Ezra shrugged. "Riding horses."

Josiah tamped down a surge of frustration. "But what breed? Are they Thoroughbred? Arabian? Morgan? Quarter Horse?"

Ezra raised both brows. "You'll have to ask Zeche or Mara. They're in charge of the stock, I just train the ones I'm assigned."

Josiah slumped against the ladder back of his chair. How could this kid not care about the horses?

Josiah pulled open the barn door and almost collided with Zechariah, leading a small brown horse. The animal let loose a high-pitched whinny that vibrated its body.

"Easy," the man crooned, stroking the horse's neck. "Get back. This filly's rarin' to go."

Josiah stepped out of the way, and the horse charged forward. She wasn't a large mare, but the man's stride lengthened to keep up with her jigging. Her head tilted as they moved, displaying her impatience and the firm grip he held on the reins.

The pair halted in the courtyard, and Josiah eased toward them. The mare dropped her head to nibble at dry shoots of grass poking through the snow. But when he reached a hand to stroke the thick chestnut hair on the horse's neck, she startled, sending them both a couple inches backward.

"Easy there, girl." Josiah kept his voice in the same crooning tone Zechariah had used. The mare's ears twitched, and one swiveled toward him while the other faced behind her. She dropped her head back to the ground and tore into the clumps of brown grass.

The door from the main house opened and Mara appeared with a bundle in her hand. It was a little easier to think of her as Mara instead of the formal Miss Reid when she was there before him, standing out from her drab surroundings like a Cardinal perched on a pile of sticks. He'd like to get to know her better, although he couldn't let her distract him from his goals. As she strode toward them, the somber tone of her navy gown couldn't hold back the light that resonated from her eyes. Her full lips parted in a smile that could've melted the snow. In the distance, a bird sang. Or maybe that was in his mind.

"You all set?" Her pretty brows raised.

He nodded. He should probably say something, but his mouth had filled with cotton. He forced a swallow.

The mare jerked her head up, providing a welcome distraction. She let loose another ear-splitting whinny, this time focused into the distance. Josiah followed her attention to a horse and rider cantering from the west.

"Your ride's here."

Zeche's words brought much needed focus into Josiah mind. He turned to the man. "Anything I need to know?"

But it was Mara who spoke up, pulling his attention once again. "I've got a bundle of food here, biscuits and cheese to carry you through. Once you move the mail mochila over, I'll hook it on your horn while you mount."

He nodded, putting forth effort not to look directly at her. But his traitorous gaze found her face for one final glimpse, and those luminous eyes caught him for a moment before he could pull away. "Thanks."

And then the rider was upon them. As the other man reined his horse to a stop and jumped to the ground, Josiah had to look twice. He was just a kid—maybe fourteen, if that. Horse and rider stood blowing while Josiah grabbed the mail bag and tossed it over his own saddle. He'd watched this routine closely at the stage stops on the way from Missouri.

As soon as the mochila was settled over his saddle, Mara slipped the loop of her bundle on the horn, and Josiah placed his foot in the stirrup. This was the part he hated to do in front of an audience. The mare sidestepped away as he pulled himself into the saddle, leaving him hanging sideways. He clamped his jaw and gripped the horn tighter. He'd get in the saddle if he had to pull himself up with his teeth.

Another shimmy from the horse, and he almost lost his hold. With a mighty effort, he heaved himself up, straddling the animal under him. He clung tight with hands and legs, so she couldn't shuck him if she tried. At last, he thrust his right foot in the stirrup and gathered the reins.

"You ready?"

Zechariah scrutinized him, and Josiah had an urge to get far away from these people. His clumsy effort to mount had just proven him a novice.

He forced his body to relax, inhaling a steadying breath. "I'm ready."

The man released his grip on the reins, and the horse bolted forward like a fish tossed in a river.

Josiah kept a hand tight around the horn, while the other gripped the reins. He hunkered low over the horse's neck. She started off at a gallop, releasing raw energy underneath him as her muscles flexed with each lunge. The scenery flew by in a blur.

Snow still covered much of the rocky ground. Would she slow down when they started into the mountains? He applied pressure to the reins to test her response. The mare didn't seem fazed, as her legs covered ground with dangerous speed, churning the powder beneath.

He pulled harder. The horse's head came up and she slowed a bit. Then she jerked her mouth, yanking the reins so they slid through his fingers. He gripped the leather tighter.

This one would be a handful.

Chapter Three

*D*arkness coated the land by the time Josiah reined in at the Three Crossings station, his last stop on the eastbound ride. He'd long since traded the wiry chestnut mare for a muscle-bound bay who took the bit in his teeth and ran for a solid twenty minutes. And each of the other six horses he'd ridden over the past ten hours had been similar, covering ground like they'd been locked in a stall for a week. The minute they were turned loose, there was no holding 'em back. But he'd finally arrived at the last stop.

A middle-aged man with a shaggy brown beard met him in front of the barn. "You the one takin' Henry's line?"

"Yep." Apparently, each route was known by its rider. "The next man not here yet?" Josiah eased his feet from the stirrups, rotating his ankles even though agony shot through his legs.

"Nah. A couple of the buttes get icy, so Neil's usually late when there's snow on the ground."

Josiah nodded. He needed to dismount, but experience told him bullets would shoot through his legs when he landed on the frozen ground.

The man shifted from one foot to the other, and then back to the first, wrapping his coat tighter across his girth. "Coffee's on the stove an' some beef an' taters under the cloth." He probably didn't appreciate standing in the cold while Josiah worked up the nerve to climb off the horse.

Better get to it.

Josiah gripped the saddle horn as he lowered himself to the ground. But his legs had bowed from holding the bent position so long in the chill, and they almost didn't support his weight. He leaned against the saddle until his limbs reawakened.

And, oh, did they come to life. Pain shot through his lower half like knife slashes, but he gritted his teeth and reached for the mochila that held the mail. With it draped over his shoulder, he dragged himself toward the house while the man led the horse away.

As Josiah pushed open the door, he found himself looking for Mara's pretty face, with those doe-like eyes and the smile that could cut through the thickest darkness. But she wasn't here.

Anyway, he had a job to do, and soon the relief rider would show up with the westbound mochila. Then Josiah would mount up and be off again. Ten more hours back the way he'd come with a new mail bag. More bone-jarring rides on crazy horses over icy hills. In the dead of night, to boot.

A lonely plate sat on a small table near the cook stove. Josiah poured himself a cup of coffee, then eased down on the bench in front of the food. No fork or knife, just a burned chunk of beef and some shriveled potatoes. He poked the meat. Cold.

He drew in a long breath, then exhaled. Before long, he'd have enough money saved to find good land, build a house, buy some stock, and raise the finest Arabian horses in the west. He could do whatever it took for his dream.

Mara kept steady tension on the rope until the filly bobbed her head and stepped forward, releasing the pressure on her halter. Stubborn thing. At eight months old, with steady handling from birth, she should be leading easily by now and learning to stand quiet when tied. But not this sassy gal.

"Good job." Mara kept her voice soft and crooning as she stroked Bandita's neck. With horses, you had to reward good behavior every time, even when the mare was working on her last thread of patience.

She straightened. Time for another lap around the corral. Squaring her shoulders, she spoke a loud, two syllable, "Wa-alk." Bandita moved forward and Mara fell into step beside her.

Their new Express rider had made it back that morning in one piece, but with dark hollows under his eyes. After riding hard from Kansas to get here, he'd had to turn back around and pull a two-hundred-mile mail run in less than a day. That was more than most men would take on, but he hadn't complained. Just took the ham and biscuits she offered and dragged himself to the bunkhouse.

Mara's eyes drifted in that direction. The door was still closed, even though the sun had passed the noon mark a few hours ago. He'd missed lunch, but he probably needed sleep more than food right now.

A tug on the rope stopped her. She turned to face Bandita, who stood with feet planted and head raised. The rascal. Mara kept steady pressure on the rope as the animal's wide eyes flashed white around the edges. The feisty thing hadn't yet learned Mara could outlast her. Just a bit more patience.

A chuckle drifted from the fence, and Mara peered over the filly's head at Zeche sitting on one of the two-year-old geldings.

"She's a tough one." His voice hinted at amusement.

Mara squared her shoulders. "I'll get through to her."

"I've no doubt."

She gave him a look that expressed a little of her frustration.

"You've never met a horse you couldn't win over to your way of doing things, whether you coaxed it out of them or just plain outlasted the animal."

28

Mara eyed the filly. "Well, Bandita definitely requires outlasting, but I think we're close to an understanding."

Zeche nodded and signaled his horse forward, holding the reins high over the palomino gelding's neck so the young horse could feel his directions. Typical of his usual gentle touch, coupled with firm direction and patience. What Pa used to call the *common sense* approach.

They worked with the animals from birth, so by the time each horse reached three years old, it handled like a seasoned saddle horse. Their horse training had always been a family operation, but the hole left by Pa's passing hadn't been so easy to fill in.

Mara worked in silence as she put the filly through her paces, and on the other side of the pen, Zeche did the same with his gelding. He seemed aware of her presence, but was engrossed in the interplay of training—the one-on-one interaction that built a measure of trust and respect between man and beast.

Mara's gaze drifted to the bunkhouse. Again. But a hard pinch on the back of her arm jerked her back to her surroundings. In a reflexive action, she shoved her elbow back, catching the filly on the side of her mouth before the animal knew what had happened. Bandita threw up her head, white flashing around her dark eyes again.

Mara eyed the horse, rubbing the soft flesh on the back of her arm where the horse's teeth had connected. "Brat." From the sting, she'd see a bruise there tomorrow.

The filly only blew on her.

"Don't ever trust a horse that shows the whites of their eyes." Zeche's voice drifted from across the pen. A saying she'd heard from Pa more than once.

She squared her shoulders and pulled on the rope again. She had to get Pa's voice out of her mind. The horses had always been her safe place, her love. But hearing him in everything just made the work harder.

Keeping her voice steady and controlled, she said, "Wa-alk." She would have this animal leading and tying if it killed her.

Zeche watched from atop his mount on the far side of the pen. "I got a letter from Uncle Martin in today's mailbag."

Mara kept her body moving, face forward but eyes on the filly beside her. Why did he bring this up again?

"He and Aunt Greta are excited about you coming to stay with them in Washington, D.C. Says Greta's already planning your welcome reception. She wants to make sure you come before they leave town for the summer."

A pulse ticked through Mara's jaw. How many ways could she say no before her brother would let this go?

"I'm thinking you could wait until April, after most of the foals are born. I can spare Ezra long enough to travel with you."

She inhaled slowly, then released the spent air. "I thought we talked about this." She glanced over to study his reaction. The last thing she wanted to do was hurt him, but she wasn't leaving this place. Now more than ever, they had to stick together.

"You know that's what Pa wanted. And it's what I want." His voice strengthened with that last sentence.

Did he think she could trade this wild, wonderful land for some eastern city, where her aunt would do everything possible to match her up with a high-society dandy? As nice as it would be to see her mother's family, she wouldn't put herself in that position. Nothing good could come of it.

Zeche's hard expression softened. "It's best, Mar. You have to see that."

No, she didn't, but arguing with Zeche wouldn't get them anywhere. Her brother was as hard-headed as this filly.

Mara ran her hands over the horse's back and sides. Down her legs, under her belly. The young animal had to get used to human touch. And it gave a good excuse to keep her face and her focus away from Zeche.

If she had to marry—which she didn't—it would be to a man who loved this territory as much as she did. Someone who would help her carry on her father's legacy as a breeder of high-quality, highly trained steeds.

An image of the new Express rider flashed in Mara's mind. Loose curls of brown hair, crystal blue eyes. A hint of sadness lined the corners of those eyes. What was his story? Most of the Express riders had little or no family. No one to talk them out of the dangerous work. No one to miss them if they never came home. The pain that had stiffened his movements when Ezra mentioned the sea… Something deep within her ached at the thought of his past. It had to be tragic.

When Josiah opened his bunkhouse door the next morning, huge flakes fell from the sky, so thick he could barely make out the semi-circle of buildings forming the courtyard. A hunched figure strode from the barn toward the main house. Josiah trudged the same direction.

He stepped into the cabin behind Zechariah, a tug of guilt pulling at his chest. The other man had a solid layer of snow covering both shoulders and his hat, compared to the handful of flakes that had gathered on Josiah's coat. Red splotched the man's cheeks and nose. How much work had he already done out in the weather this morning?

When Josiah shut the door against the cold, the warmth of the cabin crept through his frozen shell. He reached for the buttons on his coat, a savory aroma drifting through his senses. Coffee. And not burned this time. He turned to the table where Mara poured the dark brew into cups.

Against the plain backdrop of the wooden cabin walls, she stood out like an angel. Making his heart stutter, even in a plain white shirtwaist and brown skirt. Her hair was pulled back in a simple ribbon, leaving the length of it to float halfway down her back. Full lips pursed as she poured the steaming liquid, and her eyelids were lowered to reveal thick black lashes. She snatched his breath every time he saw her, which accounted for the tightness in his chest now. It wasn't good that she had such an effect on him. He'd have to work harder to control his body's reactions.

Mara stopped pouring long enough to look up, and her luminous brown eyes found his. A dimple formed in her right cheek. She'd caught him staring.

A new heat crept into his neck, and he moved his attention to Ezra, who added logs to the fireplace. A flurry of sparks shot up as he dropped a big chunk in the center of the flame.

"Breakfast is ready." Mara's soft voice drifted from the cook stove, pushing all three men into action.

Josiah ambled to his chair and stood behind it while Mara stirred something at the stove. He may be deficient in many things, but at least he knew better than to sit while a lady still stood. Pa had drilled that into him when he was a child. Then after his parents' deaths, his time as kitchen runner, and then chef, at the John Wesley Hotel in Savannah had only reinforced that habit. Of course, he typically hadn't been able to sit down *at all* during meals at the hotel, but especially not while a lady still stood. It was a habit he hadn't lost in these last few years of wandering.

After Ezra said grace, Josiah started into his eggs, fried beef, and biscuit. The eggs needed salt, and the beef might be hardtack in disguise, but they were both edible compared to the biscuits... The hard lumps seemed to be nothing more than flour, water, and enough soda to douse a campfire.

He scanned the table. Blackberry preserves. He heaped on a healthy coating and closed his eyes as he bit down. The berry mixture had a tangy aftertaste, but it did help mask the floury texture of the brick biscuits.

"You think it'll snow all day?"

Josiah opened his eyes as Ezra waited for his older brother's response.

Zechariah glanced at the cabin door, as if he could see through to the clouds outside. "Probably just this morning. I don't think we'll be snowed in yet."

"Davy said they already have three feet up in the mountains above Salt Lake City." Ezra glanced over at Josiah. "Davy's the Express rider to the west of us that runs your mail from here to Rock Creek station."

Josiah lifted a brow. "The kid who gave me the mochila on Friday? He's a full-time rider?" He'd assumed the boy was just filling in.

Ezra nodded. "Yep. He's young, but he gets the job done. And there's plenty more younger than him that rides for the Express."

Did that make Josiah the old man in the group? At twenty-eight? "Do his parents approve of him riding? With the Indian trouble and all?"

Ezra's mouth formed a pinched line before he spoke. "No parents to worry about him. I think he said they died in a mining camp. Cholera, maybe."

A pang shot through Josiah's chest. An orphan. Like him. He grabbed a hunk of beef and worked to bite off a piece. His teeth were no match for the stuff, but it gave a welcome distraction.

The Reid brothers continued to discuss the weather, and Josiah kept an ear to the conversation. It sounded like the winter would get worse before it grew better. Throughout the meal, Mara stayed silent. Josiah braved a glance and saw her intelligent eyes tracking between speakers, absorbing everything said. Did her silence have something to do with his presence, or was she always this reserved?

When most of the plates were empty, Mara rose to get the coffee pot from the stove and refill their cups. It didn't seem right having her wait on him. After filling Zechariah's, she came near enough to pour into Josiah's tin.

"Thank you," he whispered, just loud enough for her to hear.

Her eyes shot to his face, and the force of them sent a jerk through his chest. Her right cheek dimpled again as one side of her mouth curved. That half smile was a killer. Made a man want to reach up and stroke her cheek, trace her lips. Maybe touch them with his own.

She turned away and moved to fill Ezra's cup. Josiah released a long, quiet breath. These reactions weren't good. He couldn't let her get to him like this.

The men downed their mugs quickly this time, a pulse of anticipation tightening their posture. Josiah tried to do the same, but he had to force down the bitter stuff. Would he ever get used to the sad excuse for meals these Express stations served? Did he want to?

Zechariah plunked his cup on the table. "Ezra, you start cleaning stalls. I'll let the stock out, then hay and break the ice."

The man didn't mention Josiah, so he spoke up. "What for me?"

All three pairs of eyes turned to him, and he had to fight down the heat that crawled up his back at the attention.

"The Express riders don't usually help with the chores." Zeche's words came out laced with the tiniest bit of British accent.

"I'm not used to sitting around while everyone else works."

The other man studied him, and Josiah met his gaze. The lines around his eyes—or maybe the color of them—softened the smallest bit. "You can help Ezra with the stalls."

Josiah's chest relaxed and he nodded. "Will do."

Chapter Four

*A*t noon the next day, Josiah settled into the saddle of the same sorrel mare he'd ridden three days ago. She was just as jittery as before, too.

Ezra had a tight hold on the mare's reins, and handed up the package of food Mara had packed. He raised a hand to shade his eyes against the bright midday sun. "Snow'll have the trail covered, but watch for your landmarks. You should be within sight of the river most of the time."

Josiah nodded.

The mare danced, and he kept a white-knuckle grip on the horn with one hand and on the reins with the other.

Ezra patted the animal with this free hand. "This girl will wear herself out soon, but don't let her go too fast over the ice on the buttes. A trot will do in the slick spots."

Josiah nodded again, pulling back the reins as the mare's neck bowed.

"Off you go then." Ezra released the bridle and the mare spun, then lunged into a canter.

Across the open valley, snow reached the horse's knees, and her run was more of a bounding, like a deer or rabbit. Josiah kept his grip on the saddle even after he settled into the rhythm. She'd worn off some energy by the time they climbed their first butte, and he pulled her back to a trot as Ezra had said. The slower pace was a relief, but the mare's bouncy trot could jar his teeth loose. He hung on with both hands, but his hold made it harder to steer the horse.

He lost the trail in spots, but kept the Sweetwater River in sight and picked his way as best he could. When Warm Springs Station finally appeared around the bend, he pursed his lips and released his incoming whistle. Relief sapped the last of the strength from his muscles.

His reprieve was short-lived, because he was back in the saddle within minutes for the nine more grueling hours it would take to finish this direction of the route. Halfway through the trip, darkness fell, and he had to pick his way by the light of the quarter moon. After that, each horse he rode stumbled several times, and Josiah did his best to keep the animal's head up while he sent a desperate prayer heavenward. This new job just might bring him and the Lord close again.

If he lived through it.

The next horse and rider stood waiting when Josiah arrived at Three Crossings, his final destination. At least he'd get a night's sleep this time before heading out again. The station master stood nearby, holding a lantern to help with the switch-out.

"Glad you made it." The keeper's gruff voice echoed in the still night.

Josiah could only nod. He grabbed the cloth that held Mara's last biscuit, and slipped off his horse so the fresh rider could take the mochila. The man bounded onto his own horse and cantered off into the night.

"There's food on the counter and an empty bunk on the other side o' the canvas. Yours is the top." The stationmaster turned the weary horse and ambled toward the barn.

Josiah trudged into the long stone building. The wooden door slammed behind him, and he eyed the plate on the counter to his right. Something black and shriveled lay on the tin circle. Probably cold, too. His focus shifted to the bundle in his hand. Every bone and muscle in his body ached. He had no energy left to sit at the table. Mara's last biscuit could hold him over a few more hours.

Turning toward the tarp, he pulled back one side. His eyes took a moment to adjust to the dark interior, but he finally made out two sets of bunks. A steady snore drifted through the makeshift room. Josiah stepped inside. The upper and lower beds in front of him were both occupied. He turned toward the set on his right. The bottom held a blanketed form, but that top bed was looking better by the minute. Anything that allowed sleep.

Josiah pulled himself up to the bunk, found a wool blanket wadded in the corner, and stretched out, boots and all. The room contained no stove, but maybe body heat would keep them all warm. Body heat from perfect strangers, but he was too tired to care.

It might've been the growl of his stomach that woke Josiah. Or maybe the need to relieve himself. He didn't even try to bite back the groan of his muscles as he rolled out of bed. But his legs kept dropping where the floor should have been. He grabbed at the side of the mattress, but missed. His backside hit the floor. Hard.

Top bunk. Wouldn't forget that next time.

Josiah ran a hand through his unruly hair, then gathered himself and pushed up to his feet. He still wore his jacket and boots from the night before, but sleeping next to the cold stone had embedded a chill in him. As soon as he attended to personal things, coffee would be next on his list.

When he stepped from the cold outside into the main room, a man was seated at the table, and the station master stood by the cook stove. Brantley was his name...maybe.

"Here's yer coffee." Brantley held out a tin cup. "Lunch is ready enough."

Josiah took the cup with reverence, letting the heat soak through his frozen hands. He braved a swallow, then summoned every bit of self-control he possessed not to cough it back up. It had to be at least three parts burnt beans. He took another sip, and his eyes watered. As an exercise in willpower, he kept the brew in his mouth and let his mind wander through how it could have been ruined so thoroughly. The ground beans must have been exposed to the air long enough to kill the aroma. Then it was probably placed on the stove to simmer till every decent flavor was extracted from it.

He swallowed the drink and turned to sit across from the other man at the table. The fellow was a little younger than Brantley. At least, it appeared that way, because not much gray salted his brown beard. The stranger had been staring at the door, almost in a stupor, but now turned his focus to Josiah.

"You the new Express rider?" His voice was heavy with gravel, and he raised a cigar to his mouth.

He nodded. "Josiah English. I've taken Henry's line."

The end of the cigar glowed red as the man still eyed him. The fine hairs on Josiah's neck rose, but he held the fellow's hard stare. The cigar lowered, replaced by a cloud of smoke, as he nodded. "Hellman. Ben Hellman."

With that, Hellman turned his gaze back toward the door. Every so often, he lifted the cigar to his beard, then blew a puff of aromatic smoke. His eyes stayed trained on the door, apparently lost in his own world. Strange fellow.

Brantley placed a bowl in front of each of them, then came back with his own and sat on the same long bench as Hellman. Silence slipped over them as food consumed their focus. The soup was mostly water, but Josiah found a few chunks of meat and potatoes. It took a second helping before his stomach relaxed its pangs. It would've been nice to have some of Mara's biscuits to go with it. At least they had substance and padded his backbone.

When darkness fell, Josiah stood in the station yard next to Brantley and a paint gelding. The shrill whistle of the incoming rider pierced the frigid air, and the horse beside him nickered into the darkness. No answering whinny sounded, but that wasn't so unusual. After riding twelve miles at a fast clip through the snow, the horses were usually too worn out to socialize.

Josiah blew into his gloves and shifted from one foot to the other. Was it colder now than last night? Being on horseback warmed him, so it was hard to tell. One thing for sure, it had never been this frigid in Savannah.

After he transferred the mochila to his saddle, Josiah mounted and signaled the bay gelding into a lope. The snow didn't seem quite as deep as before, but darkness cloaked their path so it was slow going. At least he could see a few of his tracks from the night before. And this horse handled easier than some. So far.

He'd asked Brantley the gelding's name, but it seemed the Express horses weren't christened like normal riding animals. *Too hard to keep the names straight with 'em movin' from station to station,* the man had said.

42

Josiah released his grip on the horn long enough to pat the gelding's shoulder. "Good, boy."

They settled into a flat section away from the trees. The day's sun had melted several inches of snow here. The gelding had a nice rocking-horse gait, and Josiah relaxed into it. After a few minutes, he allowed his eyes to drift closed for a second. It had been days since he'd gotten a decent night's sleep, and his body longed for even a quick rest.

A hard slam to his back brought Josiah to full alert. The world didn't look right, and he struggled to make sense of what had happened.

He lay in the snow, on his back.

Blinking, he turned his head, and frigid moisture touched his neck. He sucked in a breath. Struggling to sit up, he glanced around. His horse stood a few feet away, eyeing him with a wary look, reins hanging to the ground.

How had he fallen off?

He rubbed a gloved hand over his eyes, and a yawn forced its way through his open jaw. He must have fallen asleep.

Josiah blinked and grabbed a handful of snow, then swiped it over his face. That brought his nerves back to life. Might bring on frostbite, too, if he didn't get a move on.

By God's grace, the mochila was still on the saddle. The gelding stood quiet for him to mount. This really was the best Express horse he'd ridden yet. He nudged the animal with his heels and it moved off into a canter.

He had to stay alert this time. Focused. The route ahead wouldn't be too long if he thought about it in sections. Their next stop would be coming up in about twenty minutes. Or maybe less, depending on how long he'd slept. Then one quick horse change after another, about every hour if he stayed on schedule. At the end of it all was the Rocky Ridge — his home station. And Mara.

It'd be four o'clock in the morning if he was on time. Would she be up yet? Or would her brothers handle the relay and take his horse? Maybe she'd get up just to see him. That was surely wishful thinking. And he wasn't even certain he wanted it. But out here in the icy darkness, he clung to the pretty face that smiled at him in his mind. A smile he'd see in just a few hours.

It was that hope that drove him forward.

Mid-morning the next day, Mara dumped the last cup of flour into the dough on the counter, then worked her hands into the pile of powder and liquid. The door squeaked behind her and she turned to look, but kept her hands in the mixture. Bread dough could make a mess faster than a horse's tail could flick a fly.

Josiah stepped into the room, his presence filling the space in a way no other man could do. He scanned the interior, and when his eyes rested on her, they softened so much she could see the change even across half the room. One side of his mouth quirked in a sort of half smile that did funny things in her chest. He unbuttoned his coat and hung it on a peg. "Hey, there."

"Hello." A mindless word. And she wasn't a mindless woman, yet every time this man neared, she seemed to lose the ability to speak sensibly.

"I was hoping I'd find you here. Hoping you'd put me to work." That tilt of his mouth again.

"You were?" She sounded like a mockingbird, repeating everything he said.

"Yep. Can I help with lunch?"

Help? That must be his way of saying he was hungry. She glanced toward the table. "Have a seat and I'll get you some coffee and a biscuit." Wiping the mess from her hands, she shifted over to the bucket of water in the sink.

"I'd rather help, if you don't mind. I've done a bit of cooking before. Put me to work."

She stalled, then turned to eye him. Help cook? But his blue-green eyes shone back at her, earnestness shimmering in their depths.

She had to pull herself away before she lost herself completely in that look. With a deep inhale, she scanned the dough and ingredients scattered across the work counter. "I was just making bread for the stage."

"What time does it arrive?" He stepped into the kitchen area. He was so near now. Just feet away.

45

She dared not look at his face. "Around three o'clock." She moved back to the dough, and continued kneading. Working the mixture between her fingers had a calming effect, and she focused on the sensation. She needed to get him out of the kitchen before she did something really simpleminded.

"It's too early to start on the meat and gravy for lunch, and I'm just about ready to let the bread rise. I don't think there's anything you need to do. Thanks for asking, though." Mara waited with her back to the man. Waited for the sound of his footsteps leaving the kitchen. After a few moments, the tightness in her chest told her she wasn't breathing. She released her spent air in a slow, silent stream.

"How about I make cinnamon crisps?"

She turned to find him watching her, and she couldn't quite wipe the shock off her face. "I...don't have any cinnamon." Did he really know how to cook? Cinnamon crisps weren't hard, but they were more than either of her brothers would attempt.

"Sugar crisps, then." His mouth quirked on one side again, sending a surge of heat through her chest. "I won't use many supplies, but I think your guests will like them."

She didn't have the power to say no when he looked at her like that. "All right."

He rolled up his sleeves and moved to the washbasin. "I just need flour, butter, sugar, and a flat pan."

Mara pushed the ingredients he specified to the far corner of the work counter, then went back to kneading in earnest. By the time he stepped to the spot she'd prepared, she'd divided her dough into loaf-sized sections.

She kept an eye on him while he focused on his task. He didn't speak, working with efficiency as he doled out ingredients and mixed them together. Who'd taught him to cook like that? He'd obviously done this more than once.

Mara placed her dough sections in the bread pans, then draped a cloth over it all. She turned to the washbasin, keeping her eyes focused anywhere except on Josiah. As soon as her hands were clean, she dried them on her apron and reached to untie its strings.

"I need to work with the horses." She had to get away from his unsettling presence. Draping her apron over a peg on the wall, she grabbed her coat and slipped out the door before Josiah could respond.

Chapter Five

ara pulled the corral gate closed as Bandita kicked her heels and cantered toward the rest of the herd. The filly had been extra challenging today, digging in her hooves when Mara gave a command, and spooking at imaginary ghosts just to break up the monotony. The obstinate streak that ran through that horse was wider than the Sweetwater River during spring flooding.

She stopped in the barn to hang the halter on the wall, then headed toward the house. The stage was due any time, and she needed to check on the bread in the oven. She'd caught Ezra walking toward the house earlier and asked him to put the loaves in when they finished rising. The stage driver and passengers, if he had any, would be thankful for warm bread and butter to go with their fried buffalo steak and gravy.

As she crossed the courtyard, a rumble sounded in the distance. Mara stopped and shaded her eyes. The stage was early today.

She jogged toward the house as quickly as her skirts would allow, unbuttoning her coat as she went. The steaks were cut and parboiled already, just needed to be fried and gravy made from the drippings. She would pull the bread from the oven first, so maybe it would be cool enough to cut when the gravy finished. And she needed to brew another pot of coffee before anything else. The people would wait more patiently if they had warm coffee to tide them over.

Mara pushed through the cabin door and stalled there on the threshold.

Josiah stood in her kitchen. Just like she'd left him hours ago.

He sliced bread, and glanced up at her unceremonious entry. A touch of that grin took over his face, the one that tipped his mouth. And this time it added a roguish sparkle to his eyes.

She pushed back the butterflies in her chest. "What are you doing?"

"The steaks and gravy are ready, the sugar crisps should be coming out of the oven any minute, and the bread just cooled enough to slice. Any sign of the stage yet?"

"It's pulling in now." A feeling washed over her like she'd walked into the pasture and found someone else riding her horse. In a way, that's what *was* happening.

"Good. Would you mind setting out plates and cups?" He looked so perfectly at home there, as though the tiny cooking space had grown to fit his broad shoulders and rugged presence.

As she struggled to make sense of what was happening in her own home, she moved forward to gather the dishes he'd mentioned. She couldn't help but dart glances at the man as he leaned over to open the oven door, and used the leather pad she'd stitched to pull the pan from the heat.

She'd finally found the words to ask him where he learned to cook, when the cabin door opened and three men ambled into the room.

She recognized the man bringing up the rear. Mr. Campbell, one of the usual drivers who came through here. She poured coffee as they found places around the table.

Josiah had filled two plates with steaks and gravy by the time she returned the coffee pot to the stove. And by the time she'd carried those platters over to the table, he had the third ready, along with a plate of sliced bread. It smelled heavenly, even if she had done most of the batter work. He'd pulled it out of the fire when the top was perfectly browned.

"This your new hired hand, Miss Reid?" Mr. Campbell's voice carried across the room.

Mara glanced from the stage driver to Josiah. "This is the new Express rider, Mr. Josiah English. Mr. English, may I present Mr. Gus Campbell with the Butterfield Overland Stage." For once, she was thankful Pa had insisted his children learn proper introductions, even after they'd left England.

"Likes to work in the kitchen, too, I see." It wasn't clear from Mr. Campbell's tone whether he was teasing or jeering, although she'd not known the man to be rude. Still, he was hardly a close friend.

Mara watched Josiah. Would his hackles rise against the implied insult?

His expression took on an enigmatic look, but he nodded. "Used to cook in a hotel in Savannah. Old habits stay with you."

She tried to keep her own expression as neutral as his, but she probably failed at the effort. He'd cooked in a hotel? No wonder he had an easy confidence in the kitchen. Heat crept up her neck as she thought through the food she'd prepared for him these past days. It had been passable, but probably not up to the variety or skill level he'd been accustomed to.

Still, it was the best she could do given her other responsibilities. Especially with the limited supplies she had to use.

Mr. Campbell had turned to his food, and Josiah was back at the stove, working at something in the pan. What else didn't she know about this man? Maybe it would be better not to find out. The more she learned, the harder it was to keep her attraction at bay.

The next morning, Josiah stepped out of the bunkhouse and glanced around for any sign of activity. After breakfast, he'd written a promised note to Albert Chambers, the owner of the hotel where he'd lived and worked for a third of his life. But now it was time to get to work. He checked the back corral first, and the sight of Mara's elegant form riding a leggy paint horse did funny things to his breathing.

He approached the rail and leaned against a post. She was graceful. Poised. She and the animal beneath her moved in perfect harmony, as if it read her mind.

Mara saw him right away, and gave him the hint of a smile as they moved in his direction. He was falling for this woman. Faster than he liked.

He forced his focus down to the horse she rode. The long-legged mare was flashy, with patches of white and brown splashed across her body. She moved in a graceful jog across the pen under Mara's smooth direction.

As she eased the horse to a stop in front of him, her face seemed to light from within. She reached down to stroke the mare.

A tickle of jealousy caught him off guard. Was it Mara's affection for the horse he envied? Or the effortless way she handled the mare? Probably both.

He met those luminous eyes. "Nice mare."

Mara's smile widened as she looked down at the thick brown coat she stroked. "This is Rose, one of my three-year olds. We've been together since she was a newborn."

"Seems like you understand each other. Will you keep her?"

Mara's lips met and her eyes lost their sparkle. "No, she'll go with the next batch that are sold."

"You would let her go? I can tell in five minutes she's special."

She shrugged. "I don't have a choice. We raise and train them, then they leave. It's how we earn a living."

He didn't miss the grief in her eyes, even though she tried to mask it. Her pain pulled at something near his soul. What he wouldn't give to tell this woman she could keep her horse—this animal she'd bonded with.

Mara signaled the mare and they walked along the fence. Then Rose moved into an easy rocking lope. Mara turned her through the center of the pen. Halfway across, Rose's rhythm changed, and she raised both front feet in the air for a split second, like the steps of a dance. At the fence, Mara guided her the other direction.

They were amazing to watch, and Josiah's chest pulled tighter the longer he stood there. Mara put Rose through her paces for a few more minutes, then allowed her to walk on a loose rein. She stroked the horse's damp neck, and her lips moved, but he couldn't make out any words. Maybe they didn't need sound to understand each other.

She dismounted in the center, then led the mare toward the gate.

Josiah met them there, and fell into step on Rose's other side. "I can untack her."

Mara glanced at him over the horse's neck, but didn't answer. They entered the barn in silence, and she led Rose to a tie ring where a halter hung. Should he offer again?

Mara finally spoke. "Why are you doing this?"

He looked up to find her brown eyes watching him, intensity rendering them even larger than normal. Her gaze was so powerful, it was hard to hold onto it. "Untacking the horse?"

She jerked her hand in a sweeping motion that encompassed the barn. "This. Why do you keep trying to help? You have a job here, but doing the grunt work in the barn or the kitchen isn't it."

Did he have to have a reason? Truthfully, he couldn't say what possessed him these days. It was just a driving force inside him. Shrugging, he glanced at the mare. "I don't like to sit around. And it's good experience."

She slipped the bridle off Rose's head, leaving her without a restraint. But the mare just dipped her head and blew out as Mara moved back to untie the cinch strap. "You don't get enough horse experience when you're riding a two-hundred-mile route?"

The sardonic tinge to her words tugged at the corners of his mouth, and he sneaked a sideways glance at her as he lifted the saddle from the mare's back.

She met his look with raised brows and maybe a little sparkle in those expressive eyes.

He shrugged again, acknowledging the truth in it. "It's more the care and training I was thinking about."

She was silent as he carried the saddle to the bar mounted in the corner of the barn. When he returned to Rose, the horse had her head draped over Mara's shoulder, eyes drifting shut as Mara scratched a spot on the mare's chest. It was almost like an embrace as the two of them melded together. The bond between them was almost strong enough to touch.

Mara finally stepped away and slipped a halter on Rose, then turned to look at him.

"So why do you want to more practice doing barn chores?" It was hard to read her expression as she studied him. Not disdain. Maybe...curiosity?

Her silence must have stripped away his good sense, because his mouth started running. "One day soon I'll be raising horses of my own. Arabians. Working here is good experience. And if I can lighten the load a little, too..." He raised a shoulder again as he turned and gazed toward the open barn door. What was he thinking to share his dreams like that? He knew better than to open himself to the ridicule.

"Arabians?"

He jerked at the word, his wayward gaze finding her face. Her head was cocked, brows gathered in definite curiosity.

"Yes."

She seemed to consider this for a moment. "I think half-Arabs would sell best. At least in this part of the country. If you mix them with Quarter Horses, you'll get a better temperament and calmer head, but still the endurance and beauty of the Arabian."

Josiah swallowed down the words clogging his throat. He'd trusted her with his dream and she'd given back something he'd never had before—belief.

Josiah sped out of Ice Springs Station on another fresh horse. He tightened his right hand around the reins, and pulled back a little toward his chest. The gelding threw its head, never slowing. He was only a fingertip grip away from out-of-control. Josiah forced himself to breathe, then strengthened his hold on the horn and hunkered down for the ride.

Soon, the rocks became bigger, and they reached the base of a rough ascent, the steepest stretch in his line. The gelding lunged up the first section. His speed slowed by a hair, but the animal exerted more effort, his body moving almost faster than his legs. Josiah kept the reins tight.

"Easy, boy. Easy." His crooning did no obvious good to slow the horse. Maybe because his voice wobbled like his heartbeat. For a split second, he remembered the image of Mara on Rose, moving together in unison as the mare understood her every request. He wanted to ride like that.

An extra strong lunge brought Josiah's focus back to the horse beneath him. He leaned low over the animal's neck as they ascended. Should he give the gelding his head so he could focus on climbing? Maybe. But he couldn't quite bring himself to loosen the reins as the horse surged forward.

And then they were falling. The gelding struggled to find his footing. Josiah pulled hard on the reins. It happened so fast, yet everything in slow motion. The horse went down on one knee, then swayed. For a long, breathless moment, they sprawled there. Motionless.

Then with a mighty effort, the horse raised himself back up on all four hooves. The animal stumbled to a stop, and Josiah released a breath. He slipped his feet from the stirrups and slid to the ground. His legs quivered as he took deep breaths to still his racing heartbeat.

The horse heaved, gulping in air as he stood straddle-legged. A glance at his knee showed blood seeping from a gash. It wasn't gushing, though. Josiah stroked the gray neck. They were both alive. And the horse put weight on all four legs, so maybe nothing was broken.

He ran his hand down the gelding's shoulder and forearm. When he came near the knee, the animal flinched and shifted his leg backward.

"Easy, boy." He kept his voice low and calm.

Should he tie something around the wound? Leave the horse here and send someone back for it? But what good would that do? The horse would still have to walk to the Express stop.

Josiah looked up the hill. They were about twenty feet from the top. It was much farther to the bottom, and going downhill would put more stress on the animal's front legs. Up they'd go.

He slipped the reins over the horse's head and gave an encouraging tug. "C'mon, boy."

The horse took a tentative step forward. He limped, but progressed a few paces before stopping. Josiah tugged again, and this time the gelding kept moving. He seemed to put more weight on the leg as they climbed.

At the top of the hill, Josiah allowed the animal to blow while they both rested. He stroked the gelding's neck as he thought through the rest of the path to the next station. It was an easy slope down from here, then the ground leveled off for a while. They would have to cross the river before they finally arrived at the next stop. Too bad he didn't have time to let the horse stand in the icy water. That'd help the swelling that already showed in the knee. But maybe the station master would come back and do it.

Josiah gathered the reins and stepped forward. They'd better get to it.

Chapter Six

Mara ran her hand down the colt's front leg, squeezed the long, narrow bones below the knee, and picked up the hoof. It was full of mud, but she had no plans to clean it out. Instead, she tapped the bottom a few times, and lowered the hoof back to the ground.

"Good, boy," she crooned, stroking the dark neck. "You're getting the hang of this, aren't you?"

Jericho shook his head and chewed on the rope that held him to the barn wall. He was so calm and affectionate, the exact opposite of Bandita's vindictive ways. One would never imagine they shared the same sire. It seemed the mother's temperament had won out in both cases. She pinched her lips against a smile.

A whistle pierced the air, quickening her pulse more than it should have. Josiah was back.

Mara gave Jericho a final pat. "You wait here, boy. I'll be back." Then she headed for the stall that housed the Express horse she'd saddled a few minutes before.

Zechariah met her at the barn door as she led the bay mare out. "I gave Davy the food you packed for him."

Mara nodded. "Thanks."

Josiah was close now, the outline of his broad shoulders clear against the pale background of patchy snow and tan grass. As he neared, the thunder of the horse's hooves was almost overpowered by its heavy breathing and the squeak of the saddle leather. As Josiah slowed the mare to enter the courtyard, his blue eyes locked on her with the power to capture. But it was the rakish tip of his mouth that really undid her. She swallowed down the butterflies in her stomach, but it did nothing to still the surge of her pulse.

When he slid from his horse, things moved quickly. Zeche took Josiah's mount, and Davy transferred the mochila to his horse. Then the boy was mounted, and away at a fast canter within a matter of seconds. Zechariah took the sweaty horse Josiah had ridden without a word and ambled toward the pasture. He'd walk her out for a few minutes until the mare caught her breath and her muscles began to cool.

Mara looked back at Josiah as silence settled over the little clearing. A horse nickered from the pasture, probably greeting the new Express mount. Josiah met her gaze with that quirk of his mouth she was coming to love. Just a pulling of one corner really, but it pressed into his cheek in what could almost be called a dimple.

She forced herself to look away from his mouth, moving her focus up to his eyes. Their clarity was shadowed some by the tired lines that framed them. He must be exhausted. "Are you hungry?"

"Starved."

Good. That gave her something to do. Mara turned toward the house and started walking. "Come inside. I saved you breakfast."

Once in her kitchen, she worked fast, shifting the pan of meat gravy to the front of the stove and pouring a cup of coffee. She'd left it on low heat, but hopefully it hadn't been there long enough to scorch.

"Can I help?"

She glanced up at the close proximity of Josiah's voice. He stood beside the stove, close enough to touch. Close enough for her to take in every detail of his face. The stubble on his jaw hadn't grown long, but enough to give him a roguish look. She found his eyes, the weariness in them tugging at her chest.

Mara touched his arm before she could stop herself. "You're tired. Sit."

He met her gaze and held it, stilling her breath with the power of his eyes. Her chest tightened with a longing she'd never experienced. He looked like he would reach out to her, but he didn't.

She had the sudden urge to step closer. But she didn't.

Instead, they stood staring at each other as time suspended and the rest of the world stopped. A second. An hour. She had no idea how much time passed.

Finally, Josiah released a long breath. His action broke the connection, and in Mara's chest, a prick of disappointment blended with a fragment of relief. Her hand slipped from his arm as he turned away and walked to his chair at the table.

Mara moved back to the work counter and focused on breathing. What had just happened? One moment she stood warming breakfast, and the next she was connecting with something deep in his soul.

The cabin door squeaked as it opened, and Ezra's voice sounded, greeting Josiah. Mara slid her eyes closed. *Thanks, baby brother.* Until she could figure out her feelings—and get them under control—a little buffer would be welcome.

"Supply train should be through any day now."

Josiah bit into the doughy bread as Ezra spoke. He nodded, but his mouth was full, so the younger man kept talking.

"Usually comes through to all the Pony Express stations once a month or so."

Maybe they would bring better food supplies. The bread in Josiah's mouth was gummy. Had Mara let it rise before baking? In fact, its consistency wasn't very different from the gravy she'd spooned on his plate for dipping.

His gaze drifted to where she stood wiping the work counter in the kitchen. She may not be the best cook, but she was remarkable in every other way. Heat crept up his spine as he replayed their moment before her brother had come in.

Something special brewed between them. She'd felt it, too. It had showed all over her face. And now even more by the way she wouldn't look anywhere close to his direction. He'd never met a woman who captured him the way she did. It was like she could see all the way through him.

Which could be dangerous. There were pieces inside him not decent for anyone to glimpse, especially a woman like Mara. It was hard to resist her draw, but he had to be careful not to let her too close.

He could do that. He'd gotten good at guarding himself from disappointment. He'd certainly had enough practice at it.

And if Mara took him up on the idea that had been developing in his mind, he'd need to do better at protecting himself from her powers. If he could do it, this idea would be perfect. He just needed to find the right moment to ask her.

After he slept. A long time.

Josiah tossed the load of hay into the larger pasture, then spread it into smaller piles spaced apart. The horses milled around him, and he stroked a head here and a shoulder there. A gray mare pinned her ears and charged the horses nearby, scattering them like marbles. When they were gone, she straightened her ears, meandered to the hay the horses had been eating, and settled in with a sigh. Josiah shook his head. Alpha mare.

As he headed back toward the barn, his attention drifted to the riding corral. Mara rode a lanky chestnut, its bouncy trot sending her long hair glittering in the sun. He'd finished cleaning and restocking the stalls, so he headed her direction to watch.

Her movements weren't quite as fluid on this horse as they'd been on Rose, her directions more apparent and exaggerated. But she was still graceful, and the horse obeyed what she asked. He could watch this woman ride for days. Years. The rest of his life.

Mara didn't acknowledge his presence. Her forehead creased and her focus never wavered from the mare underneath her as they worked. At last, her face relaxed into a gut-tightening grin, and she reached down to pat the horse's neck. Then the pair ambled toward him.

As they neared, Mara's face shone, her luminous eyes dancing in the sunlight. "She did well today." She reached down to pat the thick chestnut coat again.

He nodded as the mare stepped up to the fence. Josiah reached a hand for her to sniff before he scratched her forehead.

"This is Sharon, one of our two-year-olds." Mara stroked the horse, her lips touching in a fond smile. "She's learning to neck rein and adjust her speed at a trot."

Josiah nodded, although the jargon meant nothing to him. "You have a way with her." That he understood. Mara could get any animal she touched to perform just because she asked.

Her head ducked, and she continued to pat the mare. "Sharon's a good girl. Likes to please."

He studied the woman. "Mara, I was wondering." He paused, struggling to put the right words together to ask his question.

Her gaze slowly lifted, her dark brows raised in question. "Yes?"

"Some of the Express horses get a little high-strung. I was wondering if maybe you could give me tips on training them." He forced his breath to keep coming in even spurts. He couldn't remember a time when he'd had to ask for help. Had said it would never happen again. And now this knot in his stomach reminded him why.

He studied her face, but her expression had grown cryptic. For someone whose features usually showed a clear visual of her thoughts, not even her eyes gave him a glimpse of what she was thinking.

Was she trying to find a way to decline nicely? A spurt of desperation flared through him. "I could...help in the kitchen. With the cooking. In exchange."

The skin between Mara's brows pinched, and he still couldn't read her thoughts. Her silence pulled the knot tighter in his gut.

Finally she spoke. "I don't mind teaching you about the horses. But I don't feel right about the other. It's not your job to cook here." One side of her mouth pressed tight.

The tension in his neck eased. "I don't mind. Really. You'd be doing me a favor, it's the least I can do."

Mara's features relaxed a little. "I guess. We can take the horses out for a ride in the hills after lunch, then you can help with dinner. If you decide you want to stop, just say so."

A grin tugged at his stubborn mouth, and he let a little of it take shape. "I won't."

Six months ago, if someone had told Josiah he'd be riding horseback through the western hills with a woman as pretty as Mara, he'd have laughed out loud. And he might still let out a chuckle now, but for an entirely different reason.

Mara rode beside him, tall and graceful on a bay and white paint gelding. His own gray gelding jigged underneath him, and Josiah shortened his reins another inch. Both animals were two-year-olds, familiar with the basic instructions but not *polished*, according to Mara.

She looked over at him, her eyes scrutinizing. "Let's start by fixing the way you sit in the saddle."

Josiah looked down at the leather underneath him. "I'm in the middle." He had to force his tone to stay even.

He'd asked for her to critique him, although he'd expected more focus on the horse.

"First put your shoulders back, then rock back in the saddle like this."

It felt a little wrong to study her form, so he tried to keep his focus on the parts she'd probably meant. Her shoulders were squared, back straight in a way that looked relaxed enough to be natural. Perfectly balanced.

Pink touched Mara's cheeks and she spoke again quickly. "Now put all your weight down in your heels."

He pushed down on the stirrups.

Mara's brow puckered as she watched his feet. "Try this. Stand in the stirrups." She demonstrated. "Now lower your heels so all your weight is pushing down the back of your legs."

The back of his calves burned as he stretched the muscles, but his legs seemed to lock solidly in place.

"Now keep that feeling as you bend your knees and sit back in the saddle."

That was easier said than done, but Josiah worked to keep the tight stretch in his legs as he sat.

"Great." The smile she flashed made him wish he really could do something great for her. The horse underneath him jigged again.

"Now, bring your hands down so your wrists rest on the saddle."

Josiah shot her a look. If he did that, he'd be giving this gelding its head. He and the horse would be on top of yonder butte in three seconds flat.

"I'm serious." The edge of her lip slipped under her teeth, giving her a bit of an impish look. "The horse is listening to what your body's telling him. If you're hunched forward and tightening your legs and reins, he thinks you're getting ready to tell him to run. If you're sitting deep with your weight in your heels, shoulders back, and hands loose, he'll relax."

Her point sounded valid, but loosening the reins for a jittery horse didn't seem like a good idea. Still, she was the teacher.

He concentrated on sitting back with his heels down as he dropped his wrists to rest on the saddle front. Tension eased from the horse like water through a strainer, and the animal extended his neck, breathing out a long snort.

Josiah glanced at Mara. "I guess you do speak Horse."

Her eyes danced, then a soft laugh drifted from her like the rustle of leaves. It was the first time he'd ever seen her laugh, and the image of her was worth every bit of embarrassment in asking for her help.

The breeze feathered loose tendrils of brown hair across her face. Her eyes were bright, skin a perfect cream, and lips brushed brilliant red by the wind. She glanced up and caught him staring, then slid her eyes away.

He should probably apologize, but couldn't bring himself to do it. He wasn't sorry he was given this chance to watch her. She was mesmerizing.

Pink flushed her cheeks again. She opened her mouth as if to speak, but something in front of them caught her attention.

Disappointment pressed him as he turned to follow her gaze. But then his chest seized, and he blinked twice to confirm the image in front of them.

Indians.

Not twenty feet away, three Indian women stood. The older was wrinkled and silver-haired, while the other two had long black braids and slender forms. All carried armloads of firewood.

Josiah jerked back on his reins and stretched his arm sideways to block Mara's forward motion. Where there were women, Indian braves must be close by. His eyes scanned the landscape. No other signs of life. Were the women armed? From the stories he'd heard, Indians were savage, no matter what gender.

Mara pushed his arm down, but she kept her horse positioned behind him. He didn't dare take his eyes off the squaws, but his hand crept down to the flap of his saddle pack. His fingers closed around the butt of his Colt and he pulled it from the satchel.

"Leave it," Mara hissed. Then in a louder tone, she spoke a quick mixture of sounds, high then low, then high again. It caught him so off guard, he turned to make sure those noises came from her, although he'd have known the softness of her voice anywhere.

The oldest squaw responded in the same language, and Josiah scrutinized her.

She motioned with a wrinkled hand, and then all three women started shuffling the same direction they'd been headed. He didn't know whether he should ride after them or grab Mara's reins and high-tail them back to the station.

He compromised by doing neither, but kept his focus on the women until they disappeared around the base of a butte.

The moment they were gone, he released the clamp on his jaw and forced air to flow in and out of his chest as he turned on the woman sitting beside him. "What was that?"

Mara looked at him as if he'd just asked her to pass the butter. "They were Cheyenne squaws, out gathering wood." She didn't meet his gaze, but raised her reins as she started to guide her horse forward.

He reached out and snatched her reins, stalling the horse mid-stride. "What did they want?"

She raised both brows at him. "Nothing. I'm still learning Cheyenne, but I think she mostly said hello." Her tone held an arch to it that he'd ever heard from her. And when she jerked her reins from his grasp and kneed the horse forward again, he let her go.

But he had to find another way to get her attention. She could be riding straight into a trap for all he knew, with braves positioned around the butte to snatch her up for her pretty brown scalp. Or worse still—for other benefits she could provide.

Fire flared through his veins and he reined his gelding back the way they'd come. "We have to get back to the station." Maybe she would follow him.

"I thought you wanted to ride."

He halted his horse and looked back at her. Mara and her gelding had paused too, and she watched him. He worked to keep his tone schooled. "We just saw Indians. We need to get back and warn the others."

The tilt of her head showed exasperation, but it was nothing compared to what was roiling in his gut. "They were Cheyenne squaws. I know them. They're friendly, and their men come to trade at our station."

Josiah could only stare. She knew these Indians? "What did you say to them?"

The corners of her mouth lifted. "I told them to come visit when their men come to trade."

Chapter Seven

"What did you have in mind for supper?" Josiah held the cabin door for Mara as they stepped inside to start cooking. First an afternoon in the saddle, and now an evening in the kitchen. Except for the little run-in with the Indians, this might easily be one of the best days he could remember. There hadn't been that many to choose from in the last fifteen or so years.

"I was planning flapjacks and sliced ham." She hung her coat on a peg and stepped toward the washbasin.

"I'll start on flapjacks." And they'd be the fluffiest, tastiest batter cakes she'd ever imagined.

After washing up, he placed the griddle on the hot part of the cook stove and added another log to the fire from the nearby pile. From shelves, he pulled out the eggs and flour he'd used before, then found a couple of bowls and started to work. He broke the eggs and separated the whites from the yolks.

As he beat the yolks, the room grew quiet. He turned to find Mara watching him, brows knit and her cute little chin tilted.

"What are you doing?"

"Separating the eggs. It makes the cakes lighter."

He poured in a generous portion of milk while the burn of her gaze crept up his neck. He forced his shoulders to relax, then scooped flour into the mixture.

Mara didn't speak again, but the feel of her watching was hard to ignore. He spooned a dab of cream from the crockery.

"Do you have any saleratus?" He knew she did. He'd tasted the sodium bicarbonate in her soda biscuits.

Mara pulled a small tin from a shelf and set it out for him. She still didn't speak, and it made him want to say something to fill the silence. He must be going off his rocker.

But maybe this would be a good time to learn more about her. "Have y'all been in this territory long?" He poured in the egg white and whipped the mixture.

"We moved here last year from Maryland. Pa negotiated a contract with the Express, and they paid for us to build the station. He'd always wanted to move out west."

"Your pa?" The question was out before he considered it. Before he realized what the lack of the man's presence now must mean.

"He died last spring."

Her voice held a weight of sadness that clenched his chest, and the pain of it flared the defenses he'd honed so carefully for the last fifteen years. He didn't want to feel sorry for her. Didn't want to feel anything for her.

But how could he not? He knew what it was like to lose the parents he'd thought would always be there. His stubborn gaze flitted over to catch a glimpse of her. To see how she was handling the sharing of the news.

She'd wrapped her arms around her waist, making her look even smaller than her willowy form. She didn't meet his gaze, only stared at the bowl in his hands.

She was close enough that he could reach out and brush her arm, and his traitorous hand did just that, resting on her sleeve. "I'm sorry." His voice came out hoarse. "Nothing makes losing any easier."

Mara's eyes softened then, glistening as their amber depths widened. "You've lost a parent?"

She searched his face, and he had to harden himself against the burn in his throat. He hadn't let himself get this soft since he was a kid. But it was the way she looked up at him with those big, glassy eyes.

When she stepped into his arms, he couldn't bring himself to push her away. Might have even pulled her closer, it was hard to tell. He only knew this felt so right it made his arms ache. Made his chest hurt.

He buried his face in her hair and pressed his eyes shut.

Until the sizzle of flapjacks broke through his focus.

Josiah settled into the rhythm of the gelding beneath him, as he rode out of the Rocky Ridge station. For once, he wasn't on that unruly bay mare. He checked his posture and forced himself to sit back in the saddle more.

Mara had been there to see him off, with that smile curving her lips. His arms still remembered the feel of her yesterday, when he'd held her. He could almost taste the scent of roses in her hair. The softness of it against his fingers. But she'd stepped out of the embrace as quickly as she'd come to him. After a few more tense moments cooking, she finally escaped out the door with some excuse about needing to talk with her brothers. Probably a good thing. He knew better than to let himself get so close to her.

He'd done well to keep his distance since then, except for that look she gave him right before he left on this ride. He'd been trying to bring back the same feeling of secure legs with his weight in his heels, so he stood in the stirrups, then lowered himself and kept his legs in the same position while he sat. Mara had been busy talking to the incoming rider, so he didn't think either of them had seen. But the tip of her pretty mouth when she'd shot him a sideways glance told him she'd noticed the whole thing. At least she saw he was getting good use out of her lessons.

They reached the stretch where the ground became rocky, and Josiah tightened his reins. The horse didn't slow a bit. Did these Express horses have no common sense when it came to the terrain? Seemed all they ever wanted to do was run full out. Made little difference whether they were on flat prairie land or going over the edge of a cliff.

Josiah pulled the reins again. No response. Maybe he should try a different approach. He gave a swift sharp tug while leaning back, then released. The horse slowed a tiny bit. He gave the same jerk again, then repeated it a few seconds later. Wonder of wonders, the horse slowed down.

They made it over a low butte, and a movement in the distance caught Josiah's eye. Riders. He slowed the horse even more to get a closer look. They were maybe a half mile away, so it was hard to see more than tiny figures. He could make out silhouettes, though.

Indians.

Should he rein in? Turn around? The riders moved to his left, away from the Express route. And they were almost out of sight completely.

He touched the revolver tucked inside his waistband. He had an obligation to fulfill for the Pony Express. Loosening his reins, he pushed his horse into a canter as they maneuvered down the slope.

The next day, Josiah sat at the rough wooden table in the Three Crossings station, watching Brantley fry strips of meat at the stove. The man's rough exterior and jerky movements were a better match for a cowpoke or freighter, someone who lived his life out in the elements. Not cooking breakfast for the men in his charge. Brantley used his fingers to flip a piece of meat, and Josiah cringed. Maybe the heat would fry off the dirt from his grubby hands.

He looked away. "You live in this area long, Brantley?"

"'Bout a year." The man didn't look up from his project in the frying pan. "Prospected in Californy before that."

Prospecting. Perfect occupation for this chap. "Did you strike it rich?"

"Did all right."

Something about the man's response hinted that he'd done more than all right. But then, what man in his right mind would admit he had a stash of gold laying around the cabin?

"I'm surprised you're not set up in a town, where life is a little easier." An image of this rough miner in a suit and bowler hat flashed through Josiah's mind. No, town wasn't the place for this fellow.

Brantley never looked his direction, but his wide nose flared. "Too many people."

"You ever think about takin' a wife?" He shouldn't keep pushing, but Brantley was an interesting personality. And maybe he was still adjusting to the silence around this place.

"Can't abide a woman tellin' me what to do."

Josiah pinched back a grin, but he had to confess he'd had the same thought at least once. Not that he'd ever gotten close enough to a woman to give her the chance.

He let the conversation lie for a few minutes while Brantley forked meat onto two plates and brought them to the table. A tin of biscuits plopped down next, then the man sat across from him. He shoveled food in his mouth before Josiah could bring himself to pick up his fork.

"You see Indians out on the trail yet?" Brantley raised his face from where it hovered over his plate.

Josiah forced down a bite of the tough meat. "Yesterday. Didn't get a good look, though."

"Where at?" Brantley spoke around a mouthful.

"Just before I reached Warm Springs station." Josiah told about his distant glimpse, and Brantley seemed to study every word while he consumed his food.

"Were they wearin' war paint?"

"I couldn't tell. Just saw a silhouette more than anything." Josiah bit into a corner of his meat and tugged. Nothing. He yanked harder. This stuff was tougher than the leather on his saddle.

Brantley's gaze drifted into the distance as he chewed. "Had trouble with the Indians last summer. Burned down a station up near the Carson River. Killed five people in cold blood. Attacked six or seven other stations, too."

Josiah tried to push back the tide of unease that washed through his belly. "Did the soldiers come to stop them?"

"After a month or two. Lost close ta twenty good men, though. Riders and stationmasters both. Seemed like they targeted the Express."

Josiah focused on his food, allowing silence to settle over them. Had the riders been ambushed? Attacked in passing? Killed at the stations?

He had his Colt, but to be honest, he wasn't all that great of a shot. Hadn't had much practice in the hotel kitchen. Still, he could usually hit his target if he had time to steady and aim, although that might not be good enough out here. Most likely he'd be aiming from atop a running horse.

Josiah stood and carried his plate to the dry sink. He was due for some target practice.

Mara pinned Zeche's undershirt to the clothes line, humming a Christmas carol as she worked. She always loved the dissonant sound of "God Rest Ye Merry, Gentleman," and she needed to kindle a little Christmas spirit in her chest. Ezra and Zeche needed it too, no matter how little they felt like celebrating. The holiday was less than a week away.

They'd often joined with other families for Christmas dinner back in Maryland. But with the closest neighbors being a group of grumpy old men at a station twelve miles to the East, this holiday would likely consist of a quiet dinner at home.

And Josiah's ride schedule meant he wouldn't even be here to celebrate with them. He'd spend most of Christmas day at the Three Crossings station, then leave for the trip back to Rocky Ridge as darkness fell. Maybe the boys would agree to postpone Christmas dinner until the day after, when Josiah could be here for it.

"Mara." Ezra's voice called from somewhere on the other side of the house.

"Back here." She draped the last pair of pants over the line and pinned them.

"The supply train's here." Ezra peeked from around the building.

"I'll be right there."

Mara's pulse picked up. The supply train meant fresh food stuffs, trading goods for the Indians, pay from the Express, and a few other things she hoped Ezra ordered. It might be a good Christmas yet.

She strode into the house to start fresh coffee and check on the stew. She already had soup on the stove for the stage scheduled to stop later in the afternoon. The timing couldn't be more perfect.

When Mara stepped in the door, Josiah stood at the cook stove, stirring something in the big pot. She shouldn't be surprised, but she allowed a smile to touch her lips. "Supply train's here. I should've known better than to think I needed to hurry in to get food ready."

He gave her one of those amused expressions that tipped his mouth. "I couldn't need you more."

She raised a brow. Did he mean that the way it sounded?

"Would you slice a loaf of bread? I still need to set the cups and spoons out, and the sweet rolls should be about ready to come out of the oven."

"You made sweet rolls?" Why did she never think to bake things like that? Probably because she didn't spend any more time in the kitchen than she had to. Josiah, on the other hand, seemed to *like* to cook. She should just turn over the duties to him. But cooking wasn't the Express rider's job, now was it?

Mara sliced the bread at the counter while Josiah worked nearby—moving from the stove to the counter, to the dry sink, and back to the oven. His nearness didn't steal her breath as much as it used to. Now it enlivened her. She sensed him with an awareness that woke every nerve. And at the same time, his presence wrapped around her like the warmth of a fire on a snowy night.

She was falling for him. No matter how much she told herself to resist him.

But why shouldn't she? He had a magnetism about him. A charisma, and it was more than just the draw of his blue eyes or the way the tip of his mouth made her stomach flip. The two of them even had the same goal of owning their own horse ranch. Wasn't that what she'd always wanted in a prospective husband?

"Would you mind pouring the coffee?"

Mara jerked up to find the subject of her musings watching her, one brow arched. Had he guessed her thoughts? The heat climbing her neck would be a sure giveaway.

Voices sounded outside the cabin door, and it swung wide. Mara grabbed a corner of her apron and used it to hold the coffee pot while she poured, burying her face in the steam that rose from the brew. Ezra entered first, followed by a roomful of men, each talking louder than the next.

Josiah and Mara worked quickly. While he filled bowls with stew, she set them around the table. He was all business, ignoring the cacophony around them as he worked with quick efficiency, thinking ahead to the next need. He'd definitely served crowds before.

And she was getting used to the sight of his broad shoulders filling her little kitchen. Or maybe she wasn't getting used to it exactly, but he no longer seemed out of place in the area. Even when he played the part of a servant, it didn't diminish his manliness in the least.

This man was something special.

The next morning, the Reid men didn't linger around the breakfast table like usual. The supply wagons and stage had disrupted their normal activities the day before, so now there were extra horses to work, trap lines to check, and all the normal chores to do.

Josiah piled the used plates in a stack, consolidating the leftover scraps into one lump.

"You don't have to do that." Mara's voice drifted from the sink. He looked up to find her pouring water into the wash bucket.

He shrugged. "It's a job I know."

She wrinkled her cute little nose. "You said you were a cook in a hotel?"

Wariness threaded in, and he kept his focus on the plates in his hand. The last thing he wanted was to relive his past. So he only nodded and let the dishes sink from his hands into the water she'd prepared. "If you need to get started with the horses, I can take care of things here."

She picked up a cloth from the counter and pulled a tin cup from the water. "I'll stay and help."

She stood near him. Very near. With only inches separating them, the scent roses drifted to him, taking him back to the other day when he'd held her. Sure, she'd only come to him for solace, but he'd breathed her in so deeply he could touch and feel her again right now.

He forced himself to step back. To turn away. He scanned the room, his gaze landing on the plate of scraps still on the table. Stepping forward, he grabbed the load and headed toward the door to dump them in the slop bucket outside. The blast of winter air helped clear his head, and a few deep breaths did the same for his emotions.

But he'd have to face her again soon if he was going to ask for another riding lesson.

Chapter Eight

osiah leaned low, tightening his legs to push the tired horse a little faster in the darkness. Just one small hill and Three Crossings Station would be in sight. Brantley would be standing in the yard with a lantern, and his relief rider would hold a fresh horse.

It was the day before Christmas. His ride out tomorrow wasn't until twilight, which meant he'd spend Christmas day with those two cranky former miners. But it would give him a chance to finish his present for Mara. He'd never been good at whittling, probably because he'd not had much time to practice. But the horse head was shaping up better than he'd expected. Hopefully she'd see past the simple craftsmanship to the sentiment behind it. Although what that sentiment was, he'd rather not consider.

When his horse topped the rise, Josiah released the long whistle to signal his arrival. He could make out the shapes of the Three Crossings buildings in the moonlight, but no lantern in the yard.

He whistled again.

A dot of light appeared by the barn, illuminating a man and horse as Josiah reined into the yard.

He slid to the ground and pulled the mochila off his saddle. "Where's the next rider?"

"Got 'imself shot."

He spun to face Brantley. "What?"

"Shot an' killed. Got in a drunken row with a drifter. Said the vagrant was cheatin' at twenty-one, but the fellow didn't much like bein' called names. Seems our man found the hot end of his gun."

Josiah's mind spun. His relief rider was dead. "There's no one else to take this pack?"

"Nope. Hopin' you will."

He inhaled a deep breath. *God, give me strength.* "Let me have that fresh horse."

Mara whipped the flapjack batter again, then draped a cloth over it and scooted it away from the edge of the work counter. Ten o'clock and Josiah wasn't up yet.

She turned back to the table and straightened his fork and cup. She centered the jar of molasses in front of his place setting. It had come on the supply train, and she'd been saving it for this special day-after-Christmas breakfast. Except Josiah hadn't been up to eat with everyone else. She should've planned the special meal for lunchtime.

Zechariah said Josiah'd looked like death warmed over when he rode in at four o'clock that morning. He must be exhausted. Riding at a high speed for ten hours in the dark would do that to anyone.

Or was he sick? The idea niggled in her mind, planting a vine of worry. Maybe she should send Ezra in to check on him. Make sure he wasn't feverish. They'd not had snow in a couple weeks, but spending so much time on horseback in freezing temperatures couldn't be healthy.

The hours drifted by like watching a rock grow. Mara didn't stray far from their main cabin so she'd be ready when Josiah appeared. Of course, she kept the front door open so she would see him exit the bunkhouse. Keeping her coat on in the chilly room was a small price to pay to make the day special for him.

Zeche and Ezra came in for lunch a little after noon. She placed the plate of sliced cheese and sourdough bread in the center of the table. "Do you think you should check on Josiah? He's not stirred yet. Maybe he's sick."

Zechariah gave her a look. "He's fine, Mara. The man's tired. Let him sleep."

She gripped a fold in her skirt to keep from slapping her big brother.

Ezra nodded, apparently agreeing. But he had that impish smile that said he knew there was more to her question than she was letting on. Her fingers itched to wipe that smile from his face the way only a big sister could, but instead, she forced herself to sit and put a piece of bread on her plate while the others ate.

Two long hours later, the bunkhouse door finally squeaked open. There'd never been a more perfect sight in all the territory than Josiah stepping from that doorway.

But she didn't stop long to admire the view. Instead, she slid the coffee pot onto the stove so the fresh grounds could percolate, laid strips of bacon on the frying pan she'd kept heating—all day—and whipped the flapjack batter into a light mixture. Josiah would have a nice Christmas breakfast if she had to pick him up and carry him to the table herself.

He stepped into the cabin, his presence filling the room like it usually did. "Smells good in here." His voice was rich and gravelly from sleep, and the sound did funny things in her chest.

Mara stopped her activity long enough to give him her brightest holiday smile. "Happy Christmas."

He stood tall and lean, his outline silhouetted by the light from the doorway. His broad shoulders tapered to a trim waist. His hair was a bit tousled, but she couldn't make out his face with the cabin's shadows.

"I'm fixing you Christmas breakfast. Have a seat. It's almost ready." Mara turned back to the frying pan and worked her spoon under the flapjack.

"Mara."

Before she could even register the voice, Josiah's scent encircled her. The aroma of outdoors, horses, and man. So close.

She turned to face him, and had to bend her neck as she looked up into his face. The deep blue of his eyes, like a clear summer sky. The strong lines of his cheeks and jaw. The stubble on his cheeks. The dark circles under his eyes.

Her teeth nibbled the edge of her bottom lip as she studied those circles. Deep exhaustion shadowed his face. Her fingers reached up before she could stop them, touching his cheekbones and the tired skin above them. "You're exhausted."

The lines at the edges of his eyes crinkled. "I've had a long ride." He cupped her hand where it touched his face, pulling it around so his lips pressed a kiss to her palm. "I'm glad to be back."

Mara closed her eyes, the kiss sending tingles through her like she'd never felt. She opened them again and found Josiah's gaze locked with hers.

He cradled her cheek with his other hand. "You are so beautiful." The words escaped in a breath as he lowered his head, his lips brushing hers.

Mara inhaled at the touch, and his mouth came back for more. More than a brush this time. A taste. Heady sweetness.

Josiah pulled back, and Mara's mouth tried to follow. She opened her eyes and found his. They'd darkened to an indigo, deep enough she could drown in their depths.

"I have something for you."

His right hand released hers, and he fished in his pocket. Her gaze tracked his arm as she stood mutely, trying to recover from the power of that kiss.

He pulled out a small figurine, the size of his palm. A horse head, carved from the vertical lines of cedar.

Mara's chest hammered as she took the piece and turned it in her hands. Mane rippled over a strong arched neck. Wide-set eyes were centered in the petite, dished face of an Arabian. "It's beautiful."

"It's not much, but it was all I could think of to make."

Her gaze shot to his. "You made it? For me?"

He nodded, ruddiness tinging his cheeks. His eyes roamed her face.

Emotion welled in Mara's chest, then rose into her throat so she couldn't speak. It spilled over in her eyes before she could finally swallow it down.

"Thank you," she whispered. She blinked to clear her vision, wanting to see everything that shone in his amazing eyes. The look that melted her defenses. Mara reached a hand behind his neck, and pulled him down to say thank you.

Josiah sliced the chicken in chunks with a long butcher knife. Tomorrow was New Year's Day, and he'd be on another ride, so the Reid family had offered to celebrate a day early. He hated holidays those first few years he was on his own, then after he took over the kitchen at the John Wesley Hotel, they'd just made more work for him. But here, with Mara and her brothers, he'd caught a glimpse of why people liked them so much. When you had someone to celebrate with, the day could be more than just something to get through.

The door squeaked open, and Mara's head poked inside as she kicked snow off her boots on the step. "Snow's still coming down out there. Getting thicker, I think." She unbuttoned her coat and shook it off, white stuff floating all around her.

"I've got fresh coffee ready. Are your brothers coming?"

"Ezra's right behind me. Zechariah's forking down more hay first." Mara washed her hands at the basin, then stepped into the kitchen area. "What should I do?"

Just looking at her bright eyes and full lips made something tighten in his chest. "Do you want to finish the eggnog?" Last night, he'd shown her how to prep the egg yolks with warm milk. Tucked in the cold storeroom, they'd left the mixture to chill and the flavors to blend. Now it was time to complete the chef-d'oeuvre—the masterpiece.

Mara retrieved the milk mixture and the egg whites and placed them on the counter.

"Need to whip the egg whites until they turn into foam. When you get close, we'll pour in another quarter cup of sugar."

Mara took the spoon and followed his directions, her long braid rocking as her body swayed with the motion of her stirring. It was so nice that she didn't wear it like the flat styles that were popular in the East—parted down the center and plastered flat into a bun. Mara's style was graceful and unpretentious, a reflection of the woman herself.

He forced himself to turn back to his work, and scooped the cubed chicken into a bowl, then added cream and the other ingredients for chicken salad. The sounds of industry blended with comfortable silence as they worked.

"Are these the dishes you made on New Year's Day at the hotel?" Mara's soft voice barely disrupted the quiet.

"Some. Can't get ingredients for the rest out here."

"What were the others?"

"Baked turkey, oysters, venison, glazed fruit, ice cream, and macaroon pyramids."

"Gracious." A few moments of silence settled. Then, "What are macaroon pyramids?"

Josiah bit back a smile. "The best cookie you've ever tasted. They're made of coconut, with sugar, milk, and eggs. You mix it all together and bake them, and the finished cookie is so much better than any pie or cake." He could just about taste them. "Too bad we can't get our hands on some coconut."

She raised her brows. "Too bad."

Boots sounded on the step outside the door, bringing Josiah back to his work. Ezra stepped in first, telling about something one of the horses had done as Zeche followed behind him.

The brothers settled in chairs around the table and Mara motioned for Josiah to take his own. He wavered as she poured coffee in each of the mugs. He was so used to being the one up and about while others ate. And it still didn't feel right to sit while she worked.

Mara finally took the decision from him when she set the coffee pot on the warming surface of the stove and settled into her seat. She gave him a pointed look and gestured toward his chair.

He sat.

The banter flowed freely during the meal, with topics ranging from the buffalo Zechariah saw when he checked traps by the river, to the need to purchase another broodmare this spring. He'd never seen the type of camaraderie that linked the three siblings together, and they pulled him into the mix as if he'd always been part of the family. But he wasn't.

Still, this was the closest he'd ever come to filling that void in his chest. The loneliness that yawned like a chasm sometimes.

Josiah had finished less than half the food on his plate when a long whistle pierced the air. He paused mid-chew, his heart sinking to his toes. All talk in the room ceased, as if they couldn't quite believe what they'd heard.

Finally, Ezra pushed to his feet and sent an empathetic look to Josiah. "Your mare's ready. I'll get her from the barn."

It took every ounce of willpower he possessed to force himself to stand.

Mara rose too. "I'll help."

He tried to summon a smile for her, but couldn't find one. For the first time in fifteen years, he'd been part of a family. But that single whistle had jolted him from the dream, bringing a hard reminder of reality. This wasn't his family. And he had a job to do.

The blast of cold snow that met him outside the cabin door reinforced the truth with a vengeance. The wind had strengthened and the snow fell thick. None of them spoke while Ezra retrieved the pre-saddled horse from the barn. Zeche tightened the cinch, then stepped forward to take the incoming rider's horse as he vaulted to the ground.

Josiah turned to accept the food pack from Mara, and met her gaze through the white flurries. Their hands brushed in the transfer, and she gave his fingers a gentle squeeze. He fought the urge to bend down and kiss her. A sweet parting. A promise to return.

But she must have seen the sentiments in his eyes, for her own gaze returned a *Thank you*. He held her focus as long as he could. And then he had to turn away, mount his horse, and ride off through the blowing snow.

Mara scrubbed the big pot with a rough cloth, expelling her frustration with every stroke. Why did Josiah have to leave right in the middle of their meal? The day had been magical, cooking with him, and then enjoying the dinner with him and her family—Josiah just the same as any of them.

Only he wasn't the same. He was the man she'd been searching for. She could see that now. Not just the way his looks took her breath, but the way he made her feel. His kindness touched all his actions, from the way he wouldn't sit at meal times until she did, to the way he worked side by side cleaning stalls with Ezra. She'd thought he was quiet and aloof those first few days. But the moment he stepped into their little kitchen, he came alive in his element. How could she not love that…at least a little?

Not to mention that kiss. Her lips heated as if he'd touched them again. He hadn't done it again since that day last week, but her body remembered every sensation.

Zechariah's baritone drifted from the other side of the room as he read the Bible aloud to Davy, the young Express rider who'd handed off the mail pack to Josiah. The orphan boy seemed to lap up any attention they gave him.

Mara's conscience pricked. She should work harder to keep her focus on the Lord, not daydream about Josiah or let frustration take over her thoughts—especially when the culprit was outside her control. *Sorry, Lord.* Maybe counting her blessings would help. She was surrounded by a close family and animals. She had a warm house on this bitter snowy day, unlike Josiah who was out riding in this mess. She

94

was ever so thankful God had brought Josiah to them. She was thankful for Rose, and how well the mare had turned—

The front door crashed open, and Mara whirled to face it. Ezra stood panting in the doorway.

"Josiah's horse…" He paused to catch his breath.

Mara's stomach jumped into her throat. She dropped the pot and was at her brother's side within a heartbeat. "What?"

"…came back limping. Without him."

Chapter Nine

*M*ara clutched her brother's arm. "Where's Josiah?"

Ezra shook his head, breathing hard. "Don't know. The horse came back with the mochila and both front knees pretty skint up."

Mara grabbed her coat and reached for the door, but Ezra caught her arm before she stepped outside.

"I'm going out to search for him." He turned toward Zeche and Davy who were out of their chairs now. "Better get ready to take the mail, Davy."

Mara jerked her arm from her brother's grasp. "I'm going out, too."

"Mara." Zeche's sharp tone stopped her cold. Too many years of stoic obedience were ingrained in her to disregard the obvious command in his voice. "You're not going out. I'll go with Ezra and we'll find him. Stay here in case Josiah comes back while we're gone."

But Zeche didn't care about Josiah the way she did. What if they didn't find him on the trail and gave up? If Josiah was out there in the blizzard needing help, she couldn't sit here and do nothing. She set her chin. "I'm going. Josiah needs me."

He met her gaze, and seemed to realize she wasn't backing down. His own jaw tightened, but he nodded. "Ezra can stay here then."

Mara sprang into action. She slipped into her coat, then grabbed blankets from the trunk by the loft's ladder. They might be out looking for a while, so she wrapped some buffalo roast and biscuits in a cloth.

"Take drinking water, too." Ezra's voice sounded over her shoulder.

There was plenty of snow out to drink, but she obeyed anyway, filling a canteen from the clean basin.

With her hands full, Mara strode to the door, plucking her cap and gloves from a peg on the wall as she exited. The frigid wind slapped her face as she sprinted to the barn. Once inside the structure, she found Zeche tightening her saddle's cinch around Rose. She secured the supplies onto their saddles, then took the mare's reins.

Ezra opened the barn door as they prepared to exit. "Davy's off now. It's nasty out there, so you two be careful." His mouth pressed into a grim line and twin grooves formed between his brows.

"Will do," Zeche said, as he mounted.

One look at Ezra's face, and Mara reached forward to kiss his cheek before climbing astride her own horse. "Don't worry." The knot in her stomach pulled tighter. "But pray for Josiah."

He didn't answer as they rode off.

Zeche kept to a steady trot, but Mara's nerves craved a faster pace. Josiah probably wasn't in the open area so close to the house. She scanned the hills barely visible through the falling snow. He was out there somewhere.

The snow fell thick, and wind swirled it around them like a heavy fog. It didn't howl yet, but hampered their vision enough that they could only see a few feet around. Mara kept her mare just behind Zeche's bay. If they were separated, sound would be their only way to reconnect.

"Are you sure we're on the Express trail?" she called through the wind.

"Pretty sure. Once we get to the hills it'll be easier to tell."

Dear God, please guide us. Keep Josiah safe.

"Josiah!" Mara called through the snowstorm.

No answer except the buffeting of the wind.

"Keep calling." Zechariah's voice barely reached her as the wind whipped it away.

And so she did. While Zeche focused on the limited area visible around them, Mara screamed Josiah's name until her throat burned and her voice strangled like a baby goat. Tears leaked from her eyes, not quite freezing before they were absorbed into the scarf wrapped around her chin and neck.

They climbed the rocky hills, keeping to the dip in the snow that signaled a trail. Zeche slowed to a walk, and they scanned the ground on both sides. Her muscles ached in the frigid air, but at least her coat kept her mostly dry. Had Josiah found a way to stay dry too, or was he freezing to death in this icy snow?

"Josiah!" *God, please keep him alive. Let him be all right.* Her mind repeated the prayer like a mantra.

The rocks rose up on either side as they entered a ravine. "Josiah!" Her voice would have echoed if it weren't for the snow still whipping around them.

A muffled noise sounded to their right, and her eyes scanned the area. "Wait," she yelled to her brother, then turned Rose toward a scattering of rocks at the base of the cliff.

"Josiah!" she called.

The noise came again. Definitely a male voice, but she couldn't make out the words. Mara jumped from her horse and lunged through snow taller than her knees.

Something dark was partially buried in the white powder between two rocks. As she came closer, the dark mound formed a face and shoulders. Mara's heart leaped at the same time dread pressed her chest.

She dropped to her knees and scooped snow away from the face. Josiah.

His eyes were closed, but his chest rose and fell—barely. He released a moan that gripped Mara's heart and infused a greater urgency into her movements as she fought to uncover him. She shucked her gloves and touched his face. His skin was cold. So cold. And clammy. Or maybe that was dampness from the snow.

Zechariah appeared beside her and laid two fingers on Josiah's neck. Mara glanced at the worry lines on her brother's face as he stared at the injured man.

"His pulse is racing."

"That means he's alive." That had to be good, right?

The lines on Zeche's forehead deepened. "It's too fast. And weak. We've got to get him warm."

Zechariah left her side—probably to get blankets—while Mara finished uncovering Josiah's legs. She examined the length of him. His legs and arms were all straight, no funny angles. She picked up his right hand and rubbed it furiously between both of hers. His fingers were almost as cold as the snow.

She reached for his left hand to warm it the same way, but stopped when Josiah moaned, his eyes rolling back in his head. Carefully, lowering his hand to his side, she studied the arm. Was it broken? Or maybe his reaction was pain from frostbite. She couldn't see much through his coat, but maybe that was a bump that raised his jacket at the top of his shoulder. When she touched the spot, Josiah moaned again, rolling his head from side to side. She jerked her hand back.

His eyes fluttered open. He didn't look at her—didn't seem to focus on anything—but the round centers were a cloudy gray that fed the panic in Mara's chest.

"Josiah." She touched his cheek. Almost no heat left in his skin.

He still didn't look at her, just maintained that cloudy lack of focus.

"Josiah, can you hear me?"

Zechariah appeared again with the blankets. "Let's get him wrapped in these."

"Something's wrong with his shoulder." She pointed at the lump. "He can't stand for me to touch it. And he doesn't seem to hear me."

Josiah's eyes drifted toward them, as if to prove her wrong. But still his pupils were a cloudy swirl of various shades of gray. Not the sharp focus they usually exuded.

"His body might be shutting down. We've got to get him warm." Zechariah handed her a blanket, which Mara spread over Josiah, then wrapped it around his good shoulder, rubbing briskly as she did so. They had to get his blood moving again.

Her brother leaned close to Josiah's face. "Josiah, can you hear me?" With a hand on either side of Josiah's jaw, Zeche turned the injured man so Josiah had to look him in the eyes.

But Josiah still didn't focus. His vision wandered down to Zeche's chin, up to his forehead. Had he lost his hearing?

Or his awareness altogether? Mara fought down her fears before they closed in on her.

Josiah moaned again, and Zechariah released him, then sat back on his heels. "I'm gonna sit him up, and I need you to wrap a blanket tight around his shoulders so his arm won't move. That'll help get him warm, too. It'll hurt and he might pass out, but I'm not sure we want that. He needs to stay awake if he can."

As Zechariah lifted, Mara wrapped quickly. She forced her panic aside and kept her eyes focused on the cloth in her hands as she bound Josiah's arm to his body.

A loud guttural scream pierced the air, then Josiah's body went limp in her brother's hands. Emotion burned in her chest, and she glanced at Josiah's face. It was almost as white as the snow around him, except for a bluish tint around his mouth. His eyes closed and his head lolled back. *God, help him. Please.*

Zeche scooted around to Josiah's side, then gathered him into his arms. With a grunt, Zeche stumbled to his feet. "Get on your horse. I'll hand him up to you."

Mara scrambled to obey and settled herself behind the saddle. Zeche placed Josiah in the seat and leaned him back against her. "Can you hold him? He's still out cold, but maybe we can keep him steady while I switch places with you."

"I've got him. Let's go." Mara wrapped her arms around Josiah, gripping the saddle horn with her left hand. He slumped against her, and she propped his body against her left shoulder so she could see around him and use her right hand to guide Rose.

She started off the way they'd come. Zeche mounted and maneuvered his horse into the lead. "Do you think he can handle a trot?" he yelled back to Mara.

"I think so. But go easy."

As Rose moved into a jog, Mara shifted the reins into her left hand so she could hold Josiah still with her right. The mare's normally weightless trot was bouncy as she lifted her legs high to clear the snow.

Josiah moaned, a sound that tore at Mara's heart.

"I'm sorry, love. We'll get you there as soon as we can."

The ride seemed to last an eternity, and Mara finally gave up looking for the Rocky Ridge buildings through the blowing snow. Her focus narrowed to the heels of Zeche's horse as she used all her strength to hold the man in her arms. His body sagged like he was still unconscious, but every so often a moan would slip out. She cradled him carefully, trying to infuse as much of her warmth as she could while not jarring his shoulder.

Finally, Zechariah called out through the wind, and another male voice answered. Ezra appeared at her side, then Zeche beside him as they lowered Josiah to the ground.

"Careful of his shoulder." Without Josiah's bulk in front of her, the icy wind whipped at her chest.

She slid to the ground and plunged through the snow to get ahead of her brothers. Pushing the cabin door wide, she strode toward the chest and grabbed the last two blankets.

"Lay him by the fire. We have to get him warm." She spread the blankets out and the boys settled Josiah into them.

He groaned, his eyes still the murky, unfocused gray. They looked almost like those of a blind man that had come through on the stage a few months ago. *God, please don't let him lose his sight.*

Mara ran to her room to pull more blankets from her bed, then carried them in a pile back to Josiah. Zeche settled a couple of hot rocks under the quilts and began rubbing Josiah's toes. Ezra was at his head, examining and asking questions as he poked. Her younger brother was the unofficial doctor in the family. His love of books had surfaced early, and he'd almost memorized both of Pa's medical books: Dr. Imray's *A Popular Cyclopedia of Modern Domestic Medicine* and *Dr. Buchan's Domestic Medicine.*

"Does it hurt here?" Ezra asked, his hand behind Josiah's ear.

A long groan was his only response. Josiah's eyes squeezed tight.

"Do we have any willow bark?" Ezra glanced at Mara.

"I think so. I'll make tea."

"Put extra water on to heat. I'll need it for his frostbite. Then go in your room while we get him out of these wet clothes."

Mara did as commanded, taking the opportunity in her chamber to change out of her own wet dress. They needed to get the horses settled, too.

She stepped back to her door and cracked it. "Can I come out?" It felt crazy to be locked inside her room when there was so much to do for Josiah.

"Yes."

As she stepped toward the cook stove to finish the tea, she glanced at the pallet on the floor where Ezra bent over their patient. Josiah lay buried in blankets, save for a patch of bare skin at his injured shoulder.

Ezra peered at the spot, and a groan from Josiah forced her to turn away, back to her work. He needed this tea. If there was any way she could take this pain on herself, she would have already done it.

"Can you bring some hot, wet rags, Mara?" Ezra broke into her thoughts, and she grabbed two small towels to get them warming.

Her brother wrapped the damp cloths around Josiah's hands and toes, while Mara strained dry willow bark leaves in a cup of hot water. Then Ezra held up Josiah's head while she spooned tea into his mouth. Josiah kept his eyes closed, but he swallowed the liquid. At least he was conscious now. Somewhat.

After about ten sips, he sputtered. His sputtering turned to coughs that wracked his body. The convulsions shook his shoulders and abdomen, but finally died into a long moan. He sank back against the pillow, his eyes pinching shut as his chest heaved.

"Easy now." Mara stroked his forehead, crooning like she would to a new foal. "This tea'll help you feel better."

After a few moments, his breathing finally slowed.

"Let's try to drink a little more." Mara nodded at Ezra, who raised Josiah's head again. She was able to get most of the brew into him before Josiah moaned again and fell back against the pillow.

"No." His voice came out in a rasp. It was the first time he'd spoken more than a moan.

"I need to wrap his shoulder now." Ezra reached for a long bandage. "Can you help me?"

Mara nodded, and eased her arms under Josiah's upper body while Ezra worked the fabric into place. Josiah's skin was solid to her touch, and the ropy muscles contoured in a way that made her fight the urge to lean down and press a kiss to his shoulder.

"Let me put the bone in place before we wrap it tight."

Mara leaned back as Ezra bent low over Josiah, fitting his hands around the bone between his neck and shoulder.

Josiah's face twisted, and he cried out. She jerked her head away, steeling herself from the sight. She couldn't watch the pain torment his features without jerking her brother away from the man.

After that awful cry, the only sound left in the room was Josiah's haggard breathing, as though breath was the only thing that would save him now.

She braved a glance at his face, drained of most of his color. Reaching out, she brushed a hand over his forehead, fingering back the hair that tangled there in damp curls. She let her hand trail down his cheek. It might have been her imagination, but it felt like he leaned into her touch the slightest bit. She kept her hand there, stroking the pad of her thumb back and forth over his cheekbone. The love that overflowed in her chest for this man was almost as painful as her fear for him. She would stay by his side as long as it took to make him well. And then, Lord willing, she'd have the chance to remain there forever.

"That's as good as I can make it. He's got a nasty knot on his head and his shoulder's broken. Frostbite in his fingers and toes, but I'm not sure if he'll lose 'em yet. He needs to rest now."

Ezra's forehead wrinkled as he watched Josiah's sleeping form. "I think he'll live. As long as he doesn't get lung fever. And he might lose some toes."

"What about his…eyes?" His cloudy, unfocused look had lit a flame of fear in her. Especially when their color was normally such a vibrant blue.

"I can't tell for sure. I've never read about anyone going blind from cold, but I guess it could happen. Could be from the shock of it all. Maybe temporary. We'll have to see how he is in the morning."

Chapter Ten

E verything hurt. Josiah kept his eyes closed while he took stock of his body. A sharp throbbing radiated from his left shoulder. Prickly tingles ran through his fingers like hundreds of ants biting over and over. And his head... Was it an option to just cut it off and be done? His skull threatened to explode inside his skin.

A groan sounded from somewhere nearby. His eyes shot open, just as his mind told him the groan had uttered from his own lips. The light was blinding, and his stomach roiled, sending a bitter taste up into his throat. Was he going to lose what little was left in his stomach?

He groaned again and tried to roll away from the light. His body exploded into a flashing pain and light that knocked him on his back again. He pinched his eyes against the agony in his head and shoulders. *God, what is this?*

Something rustled near his feet, but he didn't have the strength to open his eyes again. Probably, the stable boy come to tell him he'd overslept. Or maybe Mr. Chambers himself, the hotel owner. He didn't care anymore. Nothing could be as bad as the pain pounding his body into a thousand pieces.

Something soft and cool touched his forehead, like a pool of cold water in the middle of a burning house. For a moment, he relished it, not caring whose gentle hand it was, or why it was there. Something wet touched his lips, and he realized how parched they were, like they'd been in the boiling Savannah sun for days with no relief.

He forced his eyes open a slit to find a woman hovering over him. An angel? Her caramel brown hair fell around her shoulders, and firelight reflected concern in her wide brown eyes.

His mouth didn't want to move, but he forced it to form a word. His tongue was three sizes too big, and he had to push through the cotton feel. "Who...I?"

Twin lines formed between her beautiful brows. "Who are you?"

He bit back frustration, allowing his eyes to close. He knew who *he* was. At least, he thought he did. He fought through the cobwebs in his mind. He was a cook. At a restaurant in Savannah.

"You're Josiah English." The woman's voice was soft, sweet.

That's right. Josiah.

"And you're a rider for the Pony Express along the Sweetwater River."

Josiah's eyelids rose without as much effort this time. "What?" He pushed through the stickiness around his tongue. What was she talking about? "I'm a...cook." There. He'd got out enough words to set her straight. But it was wearing him out. His mind wasn't focusing again, and breathing took most of his effort.

"Do you think you can drink some tea if I spoon it into your mouth?"

Tea. Something wet would feel so good. But that would take too much energy. He couldn't push through the agony to do anything more.

"It will help your pain. And let you sleep better."

That sounded wonderful. Maybe he could drink just a little. He pushed open his lips, and felt a cool wetness pour into the desert in his mouth. So much work to swallow. But another sip of the liquid dripped between his lips, bringing with it a luxury he'd not experienced in a month of Fridays. It was a little easier to make his throat work this time. Over and over. Sweet moisture, and then the effort of swallowing.

"I think that's enough for now."

The soft hand on his brow again, fingering his hair, wiping a little of the pain away.

"Sleep. You'll feel better when you wake up."

110

Mara curled her legs tighter underneath herself in the rocking chair, readjusting the Bible in her lap. She stared again at the words in I Kings that talked about the extravagant temple Solomon built for the Lord. It really did sound like a beautiful structure, but her gaze kept drifting back to the sleeping form on the floor in front of her.

Had he lost his memory? Maybe not completely. He seemed to think he was still in Savannah. A cook. He seemed so confused, and every word was a struggle for him. *Lord, please let him remember when he wakes again.*

Ezra'd said he had a large bump on his head. Would that make him forget only part of his life? The part that included her? The vise in her chest twisted.

Mara glanced toward the single window in the cabin. The sky had lightened. She closed the Bible, rose, and placed the book in her chair. The men would be up soon, and would expect something warm on the table when they came in from the barn chores.

She placed a couple of dry logs on the white coals in the cook stove, then poured fresh grounds and water in the coffee pot.

Footsteps thumped and Mara looked up to see Ezra staring down at Josiah's sleeping body. Her brother's hair lay flat in the back, but stood straight up at his cowlick. He turned to look at her. "How's he doing?" He spoke in a loud whisper.

Mara motioned him over so she could speak without waking Josiah. "He woke one time a few hours ago. He seemed to be in a lot of pain, but did say a few words." As she told her younger brother about their short interchange, his brows knit together.

"Sounds like short term memory loss." He scratched the side of his jaw. "Might remember more once his body gets over the trauma. I'll read up on it and see if there's anything else we can do."

"So we just wait?" Desperation tinged her voice. There had to be more. She couldn't sit by and watch while Josiah struggled through so much torture. What if he never got his memory back? Could he still do his job? Would he still care about her? She pushed the selfish thought aside.

"We take care of him. Make him comfortable. And let his body heal itself." Ezra's tone was patient but firm, like Zeche's voice when he reminded her of something he'd already said at least once.

Mara nodded, looking back at Josiah's form beneath the mound of blankets.

"I'll let you know if I find anything else we can do for him." Ezra moved past her to pull his coat from the peg. "I'm headed to milk Hannah now."

Mara turned back to the kitchen and slid the frying pan to the hot surface of the cook stove, then dumped a glob of congealed grease into the pan. She cut strips of buffalo meat from the large roast, and laid them in the oily mixture to fry. Even though the savory aroma of frying meat wafted through the air, it was hard to summon any enthusiasm for the food while Josiah lay motionless across the room. The kitchen was his domain. The place where he came alive.

After slicing several pieces of bread, she scooped the fried meat from the pan and poured in a cup of flour for the gravy. Then a little milk.

Her brothers tromped back in soon after she had the table set, and Mara heaped their plates high. The mood in the room was somber, and none of them spoke while they settled around the table. It probably had as much to do with their concern for Josiah's condition, as the need to be quiet so he could sleep.

Ezra spoke a solemn grace over the food, adding a request for God's special blessing on their friend. Right before his "Amen," a stirring sounded from Josiah's blankets. He groaned, and Mara's gaze flickered from the heap of quilts over to Ezra's face. Should she go offer him more tea? Or water? Or leave him alone to rest?

They all waited as if time were suspended, to see if Josiah would go back to sleep. No other sounds drifted from the blankets. Zeche was the first to lift his fork and stab a strip of meat, and Ezra soon followed his example.

As her younger brother raised a bite to his mouth, his gaze found Mara's. "He needs broth soon."

She nodded. She should have thought of that herself. The poor man couldn't heal on tea alone, much less regain his strength.

Ezra looked to their older brother. "The next time he wakes up, we need to move him out of this room. He'll not get the rest he needs when we're wakin' him up all day."

Zeche nodded, then turned to Mara. "Do you mind if he takes your room for a few nights? It's close enough to the fire, and easier than dragging him up to the loft."

An image appeared in her mind of her brothers raising Josiah up to the loft with ropes, just like the lame man's friends in the Bible who lowered their companion through the roof so Jesus could heal his legs. She blinked it away, but the crazy thought almost relaxed the knot in her stomach. "Of course."

Josiah was restless through the remainder of breakfast, so they moved him as soon as they finished eating. The knot in her stomach tightened at the thought of them picking up his battered body and causing more pain. But her brothers must have read her mind. They picked up his blanket at the four corners, and carried him like he lay on an Indian travois. He stirred when they had him in the air, but never opened his eyes.

As soon as Josiah had settled and the men went outside to start the day's work, Mara plucked and cleaned a chicken, then simmered it for broth. Every time she checked on Josiah, his breathing was heavy and regular. Good. He needed the sleep.

After lunch, when Mara stuck her head in the doorway of her room—rather, Josiah's room—his breathing was light, and his chest barely lifted the covers.

Her stomach churned as she crept inside. But when his eyes fluttered open, the relief nearly stole her strength. It wasn't hard to infuse a smile in her voice. "Hi, there."

One corner of his mouth tipped, but the pain lines around his eyes kept the look from being called a grin. "Hi."

"How're you feeling?" But that was a silly question. Of course he felt awful, and would do better not to dwell on it. What she really wanted to say was, *Do you know who I am?* Or, *Do you know who you are?*

"Rough." His voice matched the word, as if he were dragging the sound over rocks to get it out of his mouth.

"I can imagine. I have broth ready, let me get it." She didn't wait for him to answer, but slipped from the room and out to the kitchen. Scooping a mug of the liquid, she grabbed a spoon and hurried back. She paused before entering the room and inhaled a steadying breath. Josiah needed a peaceful atmosphere to recover well.

She flashed him a smile as she settled in the chair beside the bed. "Are you hungry?"

He started to nod, but stopped with a flinch. Pain filled his eyes. "What happened?"

Mara spooned broth into his mouth, watching his Adam's apple bob as the liquid moved down his throat. He still didn't wear a shirt, but the quilt was pulled up so she could just see the top of the bandage that wrapped his shoulder. She averted her eyes to the cup, refilled the spoon, and brought it back to Josiah's mouth.

"You were riding your Pony Express route in a heavy snow. I think the horse must have slipped. It came back limping, and we finally found you half buried in snow."

He winced. "Feels like I was beat up."

"Ezra says your shoulder is broken. He's not sure if you'll lose any toes from frostbite, and you've got a nasty knot behind your left ear. That's probably why you're having trouble remembering."

His forehead pinched, as she raised another spoonful to his mouth. His lips were rosy and a little swollen. Were they chapped? She should bring some salve.

Her gaze drifted upward and collided with his. His eyes were a smoky gray now, and held a tiny hint of the sharp focus he always had, not the cloudy lack of color from last night.

His steady intensity made her stomach do a little flutter, and she dropped her focus back to the spoon as she refilled it. When she braved a glance again, his eyes still watched her. She studied the spoon as she brought it to his mouth, but the feel of his gaze stayed with her.

"You're beautiful."

Her focus shot to his face.

A light filtered through his eyes, and a dimple touched his right cheek. "Please tell me I know you."

Heat flared into Mara's face, but cooled as the meaning of his words settled in.

He didn't remember her.

She swallowed as she dipped the spoon in the broth, biting back the burn that threatened her eyes. Forcing her voice to stay steady, she answered, "Yes. I'm Mara. You're a Pony Express rider, and you've been riding out of our home station for about a month now."

His forehead puckered. "When did I leave Savannah?"

"Right before you came here, I think." Mara kept the spoon moving between the cup and his lips. "You worked in a hotel there. You haven't said much about it, though."

Josiah squinted for a moment, his focus somewhere other than the small bed chamber. "Oh."

"You were planning to start your own ranch. I think that's why you joined the Express."

"And I ride horses?" There was a hint of curiosity in his tone. Nothing like the fear racing through her own chest. But Ezra said his memory might come back, right?

She forced a bright tone in her voice. "Every Monday and Friday."

His eyes moved to her face. "I rode with you. I remember we saw Indians."

Mara met his gaze for a quick moment and sank into the relief flooding her chest. He remembered her. Oh, thanks be to God.

She spooned the last bit of broth into his mouth. "Would you like more?" She studied his face. Deep shadows had settled under his eyes. From pain or exhaustion? Probably both.

"No. Thanks."

Mara stood and pulled the blankets to his chin. Covered up like that, he looked so frail. "Are you warm enough?"

His eyes drifted closed. "Yes."

Mara swallowed the lump clogging her throat and leaned down to press a kiss to his forehead. "Rest, then."

Chapter Eleven

Josiah opened his eyes to a wash of sunlight through the window. A chill permeated the air, so he snuggled deeper under the covers, ignoring the drum of pain that thumped in the back of his head. His eyes scanned the room. Where was he? A chair sat close to the bed, with a small table next to it. A dresser stood against the wall, and in the corner was a woman's dressing table.

A woman's?

He sat up, but gasped as a knife of pain radiated from his left shoulder. He cradled his left arm, and found it wrapped against his body. What in the state of Virginia had happened to him?

He needed to get out of this bedroom, whoever it belonged to. He glanced down at the quilts wrapped around his waist. A pink flowery fabric stared up at him. Was he sleeping in a woman's bed, too? Heat flamed up his neck.

Clenching his teeth against the pain, Josiah placed his feet on the floor and pushed himself up. Everything wobbled. Flashes of light and pain shot through his head, then the room started to spin. His head hit the blankets, sending a bullet of pain through his skull that knocked his breath away.

He lay there for several long moments. Breathing in. Then out. He had to make sense of where he was. One of the hotel rooms? No, that wasn't right. He rode horses now. For the Pony Express. So why was he in a woman's bed chamber?

He opened his eyes again. Took in the rough-cut wood of the walls. A woman's face flashed through his mind. Mara. Was this her bedroom? He'd been hurt. A likely deduction based on the pain radiating through him.

Another sensation pricked through the layers of hurt, needling his awareness. He'd have to find the privy soon. He eased himself up to a sitting position again, and lowered his feet to the floor. When they touched the hard surface, needles started through his toes, turning into a fiery burn. His feet were wrapped in strips of cloth, and he almost doubled over with the pain of them. He might have, if it weren't for another fire still burning in his shoulder.

After a few moments, the pain in his feet had settled to a throb and the room's spinning finally slowed. With both hands on the bedpost, he eased up to a standing position. He closed his eyes against the whirling as it started up again. *Breathe.*

When he opened them again, his vision was a little fuzzy, but not enough to knock him down this time. Taking careful steps, he moved from the bedpost to the door, then through the threshold into the main room. This area looked more familiar, with memories tugging at his mind. Each step was a challenge, but he shuffled from one object to another, finally reaching the front door. He eased it open, until a blast of cold wind almost jerked the wood from his hands.

Josiah tightened his grip on the door, then stepped outside, and pulled it closed behind him. Icy air found the exposed skin around his abdomen. He should have grabbed a coat, but with the bandage around his shoulders and arm, he hadn't realized he was shirtless. No matter. Just a quick trip to the privy and he'd go back to bed. The pain in his body had spread so far he couldn't tell what hurt and what didn't.

He turned to descend the single step—and froze.

Indians milled around the yard of the Express station, looking for all the world like they'd taken over the place. Adrenaline sped through his veins as he reached for the door handle to scoot back inside. Where was his gun? As he turned, he glimpsed a white man speaking to a cluster of the redskins. Something made him pause mid-stride. The man looked familiar. Ezra? The name seemed to fit with the memory of him.

Did Ezra need help? He was practically surrounded by the Indians.

A movement in front of one of the buildings caught his eye. Three more Indians spilled from the doorway, then a white man and a woman.

Mara.

A flood of protectiveness sluiced through him, and he stumbled down the step before he could stop to think. But his ankle didn't hold his weight, and the buckling joint took him down to his knees.

Pain exploded in his shoulder, pulsing up to his head and throughout the rest of him. He clutched his skull, not daring to breathe as he struggled to maintain consciousness. Finally, the agony lessened the tiniest bit and he struggled to draw in steady breaths as he gathered his wits again.

Mara still stood with the Indians, but she was flanked by a white man on either side. Ezra had moved to her side, and the other man was someone else it seemed he should know. He brought his focus back to Mara. She didn't look afraid. In fact, she was speaking to one of the Indians, gesturing in wide strokes as she talked.

He would be of no good to her in his puny condition. And neither she nor the men at her side looked like they were concerned for her safety. He'd be better off going back in to get his gun.

His body took that opportunity to remind him of the reason he'd come outside in the first place. Maybe he'd be a little stronger after he took care of personal business. Moving back to the cabin wall, he propped a hand against it as he shuffled around the building to the privy.

A few minutes later, his body's complaints had lessened, and he was even able to walk faster without dropping to his knees. He followed the side of the cabin again, and almost reached the corner, when an Indian brave stepped out—halting in front of him.

Josiah froze, then straightened to his full height as the two stared at each other. The brave looked younger, maybe eighteen or nineteen, with smooth skin on his face and a hint of broadening shoulders filling out the leather tunic he wore.

Josiah's good hand went to his waistband, but there was no pistol there. Nothing. He straightened a little more. If this Indian intended a fight, he'd give it all he had.

The man made a series of sounds—words apparently, but nothing Josiah could begin to understand. Then the Indian pointed to Josiah's bandaged shoulder. Was he pointing out his weakness? He might be puny right now, but he'd still give this young buck a run for his money. He hoped, anyway. Or he'd die trying.

Then a soft, female voice drifted from behind him.

Mara.

Josiah's nerves tightened. He had to keep her away from this danger. "Stay back." He growled the words, the effort almost using up all his breath.

She answered, but her words didn't register. Finally, he realized she must be speaking the Indian's language, the same kinds of high-low sounds as the brave had.

The man answered, never taking his gaze from Josiah. The look in his eyes changed, though. They no longer challenged or goaded, but seemed to hold a hint of respect. Or maybe he was reading them wrong.

Mara stepped closer, coming up beside Josiah on his right. He reached out to grab her arm. He meant it to stop her, but the shift in his weight put him off balance and he found himself clutching tighter just to stay upright. Some protector he was.

She spoke again to the Indian, as if Josiah weren't gripping her arm to keep himself on his feet. The pounding in his head was threatening to take over his mental capacity now, and he squinted against it, focusing again on the Indian.

The brave looked at Mara with a twitch in his cheek. Almost like…a grin? Then he turned the same look on Josiah, although maybe a bit of derision mixed in. He was getting the feeling he'd been left out of an inside joke. Not fun…this being the outsider.

The brave spoke once more, then turned and strode away.

Josiah gripped Mara's arm harder. "What…was that?" It was hard enough to breathe through the pain, much less speak, but he needed an answer.

She gave a demure smile, filled with nothing but sweet innocence. "He asked who you were."

"And…you told him…?"

"I told him your name, but he gave you a new one."

He tried to raise his brows at her. "What?"

"He called you Wounded Arm."

He squinted, clenching his jaw against the agony pulsing through his body. "That's why you laughed?" The world spun again, and Josiah released her arm to ease back against the cabin wall. He would not faint out here in front of everyone. In front of her.

Mara stepped forward and slipped herself under his good arm. He let her, turning as they shuffled around toward the front.

"No, silly. I told him you'd earned a better name. Your new name will be Brave Rider."

Josiah blinked to clear the spinning, then turned to eye her. "What?"

"You heard me. From this day forward, you'll be known among the Cheyenne and the Reid family as Brave Rider. Now let's get you inside."

Mara hung her coat on the peg and moved toward the wash basin in the kitchen. She frowned at the image in the mirror over the basin. Her hair was a mess. And she really should do something different than a simple braid all the time. Josiah had grown up around all those city women with fancy hairstyles and gowns. He had to think she was the plainest woman he'd ever met. She brushed down the fly-away hairs on top, then dried her hands on the cloth.

Now to start the bread.

A shuffle across the room grabbed her attention. Josiah. Four days had passed since his accident, and he was moving so much better. Seemed to be remembering most things, too. He wore a navy shirt now, and his short hair stuck out in several directions, like the tail feathers on a male turkey. The familiar tightness encircled her chest.

"Wat'cha doin'?" His voice was husky, matching his sleep-ruffled look. He stepped closer, looming over her small five foot, two-inch frame. Wouldn't she love to slide herself under his arm like she'd done when the Indians were here? Of course, she'd been worried about him falling then. Mostly. Now she just wanted to be close to him.

Her conscience pricked. She should be more concerned about his healing than her attraction. Besides, she had baking to do.

She stepped toward the flour bin. "I have a sourdough starter ready to make bread."

Josiah stopped at the edge of the kitchen area. "Mind if I help?"

She eyed him. He'd seemed more like the old Josiah at breakfast, but he still moved slowly. Probably because of the pain in his shoulder. And maybe lingering pain from the frostbite in his toes. Ezra had said it looked like he wouldn't lose any. She brought her focus up to his face. "I guess so. If you'd like to work on the bread, I'll start the meat boiling for stew tonight."

She pulled the bowl of starter from the shelf and placed it on the work counter. When she lifted off the cloth, it released a sour, yeasty odor. She glanced up at him. "You do remember how to make bread, right?" She should know better than to make assumptions about his memory.

His face tipped into that hint of a grin she hadn't seen since before the accident. Just a few extra lines around his eyes alluded to the pain he'd been through—and still carried. "I think so. I'll let you know if I run into trouble." That look still did funny things to her middle.

"Good." Mara turned back to the work counter to slice venison.

With his one good hand, Josiah added flour, sugar, eggs, and a few other ingredients to the yeast mixture, then sunk his large fingers into the dough. She couldn't help but notice the smattering of short, fine hairs across his tanned knuckles. All man, no doubt about it. Even for all his skills in the kitchen. She glanced up at his face, and found his eyes focused on the dough in his fingers. His brow furrowed as he worked.

She pulled her gaze back to her own task and sliced the knife through the fresh deer meat Zeche had brought in that morning.

"My mama used to make sourdough bread. Dozens of loaves at a time." Josiah's words brought her head up. His eyes had taken on a glazed, dreamy quality. "She sold them to the hotel and at the booths down by the wharfs. I used to go along with her, and when Papa came in on the boat, I'd help him unload his catch. Then we'd all three walk home together."

Mara scarcely dared to breathe. "Sounds like a wonderful way to grow up." She'd never heard Josiah talk so much without being prompted. And most definitely not about his past. She wanted to ask him more, but didn't want to break the moment for him.

His Adam's apple bobbed as he gazed at the dough squeezing through his fingers. "It was. Sometimes he'd take me out on the boat with him. But I didn't like to be confined on the little dingy all day, so Mama let me help her bake."

He separated the dough into pan-sized mounds. "Turned out to be a good thing, too. Cooking was how I kept myself alive when I was on my own." His voice trailed away, and silence took over. Did she dare ask more? Need burned in her chest to hear more about his past. It couldn't have been easy, but it was what made this man who he was now. Knowing what he'd been through could only help her love him more. And better.

She inhaled a steadying breath. "How did you lose your parents?"

Silence again. Maybe she'd pushed too far. She braved another glance at his face, but he still watched the dough with the same scrutinizing gaze. At last, he spoke in a quiet voice. "The dinghy they were in capsized in a storm. They'd gone to the mainland to deliver bread. Just a special trip for the two of them. The squall came up out of nowhere. They found the boat right after the storm." His jaw worked. "And my parents washed up a few days later."

"Oh, Josiah." Mara touched his arm, emotion rising in her throat.

He looked at her, sadness swimming in his gray-blue eyes. But he spoke again. "I knew I couldn't make a living on the sea, the way Pa did." His throat worked. "I hated the sea." His voice echoed the first bitterness he'd voiced yet. And why not? The water had stolen his parents. His world.

"So what did you do?" She couldn't help the question. This peek into his life had her heart in her throat.

"I sold our little house on Tybee Island and begged for them to take me on at the hotel. Ended up doing the same baking my mother had, and all the grunt work they could get from me. When their old chef left, I jumped at the chance."

"How old were you then?"

"Sixteen."

"So you cooked until you joined the Express?"

He shook his head, then stopped with a wince. "I cooked until the hotel closed down."

"And then what did you do?" This felt more like the Josiah she was used to, where she had to prod for any details he'd offer.

He shrugged his good shoulder. "Anything. Everything." And something in the way he said those two words told her they encompassed more than she probably wanted to know.

But still. To look at him now, you'd never know he'd overcome such a past. He was a fighter. Someone who made the most of a tough spot, worked hard, and came out on top.

She squeezed his arm where her hand still rested. "You're special. You know that?"

He turned to look at her then, skepticism in his eyes. And maybe even despair. "I'm not much." Then he pulled his arm away from her and pushed the pans of dough to the back of the counter. He spread a cloth over them a little awkwardly.

Her chest burned with the ache of his loneliness. Did he really not know how special he was? How much she loved him? Every part of him. She'd been right. His past had made him the strong man he was today.

"Josiah."

"What?" He picked up the cleaning cloth and wiped the flour into a little pile on the counter.

"Look at me."

He shot her a sideways glance, then stared down at his work on the counter. Stubborn man.

She grabbed his arm and pulled him, and he finally turned to face her.

"Yes?"

Without stopping to think twice, she raised up on tiptoes and slipped her hand behind his neck to pull him down. Their lips met in a soft kiss, his barely recovering from his surprise in time to offer a sweet response. Then she pulled back to look in his eyes. "That's what I think of you, Josiah. And when I said you're special, I meant it."

He raised his hand to her cheek, sliding a finger across her cheekbone as he looked into her eyes. "I'm not the special one." This time, she didn't have to pull him down. He lowered his mouth for a kiss much sweeter than the one she'd initiated. Achingly gentle.

He pulled back, and she started to protest, until the squeak of the door hinge pushed into her mind.

Her heels sank down to land on the floor just as a throat cleared in the background. She dropped her hand and turned to face their intruder, doing her best to wipe the silly grin from her face.

"Ezra."

He looked at her with a little bit of a scowl gathering in his brows.

"Came to see if I had time to ride Jester before dinner. Looks like I might need to stay and help, though."

She gave him a sweet smile. "Sure. You can bring in more firewood."

And as he grumbled his way back out the door, she turned to slice the meat in earnest. If she didn't get a move on, they'd be having a very late supper. She couldn't help but slide a look at the man beside her, though.

His eyes were already settled on her, and he winked.

More than a week later, Josiah ambled through the barn, fists in his pockets. This wandering around the house with nothing to do drove him crazy. He'd taken over cooking duties, but feeding this small group of people wasn't a full-time job like cooking for the hotel had been.

He stopped to rub the muzzle of a bay foal in the large stall that opened to the pasture. "Hey, boy." The colt snuffled against his hand, then shook its head and darted back out into the sunshine.

"I don't blame you. I'd run outside and work some energy off too, if I could."

With the horses out, an eerie quiet settled over the barn. Mara had gone for a ride near the river to check the snare lines. Zechariah hunted over the crest of the hill, and Ezra wrote letters in the house. But Josiah had spent more time than he could stand in that little cabin—the walls were closing in on him.

Just another few days and he'd head back out on his Express route. One more year of that, if everything went well, and he'd have enough saved to buy land and his first few horses. Property was much cheaper here than what he'd priced back in Georgia. If he had the money those louts had stolen in Kansas, he could probably have started in another month or two. He released a sigh. Fuming about it wouldn't change anything.

He could hang on for one more year. Besides, that would give him a year to spend with Mara. Getting to know her. Talk her into marrying him.

The thought stopped him mid-breath. Did he really plan to marry? He'd always said never. But when he added Mara's name to that question, he could see it. A little cabin at the edge of a pasture full of horses. Mara cantering across it atop a pretty Arabian mare. Cantering toward him with that huge smile on her face that only came when she rode horses. Yes, that was the picture he wanted. In his chest, a craving built.

He swallowed. Could he really wait a year to wed her? Maybe she would agree before that. Although he didn't have a house to bring her home to. And spending so many nights away while he rode his route...she deserved better than that.

The barn door squeaked open, and Josiah turned to face it. Zechariah strode in leading a chestnut, its head hanging low as it ambled forward.

"Howdy."

Mara's brother nodded in Josiah's direction. He didn't often spare many words. The man was probably close to Josiah's age, but his silence made him seem older and wiser than his years. Maybe a little hardened, too.

That made two of them.

Zechariah stopped the horse in front of a stall where a halter dangled from the post. Josiah stepped toward them and reached to loosen the cinch on the saddle. Zechariah worked on the other side, untying his saddle bags.

"No deer this time?" Josiah asked, trying to start up a conversation.

"Nope."

Josiah pulled the saddle from the horse's back with his good arm, and carried it over to the bar along the wall where several others hung. Zechariah led the animal toward the pasture, and Josiah followed them out, propping himself on the fence to watch. When the halter had been removed, the animal ambled a few steps away, then dropped to its belly and rolled. A horse's favorite post-ride exercise.

Zechariah strode back through the gate and closed it, then came to stand beside Josiah. The man didn't usually seek out his company, so Josiah remained where he was until Zeche spoke.

"You seem to like my sister."

That wasn't quite the topic Josiah wanted to discuss with him. Especially not with the way Zechariah's tone implied he didn't cotton to the idea.

He chose his words carefully. "Your sister is a special lady."

"She's special. But she's missing out on a lot here. It'll be good when she leaves to go East after spring foaling. Our Aunt Greta will take her in hand. Teach her things a lady needs to know. Help her find a suitable husband."

Josiah opened his mouth to defend Mara, but Zechariah pushed from the fence and strode away.

What did he mean she would take Mara in hand? She was already perfect in every way possible. A hard worker. So intelligent. Beautiful. An excellent horsewoman.

But then the rest of Zechariah's comment pierced his thick skull. *A suitable husband?* That would imply that Josiah didn't qualify as suitable. And the man would be right. Not a poor orphan boy who'd had to claw for every scrap he'd come by.

A heavy weight settled over his chest. Mara deserved so much better. So where did that leave him?

Chapter Twelve

"Stage is here."

Josiah glanced up from the cook stove as Ezra poked his head in the cabin door to share the news.

"Food'll be ready by the time they come in." He turned back to the work counter to mix more flapjack batter. He'd been about to serve dinner for the family, but adding a few extra place settings wouldn't be a problem.

The stage was two days late. What kind of trouble had they run into? Ezra said they didn't typically go look for it until the coach was three days past its scheduled time. Especially in the winter when it could be slowed by snow and ice.

Josiah scooped the beef stakes out of the frying pan, arranged them on a plate, and poured round circles of batter into the hot grease in the skillet. The front door banged open, and his chest surged at the sudden noise, sending a shot of pain through his shoulder. *Settle down, English.* It'd been so long since he'd cooked around a crowd. Now sudden noises spooked him?

Men filtered into the room, their baritone voices filling the space.

"Yeah, we come around Independence Rock an' seen a whole passel o' Indian teepees spread out across the valley. They stretched from one mountain to the other, no goin' around 'em." Mr. Campbell paused as he plopped into a chair at the table.

"So what'd you do?" Ezra prodded.

The light in Mr. Campbell's eyes twinkled. "The only thing we could. Turned around an' high-tailed it back the way we'd come. Took us another half day to get back to the last station. Spent the night there, then hooked up a fresh team an' crossed over the river to find another trail. Took a good bit o' windin' an' doublin' back, but we made it."

Josiah slid the plates of steaks and flapjacks to the center of the table, and the man grabbed a fistful of meat before Josiah pulled his hand back.

"Eat up, folks. We'll be hittin' the trail again in ten minutes."

The two other men from the stage settled into chairs around the table. The older fellow, dressed simply in a white cotton shirt and suspenders, loaded his plate without a word. The younger man, probably in his mid-twenties and looking like the modern definition of a dandy, scanned the simple tin place setting in front of him. Then his gaze trailed to the two tin platters piled high with food in the center of the table. His mouth pulled into a pinch and he wrinkled his pug nose.

Josiah turned back to the skillet and forked more buffalo steaks into the pan. The dishware and setting might be rustic, but the fool man would be hard pressed to find better flavor in the food of any restaurant on the East coast. Including that hoity-toity Omni Parker House Hotel in Boston people were always talking about.

As soon as Mr. Campbell had scarfed down his food, he stood and slapped his hat on his head. "Time to go, folks. Gotta make up the miles."

Both men forked final bites into their mouths and stood, the younger fellow delaying a moment longer to take a final sip of coffee. Maybe he'd learned his lesson about judging the quality of a meal by the setting in which it was served.

Ezra followed the men out, and when the door slammed shut, an easy quiet settled over the room. There was a lot to be said for solitude. Especially in this remote country without crowded streets or noisy strangers. Most of the time, anyway.

He had the second round of food on the table by the time Mara and Ezra trudged in, stomping snow from their boots and peeling off coats. Zechariah wasn't far behind, and they all settled around the table, then bowed for Zeche to say grace. Just like a family. Josiah swallowed a lump and squeezed his eyes tight.

The meal flowed in their normal rhythm, with comfortable conversation and a bit of dry humor thrown in with Zechariah's stoic tone. But soon enough, it was over and the family bundled back up to finish chores for the night.

Josiah made quick work of compiling the scraps for the slop bucket and washing the dirty dishes. He'd gotten pretty good at working with his left arm still wrapped against his side. He could use that hand, just couldn't move anything above the wrist.

When the kitchen was clean and the table wiped down, he pulled on his own coat. He'd stop in the storeroom to put the scraps in the slop bucket there, then head to the bunkhouse. After dropping off the leftover food pieces, he closed and barred the storeroom door then turned to gaze across the yard.

The moon was bright, glittering off the snow, even where heavy tracks marred the smooth surface. Horses stood in circles in the pasture behind the barn, munching hay with an occasional snort. The peacefulness of it all only intensified the longing in his chest.

He ambled that direction. The bunkhouse would be dark and cold, so maybe a few minutes watching the horses would prepare him for sleep. The barn door opened, and Zechariah and Ezra headed toward the house.

"G'night, Josiah," Ezra called.

Zeche gave a nod that seemed to say the same thing.

"Night." Josiah kept his voice low so he didn't break the tranquility hovering in the air.

He reached the back fence and propped his good arm against it. The munching of horses' teeth became the melody that trumped all other night noises. Rose was among those in the group closest to him, and he studied the white patch of hair across her face. It looked like an artist had poured paint over her, allowing it to splatter around the edges. The striking look certainly added to her beauty.

Another squeak sounded behind him as the barn door opened a final time. He didn't have to look to know it was Mara, but he turned just the same. If she noticed him, would she come and talk? Or just wave and go inside? He wasn't sure which he wanted.

As much as he'd tried to resist her draw, it was Mara who made this place wonderful. Even the majestic pull of this wilderness wouldn't hold quite the magic, if there wasn't always the chance he might catch a glimpse of her. Maybe have the chance to talk with her. See that smile that could light the darkness.

She held the milk bucket in one hand, but set it on the ground before closing the barn door. After she propped the wood rail across the latch to secure it, she picked up the bucket and looked around. Did she sense a presence in the yard? Or maybe she looked for him. Wishful thinking, probably, but a man could hope…

Shadows shielded her face, but her profile gave her away when she noticed him. Her shoulders relaxed, her chin came up, and she strolled toward the fence where he stood.

"Enjoying the night view?" As Mara neared, the moonlight pushed away some of the shadows on her face, but he could still make out only the outline of her features.

He turned back to the animals in the pasture. "It's nice out. Peaceful."

She stopped beside him, leaning against the fence rail the same way he did. The quiet settled over them for several moments before she added her voice to it. "This place speaks to me."

Josiah's chest tightened. "There's something about being so isolated, so connected to the land. It gets into your soul."

Mara's hands left the fence and settled around her upper arms. He turned to look at her. She nodded agreement with his words, but the shiver in her jaw undermined the action.

"You're cold?" He reached to unbutton his coat. Why was he letting her stand out here in this freezing night air?

"No, I'm fine." But her shoulders had started to quiver now, and she bit her lower lip.

He should tell her to go inside. But they rarely had quiet moments to talk without at least one of her brothers around. Was he being selfish? Maybe not if she wore his coat. "Put this on."

"I'm fine really."

But he draped it around her shoulders and she gripped the edges, wrapping it tighter. "Now you'll be cold."

"I'm fine." Especially if he slipped his good arm around her and pulled her close like he was itching to do. How much trouble could he get into with one hand?

Mara turned back to gaze over the pasture again.

But he kept his focus on her. Her face held no shadows now, its planes perfectly illuminated by the moonlight. Her intelligent eyes, full lips, cute pointed chin.

"I know what you mean."

He blinked. What had they been talking about? He had no clue. "What I mean?"

She shot him a look out of the corner of her eye, raising one brow. Then she focused forward again. "About the land getting into your soul."

Ah.

"This country feels more like home than any place we've lived, even though we've been here less than two years." Her throat worked, and his focus followed the movement. "I don't think I can leave it."

Her words penetrated the trance that had settled over him. Was she giving serious consideration to Zeche's plan? The knot in his gut tightened. "Your brothers want you to leave?"

She turned to him then, something welling in her eyes that looked almost like desperation. "How did you know?"

"Zechariah." He forced any trace of bitterness from his voice. "Do you want to go stay with your aunt?"

"No. I don't." Resolution laced her tone now.

He took a step forward, a magnetic force pulling him without effort on his part. His hand slipped up to her cheek. "I don't want you to go."

He'd said it. Hadn't told her everything he felt, but he lowered his mouth to hers and let his kiss say the rest.

As he tasted the softness of her mouth, memories flooded his body that hadn't yet reached his mind. He'd kissed this woman before, and she was just as intoxicatingly sweet as she'd been then. His body yearned to pull her close, secure her in his reach. But his left arm was shackled in the restricting bandage. He slid his right hand from her cheek to the back of her head, weaving his fingers into the softness of her silky hair.

Mara's hands settled on his chest, and her touch warmed him more than any coat could. They slid up until they encircled his neck. He groaned and deepened the kiss, running his hand down to the small of her back where he could pull her closer.

Sweet mackinaw, but she was amazing. Every sight and touch and taste of her. Even the scent of horses mixed with the faintest aroma of roses. She brought everything in him to life.

Her hands slipped down to his chest again, pressing flat against him. Pulling away or holding him close? He should stop. Just one more taste and he'd stop. With every ounce of his strength, he pulled away from her mouth. But he didn't release her waist. Holding her close, he settled his forehead against hers. Her chest rose and fell in almost the same rhythm as his, while he struggled to catch his breath.

Her eyes were closed but she made no move to pull away.

"Have I told you that you're the most beautiful thing I've ever seen?"

Her lids fluttered open, and her cheeks formed soft dimples. "No."

"You are." His hand itched to stroke her cheek again, but he wasn't releasing his hold on her.

"I need to get inside before the boys come looking for me."

Josiah couldn't stifle a groan.

She pulled back, and he let her go.

Mara stepped away to pick up the milk bucket, then turned back to him. Her chin dipped in a cute little gesture. "Good night, Josiah."

"Good night."

Then she turned away and strode toward the house.

His chest ached as she carried a piece of it with her.

Chapter Thirteen

*M*ara jerked the leather cinch strap until it pulled the knot tight, securing the saddle in place. The old bay broodmare pinned her ears for an irritated second, then dropped her head back to the hay at her hooves.

"Easy, girl." Mara stroked the mare's wooly neck. A lifetime of birthing foals had made this girl a bit cranky and set in her ways, but she was gentle and steady under saddle. Just what Josiah needed for his first time back on a horse after his accident.

It had been almost three weeks since that awful day. Too soon for him to be back in the saddle? Probably. She was crazy for letting him. But he'd asked, and it was so hard to say no to him, especially when he gave her one of those sideways grins. Especially since a huge part of her craved nothing more than to spend the afternoon with him. And since they'd be alone, maybe he'd give her another of those heart-racing kisses.

The memory of the one last week still rushed heat to her face. She'd been hoping every day since that he'd find an excuse to get them alone. But a blizzard had hit, keeping everyone mostly indoors, with no chance of privacy. To make up for it, Josiah had sent her sweet looks and kept her in the conversation at mealtime. She'd made a point of letting their hands brush when she passed him a dish. If only their chairs weren't at opposite ends of the kitchen table.

Today, though, she would have him to herself.

The barn door squeaked open and Ezra's voice drifted through. "...the article said they have another crew building the telegraph line from the west. They're hoping to meet in Salt Lake City sometime before the end of this year. Sounds too good to be true, huh?" His volume increased with the enthusiasm in his voice as he and Josiah ambled toward her. "A telegraph stretching from one end of the country to the other."

"Sounds like there won't be much need for the Express."

"Oh, people will still need to mail letters and catalogues. The telegraph is just for short messages."

They were near enough now for Mara to see the pinch in Josiah's brow. But he caught her gaze and his face softened in a way that set off the fluttering in her chest. He held up a small bundle. "I brought snacks for us."

"Some of your buttermilk biscuits?"

One corner of his mouth tipped. "And something sweet to go with it."

How did words as innocent as those make her face flame so? She turned to slip the bridle on the mare beside her. "Sarah here is ready for you. Ezra, can you help with mounting?"

"That's what I'm here for."

Mara looked up to catch a wink from her brother. She should be able to ignore that, but the heat surged again. She slipped under the mare's neck, dropping the reins to the ground. Striding the few steps to where Rose was saddled and waiting, she grabbed her own leathers and almost dragged the mare toward the barn door. She needed cool air.

She was mounted and waiting by the time Ezra led the old broodmare out of the barn, Josiah on his heels. Josiah's left hand was still in a sling, so he gripped the saddle horn with his right and hauled himself into the seat. The action was awkward, and the pinch of his eyes showed the pain the movement caused. This was a bad idea. She should be shot for letting him ride so soon.

She applied pressure to Rose's sides and guided her closer to Josiah's mare. "We don't have to do this yet."

Josiah's jaw tightened. "I want to."

"Maybe we could just ride around here for a while?"

"No."

The look in his eyes stopped her from arguing further. Stubborn man. She'd keep an eye on him, though. If his pain worsened, they'd come back whether he wanted to or not.

They started out in the direction of the river, following the narrow Muskrat Creek until it reached the main body of the Sweetwater. As she breathed the fresh cool air, the tenseness in Mara's shoulders slipped away, and she settled into the easy rhythm of the horse underneath her. There was nothing better.

A genial silence stretched between them, but Josiah's voice didn't seem like an interruption when he asked, "So your father taught you how to ride?"

Pleasant images filtered through Mara's memory. "Both parents really. Pa said that's what made him fall in love with my mother. Her father trained Thoroughbred racers, and she would help exercise them. It wasn't considered proper for a woman to be riding at blazing speeds in split skirts, so she did most of her riding early in the morning. Pa came to call on her father one morning, and saw Mum riding. He said he knew right then he would marry her. It only took him six months to talk her into it." She sent Josiah a smile as she finished the story. "Horses have always been a family business for us."

He gave her a look she couldn't quite decipher. Longing maybe? But there was a hint of pain in it, too.

The lapping of water sounded ahead as the Sweetwater came into view. It was about thirty feet wide here, but still fairly shallow.

"Is my mare used to water?"

She glanced at Josiah in time to see wariness in his eyes. "She's fine. Just let her sniff and drink first if she will."

He nodded and allowed the broodmare to drop her head at the edge of the water. The mare gulped for several seconds, but the crease never left Josiah's forehead and his jaw formed a tight line. She hadn't seen him that nervous before. "Did your Express horses ever give you trouble crossing the river?"

"Some more than others."

The old broodmare, Sarah, plugged across the river without incident, and Mara sent up a prayer of thanks. When they were on dry ground again, Josiah's shoulders relaxed, and he reached down to pat the mare. "Good, girl."

Warmth crept into her chest as he straightened and squared his shoulders to continue the trail. He'd been through a lot in the past few months. Going from almost no experience with horses, to riding hot-blooded Express steeds over miles of rocky hill-country. He had grit, she'd give him that.

As they wound their way through the hills and rocky bluffs, Josiah asked about her old ranch in Maryland, and how they'd found the breeding stock they used now, including the mare he rode.

They meandered through a hilly section, with Mara in the lead down one of the steeper trails. She glanced back as she finished a story about the first time Sarah had foaled a feisty colt, hoping to catch a smile on Josiah's face. Instead, his mouth pinched in a thin line, and creases dug deeper into the skin around his eyes with every bump in Sarah's stride. He was hurting.

As soon as they reached the bottom, Mara reined in her horse. "How's your shoulder holding up?"

His mouth curved but the grin didn't meet his eyes. "Not bad."

Hardheaded man. "There's a nice spot just around this butte to stop for lunch."

"Lead the way."

She almost missed the wilt of his shoulders. Relief? She should have stopped them before now.

Rose stepped forward, and Josiah's horse followed. As they rounded a large pile of rocks, Mara blinked at the sight before her.

A dozen Indian braves sat on horseback a quarter mile away. Even from this distance, war paint was visible on the lighter horses, and each man wore a large quiver of arrows on his back. And then she saw the war bonnet worn by the Indian farthest away. Her shoulders tensed. Paiutes.

Mara jerked her reins, bringing Rose to an abrupt halt, then reining the mare back the way they'd come.

"What are you—"

"Shhhhhh…" Mara hissed, as her mare backed into Josiah's horse.

Josiah turned his mare off the path to get out of Rose's way while she backed a hasty retreat. Mara had seen something that spread fear across her face. This woman who wasn't afraid of anything.

"What is it?" he whispered.

"Paiutes. A war party." Her eyes were huge. Her words clipped. "Can you handle a run?"

He'd handle whatever was necessary to wipe that fear from her features. "I'm right behind you."

Her horse sprang into a canter, then lunged up the hill, leaving him in the dust. He glanced back at the huge rock that hid the Indian war party, then loosened his reins and nudged Sarah with his heels. The mare broke into a lope. She may be an older girl, but she didn't like to be left behind any more than he did.

Fire shot through his shoulder with every stride. He clung to the horn and gritted his teeth as his mount leapt up the hill. When the ground leveled out, he focused on finding the rhythm in the horse's stride. Anything to smooth the bouncing that pushed the knife farther and farther into his shoulder. Sweat dampened his forehead, and the bite of the wind against the moisture on his face was a welcome distraction. Maybe he would pass out.

But he couldn't. Not when Mara needed him.

At last, they reached the edge of the river and Mara slowed. She glanced back at him, but he didn't have the energy to pretend he wasn't in pain. Didn't have the strength left to fight against the worry flooding her face.

"We can probably slow down now." She nibbled her bottom lip. "Let's get across the river, then I'll ride ahead and warn the boys."

There were so many things he didn't understand about this country. About this woman. But he needed to understand why these particular Indians scared her into a cross-country flight, when she'd casually talked or even joked with every other Indian they'd encountered.

He forced his teeth to un-clench. "Have you had trouble with the Paiutes?"

Her face paled again. "They've attacked other Express stations. Things got so bad last summer, people called it the Paiute Indian War. They killed dozens of Express workers, and over a hundred and fifty horses were lost. We haven't seen those Indians in this area for a while, but that was definitely a war party. I've gotta get back and worn the boys. There might be another band even closer."

The fear in Mara's eyes sent a tomahawk through his chest. "Let's go then." Pushing his pain aside, he tightened his jaw and kicked his tired horse toward the river's edge.

It took Josiah longer than usual to clean the kitchen after dinner that night. His shoulder throbbed, and the only thing that made it better was to keep his arm immobile. A loose sling gave some support, but it would feel better if he had Ezra wrap the arm close to his torso like he'd done before.

While Josiah scrubbed the stew residue from the big cast iron pot, Zechariah sat in the armchair by the fireplace, cleaning the new Sharps Carbine rifle that had come on the last supply wagon. He'd noticed the man didn't go many places without a rifle.

Especially now, after the Indian sighting.

Josiah glanced toward the door. Mara was still in the barn finishing with the animals. But Ezra was out there with her, and he carried the Winchester.

He set the pot in its place on the floor next to the cook stove, then reached for the bowl of sourdough starter and uncovered it. A pungent, yeasty smell permeated the air. Interesting something that smelled so foul could make such tasty bread. He scooped a cup of flour and dumped it in the bowl, then added some water from the drinking bucket he kept at the end of the counter. The mixture thickened nicely. A couple more days and it'd make a good batch.

The cabin door creaked open, and Josiah snapped his head around. Ezra stepped inside and closed the door behind him, then unbuttoned his coat. He was by himself?

"Where's Mara?" Josiah flipped the cloth back over the yeast mixture and wiped his hands on a towel.

Ezra glanced at him. "She was almost done milkin'. She'll be in shortly."

"You left her alone out there?"

He lifted a shoulder. "She has the rifle."

Did he really think that was all right when they'd seen an Indian war party just that day? Even with the rifle, she wasn't a match for a dozen angry braves.

Josiah tossed the towel on the counter and strode toward the door. "I'll make sure she gets inside before I head to the bunkhouse." He grabbed his coat from the peg, then slammed the door behind him.

The cold air blasted him, cooling his temper but not squelching the fear that simmered in his gut. Did these men not realize she was a woman, and needed to be protected as such? Sure she was fearless and brave and capable of more than most men. But if the Indians got their hands on her... Bile rose up the back of his throat. He couldn't even think about that.

A movement in the distance grabbed his focus—a shimmery fabric swaying in the moonlight. Mara. Her light blue skirt swished as she turned to close the barn door, then reached for the bucket of milk.

The sight of her brought him to a stop. Her head was erect, eyes scanning the shadows as she picked her way across the courtyard. If anyone could outsmart the Indians, it would be her. But still...

Protectiveness surged in his chest, pushing him forward. She saw him as soon as he moved, and the moonlight illuminated one side of the smile that spread across her face. His stride lengthened.

When he reached her, need drove his actions, and he took the bucket with his good arm and set it on the ground.

Then he reached for the rifle and placed it on top of the bucket. Her hands free, he slipped his arm around Mara's waist and pulled her close, touching his lips to the soft skin where her forehead met her hair. "You're all right?"

"Fine." Her whisper was soft, pulling his eyes closed as she sank into him.

Her hair held the faintest scent of roses. How did she smell like that, even in the middle of the winter? And after a long day's work. This woman was a mystery.

"You were coming to protect me?" Mara leaned back to look at him, and his gaze feasted on every inch of her face. Her luminous eyes with the dark brows above, her cherry red cheeks, her lips pinched in a pert little smile.

His mouth found its own grin. "You need protecting."

A twinkle flashed in her gaze and her dimples deepened. "From you."

Oh. No way could he resist that one. He tightened his grip on her waist and lowered his mouth. Her soft lips met his.

A sound pricked his awareness.

"Mara?" A man's voice drifted across the courtyard.

Josiah eased back, holding in a groan as he turned to look. The open cabin door spilled light onto the ground around them, and in the center of the beam stood a dark shadow—holding a long rifle.

"Zeche." Mara's voice dragged the word into two syllables, just like a younger sister.

"Coming in?" His tone held a hint of challenge, probably meant for Josiah.

"When I'm ready." But she slipped out of Josiah's hold, then reached down to grab the rifle and bucket.

"Good night," he whispered as she strode past him toward the open door.

She shot him a little smile.

Josiah raised a hand to his forehead in salute toward the broad profile now propped against the door frame, then turned toward the cold, dark bunkhouse. A yearning gripped his chest. He'd have all night to examine how he really felt about this woman.

Chapter Fourteen

Mara settled the saddle in place on the chestnut Express horse. She rubbed a hand along the gelding's neck. "You'll be good today, boy?" He'd better be. This ol' boy was the quietest Express horse they had. And that's what Josiah would need on his first official ride after the accident.

The barn door opened, splashing light down the aisle and across the gelding's saddle. Josiah's lean, rugged outline filled the opening. Mara's heartbeat stuttered in her chest. He was so handsome.

He allowed the door to close behind him, then strolled through the barn in her direction. "Thought I'd come see if I could help." His mouth tipped in that look only he could give.

Mara raised a brow. "I'll bet you just want to make sure I do it right."

Lines crinkled around his eyes, and she could imagine the sparkle that the shadows concealed. "I'd never question anything you did with a horse."

How did he have the power to melt her like snow in a hot kettle? This love that overflowed in her chest—it started in the deepest place and poured out so much, it hurt sometimes. Like now, when he was about to leave on another dangerous ride. It wasn't snowing at the moment, but fresh powder from the night before covered the ground, and the rocks would be slippery. He could have another accident, maybe worse than before.

Josiah stepped around the gelding and stopped in front of her. He touched her chin and raised it, until her gaze met his. Two valleys formed between his brows. "What's wrong?"

Her body craved his arms around her. Wanted the feel of his protection. The solid strength of *him*. Wanted him to stay here with her. Always. But instead of stepping into his arms, she swallowed. "Just worried."

"About?" He kept two fingers under her chin, and skimmed his other hand down the back of her arm. Goose bumps raised everywhere he touched, and a tingle shot down her back.

"You." Mara nibbled her lower lip, but kept his gaze. In truth, she didn't want to turn away. "What if something else happens? It would be so easy to reinjure your shoulder."

The side of his mouth pulled again. "You think I'm that bad of a rider?"

Heat flushed her neck. "Of course not. But it's icy out, and you never know what can happen."

He slipped his arms around her then, enveloping her in the warmth she'd dreamed of. But it was so much better in reality. His strength around her. Emotion welling in her chest. Bliss and love and terror and sheer joy. A drop of it leaked from one of her eyes. Then another. *God, please bring him back. What would I do without him?*

Josiah's arms tightened, and he held her that way for several long moments. How long she couldn't have said. She wanted him to keep holding her forever.

A whistle drifted through the air, and his hold loosened. He pulled away, then lowered his mouth to hers for a gentle kiss. It was only a quick meeting, but gave her one last memory to cling to.

Then he stepped around her and reached to slip the bridle on the gelding. When all was done, he closed her hand in his, and she walked beside him out the barn door.

A few minutes later, she stood in the courtyard watching him ride away. Man and horse in unison, cantering through the snow. A magnificent sight.

If only it didn't hurt so much.

Josiah's horse crested the ridge of the hill in the darkness, bringing the twinkling lanterns of Three Crossing Station into view. Exhaustion seeped from every pore in his body. He'd been back in the Express saddle for two weeks now, riding the two hundred mile round trip every Monday and Friday. His layup had stripped away more muscle than he'd first thought, but the rides were less grueling each time. It helped when he'd learned how to hold the reins so his left shoulder didn't take the abuse of the high-strung horses jerking on the leathers.

He released a piercing whistle as the horse descended the familiar rocky hill into the station yard. A cluster of lanterns gathered in the center of the open area, outlining the figures of two horses.

He was late. The Sweetwater River had been high from thawing snow, so it'd taken longer than usual at all the crossings. Since the relief rider now waited for him, he wouldn't get a break before climbing on a fresh horse and riding back the way he'd come.

The tired gelding beneath him slowed to a stop when they reached the cluster of men and horses.

"Ho there, English." Brantley's voice drifted above the others as the older man took Josiah's reins.

He slid from his horse, and allowed the other Express rider to remove the leather mochila from atop his saddle. Josiah took the replacement mail pack from the man and positioned it on his fresh horse.

"Nelson here brought news from the Express."

The other rider turned to acknowledge his name before mounting his horse. Was that a dark expression on his face?

"I'm off then." Dirt and mud flew as he whirled the horse and sped away into the darkness.

Josiah turned back to Brantley and reached for his reins as Hellman led the spent mount away. "What's the news?"

"The Express is closin' down."

Josiah stiffened, then stared at the man. "What?" Surely he hadn't said what it sounded like.

"Goin' outta business. Government awarded the mail contract to the stage, so the whole Pony line's shuttin' down, 'scept for the stretch from Salt Lake City to Sacramento."

Josiah's muscles wouldn't work. The edges of his vision faded blurry. What did that mean for him?

"You all right?" Brantley eyed him with head cocked, his voice a little softer than normal.

Pull yourself together, English. He pushed through the cobwebs in his head. "Did they say when they'll stop the mail rides?"

Brantley's mouth thinned. "Soon. They're cuttin' back to one run next week. It'll just be the Friday ride for you. Have to wait an' see about the rest of it." He shook his head. "Not good."

Josiah couldn't shake the daze as he mounted his fresh horse. The animal bobbed its head, jerking on the reins. He loosened the leathers and allowed it to leap into a canter.

But as they bounded up the hill and across the bluff, he couldn't stop the thoughts roiling. What now? Never in any of his plans did he expect the Pony Express to shut down. It had seemed like a gift from God. Not that God had done him many favors through the years. But he'd dared to think the Almighty might have actually helped things work out for him this time. First with the Express. Then with Mara.

But he should've realized. The accident should have been a clue. Nothing in this life was handed to him. Nothing ever came without grit, and hard work, and determination to fight his way to the top. He had to maintain control of what happened to him, or he'd never get anywhere.

So that brought him back to his question. What now? Maybe the Express would let him transfer to the line they were keeping open in California. But that line already had riders, and probably a swarm of men across the country eager to fill any empty spots.

No. He'd have to look elsewhere for a job. Maybe the stage needed drivers. Probably nothing would pay as well as the hundred dollars a month from the Express, but he'd have to start somewhere.

Mara added another log to the fire in the cook stove, then closed the iron door and brushed wood dust from her hands. She scanned the kitchen. Lunch dishes were clean and put away. Dough rising in pans on the counter to bake later. Table clean. Nothing left to do in here.

And Josiah still hadn't come out of the bunkhouse.

Ezra had helped change out horses when Josiah arrived early that morning. And the news he'd brought wasn't good. What would he do when the Express shut down? There were ranches a little farther east. Maybe he could find work at one of them. Did he have enough saved to start his own? Probably not. He'd only been working for the Express three months, and one of those he'd been unable to ride.

The sick knot in her stomach tightened. If he left, would he take her with him? She needed to talk to him. Hear what he was thinking.

But she couldn't wake him up. He'd ridden all night and was exhausted.

She started toward the door. The yearlings needed their daily workouts. Now was as good a time as any. And maybe Josiah would be up soon and come talk to her while she worked.

But after losing her temper with Bandita, and spending more time watching the bunkhouse door than the other two colts she attempted, it seemed like a better idea to head back inside to put the bread in the oven. Warm sourdough bread with dinner might cheer Josiah up. And maybe she could make cinnamon crisps for dessert. Too bad she was out of preserves. A pie would've been even better.

She released Jericho into the pasture, then hung the halter on a fencepost and trudged toward the house. Another glance at the bunkhouse showed no movement still. She refocused her gaze on the main house and didn't let her eyes stray again. It would be too easy for her feet to follow, but she *would not* disturb Josiah while he slept. This uncertainty and worry were driving her mad.

It wasn't until she rang the bell for dinner that the bunkhouse door finally squeaked open. Mara stood on the steps of the main house as Josiah emerged from the smaller building across the courtyard. She had to clutch the door frame to keep from sprinting to him and slipping her arms around his waist.

Zeche and Ezra exited the barn at the same time, and Josiah fell into step with them. As they neared the house, Mara scanned Josiah's face. Was he worried? Exhausted? Fine lines had settled around his eyes, and their depths were a dull gray-blue today. His mouth pressed tight, and his back stood rigid. Yet something about the set of his shoulders seemed like they slouched under a heavier weight than normal.

Her body craved to touch him. Rub the strain away. But she had to settle for turning back to the stove to gather the coffee pitcher. She'd find a chance to talk alone with Josiah after the meal.

They all sat and bowed for Zeche's blessing on the food. Mara peeked at Josiah once during the prayer, half expecting him to be watching her as he sometimes did. But only the crown of his dark brown hair stared back at her. She squeezed her eyes shut. She should use this time to pray for him, but so many thoughts twisted in her mind. So many emotions swirled in her chest. She couldn't fight through them to put together a coherent prayer to their Maker.

Please help us, Lord. It was the best she could do.

A solemn mood settled over the group while they piled the beef and potatoes onto plates and ate. Josiah took only a single scoop of each, then dropped his head and forked one piece into his mouth at a time.

After a few moments with only the sounds of eating, Ezra cleared his throat. "Any thought about what you'll do, Josiah?"

Josiah raised his head, shoulders still slumped. He chewed and swallowed the small bite of potatoes in his mouth, his dull eyes staring at her brother, as if from a long way away. "Thought I'd ride to South Pass City tomorrow. Maybe on to Pushroot. See if anyone's hiring." His jaw clamped for a moment before he spoke again. "Maybe I can get on with the Butterfield stage."

Zechariah stroked his chin as if he had a beard there. "Not much steady work in these parts with so few people here. The stage line is probably your best bet, unless you go farther west to California. Or back East, of course."

Mara clasped her fingers together until her nails dug into her palms. Surely he could find work nearby.

But if he did have to travel, she could go with him. It would be hard, not knowing where they would end up. But she could sleep under the stars as well as he could. And she would be a helpmate to him, just like any good wife. The best wife.

She fixed her gaze on Josiah. *Please, look at me.* If she could just connect with him, she would tell him with her eyes.

They could make this work. They could even hire onto a ranch. Maybe go south to Texas. Men coming through on the stage talked about cattle ranches in Texas all the time. She could help him. They would be all right.

But Josiah didn't look at her. He nodded, his head barely moving, his heart not committed to the motion. Then he dropped his gaze back to the plate, speared a potato with his fork, and raised it to his mouth. A strange kind of stiffness—maybe even formality—radiated from him. A sudden urge filled her to grab him by the shoulders and shake some sense into the man. This wasn't the end of their dreams. Maybe it could even be the catalyst to something more. Something better.

The rest of the meal crawled by. Mara finished long before the others, and refilled coffee cups, then started wiping out pans. Zeche shot her a frown when she must have made too much clatter, the kind of look that said he knew what she was up to and didn't approve. But there was no way he knew everything running through her mind. Were her brothers dragging the meal out on purpose? She needed a moment alone with Josiah.

Ezra finished first, and she carried his used plate and fork to the wash bucket. She had them washed, dried and put away before Zeche emptied the last forkful of potatoes from his plate.

Josiah finished at the same time, then rose and started for the door. "Thanks for dinner."

He was leaving? Mara dropped the used dishes in the bucket of water, then hurried after him, grabbing her coat from the peg on the way out. He was already several strides into the yard when she caught up with him.

"Josiah." She touched his arm and he stopped and turned to her, but still didn't meet her gaze. "Want to come help me milk Hannah?"

He ran a hand through his brown hair. "I better turn in. Need to get an early start tomorrow."

His words hit like a hoof in her gut, knocking her back a step. "I...thought it might be good to talk about things." *We need to make some decisions.* But she couldn't say that. Not when he hadn't officially asked her to marry him.

"I'm sorry, Mara." His voice was hollow, distant, as if he were walking to his own hanging. The muscles in his jaw rippled.

Another sock to her stomach, and this one left her breathless. *I'm sorry?* What was that supposed to mean?

He turned and walked away. Leaving her with more questions than she'd started with, and a nagging fear that tightened the ache in her chest.

Chapter Fifteen

*J*osiah reined his horse down to a walk as the familiar waters of the Sweetwater River came into view. A mixture of emotions flowed through him. The light murmur of water rippling over stones sounded like home, even though he'd only lived here for three months. But at the same time, a sour taste nipped in his stomach. As if he'd reached for a warm loaf of bread, fresh from the oven, and found only a hard crusty slice, not fit to eat.

He sighed and pulled the mare to a stop facing the river. Did he just love to torment himself? The tumultuous river water churned below the surface, just like his own frustrations. His mind played back through the last four days. He'd ridden from one settlement to another, covering hundreds of miles, but not a decent job to be found. Oh, there was a blacksmith who mentioned he'd be willing to take on an apprentice. And a couple of trading posts said they could use him part-time. But he could hardly feed himself on that income, much less earn enough to start a ranch.

He did find a Pony Express manager and asked about the possibility of being assigned a stretch remaining open in the west. But the man's brooding look had darkened to a thundercloud at the question. Not very promising.

The Butterfield Stage Line had all the drivers they could handle in this area, but said they might need some further west. In fact, everyone he'd talked to said there may be jobs available closer to California. But he had no desire to work in any of the frenzied mining towns he'd heard about on the west coast. Still…maybe there were some decent settlements out there, too. And there was always the telegraph line they were building to span the country. It'd be temporary work, but it was a job.

And what about Mara? Where did she fit into all this?

He released a groan, dropping his head so his brow almost touched his saddle horn. *God, why is everything so hard?* He raised his gaze back up to the heavens. The sky was perfectly blue, no clouds on the horizon. A bird soared in the distance, rising over buttes and hills that almost touched the heavens. So wild and majestic. An ache started deep in his chest. How could he leave this place?

And if he did, could he leave Mara, too? Should he ask her to go with him? But that wasn't any kind of life for her. Roaming from town to town. A drifter's wife. No real home. No place to lay down roots. She deserved a thousand times better than that. Her brother was right. A respectable husband from the city would be better for her than him.

Besides, Mara seemed to have the ability to reach through his defenses and weaken them. Now, more than ever, he had to stay in control. That was the only way he'd ever accomplish his dream. Although, would owning his own ranch really be as perfect without Mara by his side?

But see, that was exactly the problem. This was the dream he'd been working toward as long as he could remember. This would have made his parents proud. He couldn't let Mara or anyone else weaken his determination for it.

Josiah turned the horse back to the trail and kicked her into a canter. If only he could outrun his life.

Mara pulled the tray of steaming biscuits from the oven and examined them. Most were golden brown, with just a few near the back that had darker tops. Interesting how much more she cared about the food now than before Josiah came. But it was important to him, and that made it important to her. Besides, when you put the right care into cooking, the food really did taste better. Zeche and Ezra sure didn't seem to mind the improved fare.

She had to find a way to talk with Josiah today. He'd been gone four days straight, looking for another job, then arrived home just in time to ride out on his Express run. Now he was back, and it was high time they discussed the situation.

He might be avoiding her because he was worried, but that's why she needed to set him straight. Make it clear she was here to support him. She could help, and they would get through this together. Maybe this was even the chance they were looking for. The opportunity to find the place God had for them. Perhaps he'd have time after breakfast to go for a ride into the hills so they could make plans.

The door opened and Ezra shuffled in, lugging a full bucket of milk.

"Just put it on the counter." Mara nodded toward the work table as she picked up the plates of bacon and biscuits.

The others filed in, Josiah bringing up the rear, and formed a line to wash at the basin. Mara picked up the coffeepot from the stove and strode to the table.

She touched Josiah's arm as she passed, but he didn't look at her. Not even a glimmer of acknowledgement. What was wrong with him? It was one thing to be concerned, worried, or even downright fearful of an uncertain future. But his behavior this last week had bordered on uncivil.

Steam rose from the cups as she poured the hot liquid, and the pungent aroma cleared her head some. This was a hard time for him, and she had to be understanding. Hadn't Pa always said a man's dignity lay in the quality of his work? Josiah's dignity as a man was at stake here. She could overlook a little rudeness.

171

After Zeche said grace and the food was passed, conversation began about the warming temperatures outside.

"Saw some purple Indian Paintbrush blooming across the river," Ezra said, then stuffed a whole piece of bacon in his mouth.

"Probably have one more cold snap before spring hits for good." This from Zeche, their resident weather expert. He'd become so much better than the rest of them at reading the signals from the plants and animals. Some kind of a sixth sense.

"Molly looks like she's going to foal in the next couple weeks." Ezra popped another slice of bacon in his mouth.

Zeche nodded. "The two bay mares should go a week or so after that. Then Abigail won't foal until mid-April."

He turned to Mara, and something about the look in his eyes tightened her stomach. "After that, I can spare Ezra to take you to Aunt Greta."

She dropped her fork and pressed both hands in her lap, gripping her skirt to keep from slamming her hand on the table. Taking a breath, she steadied her voice. "I'm not going, Zeche."

His eyes took on that sad, almost haunted look that had flickered there more than once these past few months. "I think it's best, Mara. It's what Pa wanted."

She swallowed. Maybe, but that didn't make it right. She shot a pleading look in Josiah's direction. He didn't notice, though, because he stared at the half-eaten biscuit in his hand, his mouth steadily chewing. If she could have reached him under the table, she would've given him a good, hard kick. What was wrong with him?

Instead, she turned back to her brother. "I'm not going East. I want to stay where I'm needed. With the people I love." She was careful not to say she planned to stay here on this ranch, because that didn't look to be the case. She'd go wherever Josiah needed her.

Zeche's gaze turned wary, and his mouth pinched. He opened his mouth, then closed it. Finally, he said, "You and I can talk about it later."

Oh, stubborn boy. He'd taken on the family patron role that fit so well on him, but he would not get his way in this. It was her life, and no matter how much he thought he knew better, Zechariah was wrong in his opinion on this topic. Very wrong.

Maybe Josiah would speak with him after they went for a ride. Once her brothers saw that she'd be happily married, there'd be no reason for her to go East to find a husband. They seemed to like Josiah.

Ezra piped up then, ever the peacemaker. "There was another notice about the telegraph line in the mail yesterday. It said they're probably gonna put telegraph machines at the stage stops." A hint of sparkle touched his eye. "That means us."

Mara stared at him. Did his fascination with gadgets and technical things make him blind to the undercurrent of their conversation? For that matter, to the feelings of others?

The telegraph was likely contributing to the loss of Josiah's job, and Ezra spoke as if that hadn't occurred to him.

Her gaze shot to Josiah. He stared down at his plate while he bit into a piece of bacon. Like he was the only person in the room. As if they weren't all having a conversation around him. Was he in some kind of shock? A delayed reaction from his injury? Maybe she'd ask Ezra after breakfast. In case she should watch for other signs.

The meal was torture. Josiah's gaze kept pulling to Mara, like a compass to true North, but he couldn't let her catch him watching. Couldn't give her any false hope.

Because he had to leave.

Finally, the dinner was over, and he started toward the door behind Zeche.

"Josiah?"

He halted when she called his name, and bit back a groan. Reluctantly, he pivoted. He wasn't ready to talk about things. How did he tell her he had to leave? She was better off without him. And the more time he spent with her, the harder it would be. So he didn't answer, just waited.

The smile she turned on almost undid every bit of his resolve. "Could you help me clean the breakfast dishes?"

No. Working together in such close proximity, he was too likely to pull her in his arms. He glanced up as he opened his mouth to say no, but the hurt welling in those puppy dog eyes was enough to rip his heart. He raised one shoulder in the hint of a shrug. "All right." He'd have to keep his distance.

Josiah stepped to the table and stacked plates.

Mara came up beside him and gathered the cups and forks. "I was wondering if you want to go for a ride with me this afternoon?"

"I...don't think so." He had to push the words around the lump in his throat.

Mara watched his face, but he couldn't look at her. He was too close to giving in.

"Why?"

"I have some things I need to do here." His eyes wandered to her for just a quick glance. Mistake. Her eyes were a liquid amber, with red circling the edges. He clenched his hands into fists to keep from pulling her close and wiping the tears away.

"We need to talk." Her voice was shaky. "There's a lot that needs to be decided. Do you have any idea yet when the last run will be?"

"This Friday."

Her gasp was audible. "So soon?"

"Yes, and when I get back Saturday, I'll be heading on." He had to tell her. The truth was his only defense against his rogue heart. Against his desire to pull her close and not let go. He couldn't do that. He had to leave her here. Let her find someone good enough for her. Someone so much better than him.

"Heading where?" Her eyes widened and her tone held a bit of desperation.

"Not sure where I'll end up, but I have to find a good job. Maybe building the telegraph line."

"But..." Mara gripped the edge of the table and blinked.

He couldn't watch this. What was he still doing here with her? But he couldn't force himself to leave either. Instead, he looked down at the floor where his boot scuffed. Could he make her understand?

"Maybe you *should* go to your aunt and uncle's. You deserve someone who can give you the best." With every word, the vise clamped tighter around his chest. He couldn't take it anymore. Couldn't breathe.

He turned and fled out the door.

Mara urged Rose faster, allowing the wind to rush over her. To blow away the tangle of emotions clogging her chest, clouding her mind. They cantered over a low hill, and she leaned down over the mare's neck, loosening the reins until there was nothing holding them back. Rose stretched out over the flat ground, eating up the distance. Consuming the miles.

At last, she sat back and Rose slowed, easing down to a trot, then a walk. They both breathed hard, sucking in warm, clean breaths of sunshine. She should feel glorious. Free in this place she loved so much, riding the mare who responded to her every thought. But nothing would shake the heavy weight that smothered her chest.

Josiah had left on his last ride for the Pony Express. When he arrived back at the Rocky Ridge station before sunrise tomorrow, he would be done. No longer employed by the Express. Free to go anywhere he pleased. And the worst thing was, he seemed desperate to leave.

Tomorrow.

Why did he have to go so soon? At the very least, he could wait until Sunday and get a good night's sleep. He still hadn't said a word about her coming with him. Maybe he only planned to be gone a few months. He'd been working, saving up for the last six years. How much more could he need to start a ranch? Surely a few more months would be all it took. Then he would come back to her. They could be married and build their new life. Together.

Mara pulled Rose to a stop at the river's edge and slid to the ground. She stepped up beside the mare's neck and stared out over the serene water of the Sweetwater River. As usual, Rose draped her head over Mara's shoulder in the special way she had of showing affection. Mara returned the hug as she reached up to scratch the favorite spot behind Rose's right ear. Being with this horse always made things a little better.

If she and Josiah left, was there a chance she could take Rose with them? But as the gurgle of the river soothed out the tangle of her nerves, a burn started in her throat. How could she ever be happy away from this place? *Lord, please let Josiah feel the same way.*

Chapter Sixteen

ara glanced out the open cabin door. Still no movement from the bunkhouse. Hadn't Josiah said he was going to leave after he returned from his last Express ride today? But it was lunchtime now, and he still hadn't stirred. He was probably exhausted from riding through the night, but this wait was killing her. And with such a late start, surely he would wait until tomorrow.

She hugged her waist, and that familiar burn stung her eyes. She bit her lower lip. No crying today. She would not. The stinging intensified, and she sniffed the moisture back inside, then charged to the doorway and gave the bell a good, sharp yank. The only way to keep the tears at bay was to get things moving.

The barn door opened, and Ezra filed out, then Zeche. Still no sign of Josiah. Mara released a sigh as she turned to grab the coffee pot from the stove.

Both men eyed her warily as they stepped into the room and formed a line at the wash basin. Mara ignored them, filled the cups, and sat in her chair, hands clasped tightly in her lap. Neither of her brothers would make eye contact with her, but that didn't stop them from sending sideways glances as they settled into chairs. She bit her lip, tasting the coppery tang of blood this time.

Ezra began the blessing, and Mara focused on her breathing. In. Out. She clenched her eyes shut. In. Out. In.

"Mara."

She jerked up to find Ezra's sympathetic gaze shining at her.

"Pass the butter, little sister?"

The prayer must be over. She released that last breath and handed the plate of butter to her brother. She reached for a biscuit from the tray in front of her, then nibbled a bite from the edge. Even using his recipe, these still didn't taste as good as Josiah's biscuits.

The hair rose on the back of her neck, and Mara lifted her head. Across the table, Zeche stared at her, but he dropped his gaze the moment she returned the look.

She took another bite of biscuit, the dry texture crumbling in her mouth. Her stomach threatened to revolt, but she forced herself to chew and swallow. Her neck tingled again, and Mara realized the room had grown quiet. She raised her head, and this time both men stared at her. Ezra averted his focus to his food, but Zeche just kept watching her with his cool, calculating gaze.

She stiffened her spine. "What?" Raising her brows, she returned his look. "Have I grown an extra nose? Or maybe a set of horns?"

"No, Mara. We're just concerned. Are you all right?" Ezra's patronizing tone was the last straw.

All right? No, she wasn't all right. The man she loved was leaving within hours, and she had no idea when he'd be back. She had this sick feeling in the core of her stomach and a desperate urge to scream and cry. Was that all right?

But instead, she gritted her teeth and said, "I'm fine." Her eyes burned again, and there would be no holding back the tears this time. She dropped the biscuit on her plate, rose from her chair, and spun toward the door. "I'll be in the barn."

She escaped just in time, because the tears broke through as she sprinted across the grass. She made it inside the barn, and crumbled against the wall. Huge sobs took over, wracking her body as the anguish finally found escape.

God, why is this happening? How in the world can I handle Josiah leaving? The tears kept coming, spilling out in waves that rocked her shoulders. How could her world fall apart in one fell swoop?

Mara didn't fight the tears, but allowed them to pour out of her until nothing was left. Her muscles were spent, eyes tight and puffy. Everything ached, from her soul to her backbone cramped against the barn wall.

For several minutes she sat, knees bent in front of her, hands clasped around them. The loamy scent of the barn sank through her. Hay, dirt, a hint of manure…and horse. She breathed deep, letting the balm of the familiar smells cover her wounds.

Lord, I need Your strength. And surely Josiah would be back. She pinched her eyes shut. He had to come back.

A soft nicker sounded from the other end of the barn, and Mara raised her head. One of Rose's hugs was exactly what she needed right now. Her constant friend and solace. She struggled to her feet, shaking out her brown skirt and flannel petticoat, then started toward the stall that opened to the back pasture.

Molly, a chestnut broodmare heavy with foal, was the only horse taking shelter in the barn from the spring sun. Mara let herself into the stall and stepped through the open door into the pasture. A spattering of horses milled in the area near the barn. The rest of the animals scattered down the hill toward the creek, munching on little green shoots of grass. She scanned each animal for Rose's flashy chestnut and white coloring. Where was she? Mara stared more closely, doing a mental count. There should be sixteen horses in this pasture, including Molly in the barn. But she only counted fifteen.

Her chest pumped as she strode down the low hill toward the creek. Maybe the mare was lying in the creek bed. Was she sick? Injured? Her mind scanned through all the possible reasons why Rose might be laid up. It was too cold still for snakes, but another wild animal could've attacked her. Or maybe an injury from one of the other horses. Or maybe something internal was wrong. Lameness? A twisted gut? Mara broke into a run.

As she neared the creek, her eyes scanned the bank for the brown and white form she knew she would find. But the animal never appeared. The creek was empty.

Mara stopped short, her chest heaving from her sprint. She turned to survey the pasture she'd just crossed, counting the horses again. Fourteen, plus Molly out of sight in the barn. Where was Rose?

She focused on the fence around the perimeter. This pasture wasn't very large—maybe five acres—and was surrounded by a split rail fence. Every piece of wood seemed to be in place. Could Rose have jumped it? But why? Perhaps she'd wanted to be near Rico, their stallion. He stayed in a smaller pasture on the other side of the property so they wouldn't have this kind of problem, with animals breaking through fences.

Her heartbeat raced as new scenarios ran through Mara's mind. She struck out in a run again, over the same ground she'd just covered. Near the barn, she veered toward the house, tucking herself between fence rails, then slowing to a jog as she neared their cabin.

She was panting now, and focused on gulping deep breaths. After pushing open the cabin door, she stopped on the threshold to get her bearings and regain enough air to speak.

Both brothers whirled at her entry. Zeche paused by the table, his hands laden with tin cups. Ezra stood at the wash bucket, a rag in hand.

"Rose…" she panted, and almost choked as her dry throat tried to form more words. She swallowed a painful gulp, then tried again. "Rose is out. I don't know where."

Not a man moved. Why didn't they spring into action? They all knew how easy it was to lose a horse in this vast country.

"Come on. We need to go look for her. Zeche, can you check Rico?"

Her older brother wouldn't meet her gaze, but turned to glance at Ezra. Ezra looked back at him with raised brows. That seemed to rouse him, and Zeche squared his shoulders.

"Mara," he began, but then seemed to change his mind, and he stepped toward the table. "Come and sit." He pulled out her chair, then settled into the one around the corner.

What was he doing? Why weren't they helping look for her horse? It wasn't even her horse really. Rose was farm property. Part of their livelihood. Zeche patted the table in front of her chair, and looked at Mara with raised eyebrows and a sad smile. That look reminded her too much of Pa, which pressed the weight even harder on her lungs.

Like a puppet, she shuffled forward obediently. This couldn't be real. A fog settled over her, like she was watching someone else sink into her seat. She blinked, and clasped her hands around a piece of skirt in her lap. Then she focused on Zeche's face. The lines across his forehead were deeper than normal.

He cleared his throat. "Josiah left this morning."

She heard the sounds, saw him speaking, but it was several beats of her pulse before the words broke through her fog.

They struck her like a slap in the face, and the impact knocked her backward.

Why would he say that? Rose was missing, and instead of helping, he was giving her more bad news? Mara raked in a breath. The edges of her vision blurred, but she blinked and forced her eyes to focus. "When?"

"Early. Right after he finished his Express ride."

Mara blinked again. What he said didn't make sense. Josiah had ridden all night for the Express, then left without sleeping at all? Without saying goodbye? A weight pressed hard on her chest. Her lungs struggled to take in air. "No."

A hand settled on her shoulder, and the touch cleared a bit of the fog.

"I'm sorry, Mara."

She flinched. She didn't want his pity. She jerked back enough so the hand slid from her shoulder. She couldn't deal with Josiah right now, but she had an overwhelming yearning for her horse. She clenched her jaw. "We need to find Rose."

The Adam's apple in Zeche's throat bobbed. "He...um...took her with him."

Mara blinked. The words didn't make sense. She had to pull herself together. "Who took her?"

"Josiah." His tone was patient.

What? "Josiah took who?"

185

"Mara." Concern crept into his voice. "Josiah bought Rose. I thought you knew."

The weight pressed harder on her chest. Fog flooded her mind, her vision. Blackness crept around the edges of her focus. Josiah? Bought Rose and left? It didn't make sense. The darkness closed in. Everything inside the black circle around her vision grew blurry.

And then darkness took over.

"Mara."

A voice called to her. Josiah's?

"Mara."

Disappointment flooded. It wasn't his voice. That tone was the unmistakable sound of her little brother.

She forced open the tight skin around her eyes. She couldn't get them open all the way, but at least she could see.

"There she is." Ezra smiled from the edge of her bed. He had a contagious grin, one that always pulled a matching one from her. But she couldn't find it now.

"Feeling better?"

Zeche's voice came from the other side of the bed, bringing with it an oppressive weight of pain. She turned to him, grasping at the memories his voice brought.

Josiah. Gone. And Rose.

Anguish flooded her chest, along with confusion. She focused on her older brother's face. "Where did you say Rose is?"

His mouth formed a thin line, and he patted her shoulder with a work-roughened hand. Then he met her gaze. "Josiah bought Rose from us. Paid for her fair and square. It was time for her to be sold, and I knew she couldn't go to a better owner. I thought he'd told you, though." His face pinched. "I'm sorry. I didn't mean for you to learn about it like that."

Mara pulled in a deep breath. She couldn't deal with this now. Not in front of her brothers. She had to get them out of here.

She nodded. "I'm fine now. I'll be up in just a few minutes."

Zeche's brows furrowed, and he glanced at Ezra. Mara turned over on her side and pulled the covers up. Surely they would take the hint and leave.

After a moment, they did, quietly shuffling out of the room. Mara kept her back to the door, not moving until she heard it close softly behind them. Then she pulled the covers tight around her chin, and allowed the hot, silent tears to come.

Josiah rolled his blanket into a tight bedroll, trapping his few belongings into the center of it. He stood and stepped to where Rose grazed a few feet away. He'd not thought to bring grain, so hopefully grazing overnight would tide her over until they came to the next town. His own stomach could do with more than the biscuits and dried buffalo meat he'd been eating since he left the Rocky Ridge Station yesterday morning.

He stroked the thick winter coat on the mare's neck. "Let's get movin', girl." It hadn't seemed right yesterday, to be riding Mara's horse. But Rose was a dream—calm and obliging with everything he asked of her. She was starting to feel like his partner. Maybe even a friend.

The pinch in his chest tightened. It still didn't seem fair that Mara couldn't have kept her, though. He'd bought Rose because she was in the group of three-year-olds to be sold, and he knew for a fact she was one of the finest animals he'd find anywhere. But if there was a way he could've made sure Mara could keep her, he would've done it.

Mara. What was she doing now? Cleaning the breakfast dishes? Did she miss him? Maybe. The burn in his throat threatened to rise up and choke him. This was best. He had to keep reminding himself. She deserved so much more than he could give her. Someone better than an orphan vagabond, who didn't even have a steady job. And this was what he had to do for himself, too.

He gathered Rose's reins in his left hand, stuck his left boot in the stirrup, and swung up. He'd do something about that job part, though. After settling his right foot in the other stirrup, Josiah glanced east, then west. There was a war brewing back East. A civil war, between the North and the South. Everyone he'd seen yesterday was talking about it.

Should he go back and fight with the others from Georgia? A couple of the men had said it was all about slavery. He'd never agreed with the practice, but the thought of killing other men turned his stomach. Especially fellow Americans.

He looked back toward the west. That was the direction he'd ridden all day yesterday. If he couldn't find a job along the way, the telegraph line would be hiring men to build it in Salt Lake City.

"Come on, girl." He squeezed Rose's sides and turned her away from the rising sun.

Chapter Seventeen

ara pulled up on the two-year-old gelding's reins as his hind legs launched into the air again. She grabbed at the horn to keep herself in the saddle.

"Quit!" She popped him on the hindquarters with the end of her reins, and the horse settled into a bouncy canter. It took work to keep her body relaxed, while focusing on the animal's ears. Ezra had said this gelding was a handful, but at least he kept her focus off Josiah. And not much had been able to do that over the last two weeks he'd been gone.

The animal's pace eased, and she applied more pressure with her right leg to keep him cantering. Once around the pen. Twice. Three times. She finally allowed him to slow to a walk, and the gelding dropped his head as if he'd run twenty miles. Flecks of white foam had built up where the saddle rubbed his shoulders, and he breathed hard. She reached down to pat his neck.

A figure caught the corner of her eye, leaning against the fence. Josiah? Mara's heartbeat sped up as she jerked her head around to see.

Zeche. A wave of disappointment washed through her. And anger. She still couldn't forgive her brother for selling Rose without even telling her. And to Josiah, of all people. And how dare Josiah take her? He knew how special that horse was to her.

Mara kept the animal walking along the fence, not stopping to talk or even acknowledge her brother. Her chest burned, and she inhaled a deep breath, then slowly released it. She needed to get a handle on this anger. Zeche may not have made the wisest decision, but he wouldn't have done it to hurt her on purpose.

The next time around the pen, Mara reined the horse to a stop in front of him. He stood with his strong hands draped over the top rail, his rolled sleeves revealing ropy muscles in his arms, and a long scar that spanned the length between his right wrist and elbow.

He squinted to look up at her. "Molly's waxing over now. Baby should come in the next day or two."

Mara nodded. Waxing over. How many times had she seen the thick, milky-white coating cover a mare's udder a day or two before giving birth? "She usually does that the day before she foals. I can watch her tonight."

The worry lines around his eyes relaxed. "Good. She knows what to do, so I don't think you need to sleep in the barn. Just check on her every couple of hours." His mouth pulled in the hint of a smile, but the sadness in his eyes didn't match it. "Your woman's intuition is better than mine when it comes to the birthings."

It was nice that someone needed her. Woman's intuition or not, through the years she'd proven herself better at spotting the signs of imminent birth than the men in the family. And the mares didn't seem to mind her presence as much during the foalings.

She dismounted and led the tired gelding toward the gate. Zeche met her there, swinging it wide for them to pass through. He fell into step beside her as they strode toward the barn.

"I was thinking, next week's stage might be a good time for you and Ezra to head East."

The words slammed into her like a cannon ball, and she whirled to face their assault. "I'm not going East, Zeche." Passion fought to escape her throat. "I'm not leaving here, and that's the way it is. You can't make me go."

His face paled, but he met her gaze. His Adam's apple worked, and his eyes wore a sad, haunted look. They were almost…uncertain. It was the first time she'd ever seen that expression on her strong, confident brother.

Remorse flickered in her gut. She hated to speak to him like that, but she had to stand her ground. She held his focus, but allowed her brows to settle into their normal position

A rumble sounded in the distance, and he broke their locked gaze to turn toward the sound. Mara followed.

The stage. It was coming in fast, too. The horses ran at a near gallop, and she could see mud flying from the wheels even at this distance.

Zeche touched her arm. "I'll take your horse. You go get the food ready."

Mara didn't argue, just thrust the reins in his grip, and then used both hands to raise her skirts so she could jog across the yard. The potatoes were sliced and sitting in water, they just needed to be fried with the buffalo steaks.

The food sizzled in the pan and had started to turn brown, when the cabin door burst open. Zeche strode through the room carrying a limp mass of green muslin skirts, with a woman's blonde hair hanging from one end. Mara had to look twice before the sight registered. They'd not had a woman come through in several months. And what was Zechariah doing carrying her? Instead of setting her in a chair, he marched straight through the main room and into Mara's bed chamber. What in the world?

She used her apron to push the frying pan to the back of the stove, then scurried toward the doorway where her brother had disappeared. He stood a few feet back from the bed, staring at the woman who lay lifeless on the quilt.

She stepped inside to get a better look. The woman was, indeed, blonde, and maybe ten years older than Mara. Her face was so pale it almost glowed.

Mara moved closer. The glow was actually a sheen of sweat that covered her forehead and upper lip. A drop ran down the side of her temple.

She crept to the woman's side and touched a hand to her forehead. Before she even made contact, heat radiated from the lifeless body. At least she wasn't dead. Mara's eyes drifted to her chest. The worn green fabric barely rose and fell with each breath.

She turned back to Zeche. "What's wrong with her?"

His brow wore deep furrows. "Not sure. Campbell said he'd thought it was travel weariness. Until she passed out a few miles back, he had no idea she was burning with fever. He went to the barn to send Ezra in."

Mara scanned her memory for something that would help the woman. "Get some wet cloths. I'll see if I can make her more comfortable." She stepped to the foot of the bed and raised the green muslin enough to find two tattered leather boots. The soles were thin, but they still covered her stockings. Her fingers fumbled over the buttons, and she finally got them unhooked, then slid the leather from the woman's tiny feet. In fact, everything about her looked tiny...and frail.

Mara moved back to the woman's face and stroked blonde wisps from her temple. She stirred, and the light brown lashes fluttered open. Red-rimmed eyes stared up at Mara, and a wave of sympathy coursed through her. "Are you feeling better?"

The woman stared at her for a long moment. Then her delicate lips parted, and Mara leaned closer to hear what she was about to say. But a look of panic took over the dainty features, and the woman clawed at the side of the bed in an effort to turn over. What was happening?

194

It suddenly became quite clear when the woman vomited over the side of the bed. A foul odor spread the room, and Mara pinched her lips and held her breath. Grabbing the washbasin, she pushed it under the woman's mouth as she heaved the last remnants of her sickness.

At last, the lady eased back on the bed, but a shiver slid down Mara's spine at the sight before her. Blood ran from her nose and both corners of her mouth.

She placed the basin on the table, and Zeche pressed a damp rag into Mara's hand. She hadn't even heard him come in.

She wiped the mess away from the woman's face, but more trickled from her nose. Zeche held out another cloth, and Mara grabbed it, then pressed it lightly at the base of the nose. What was wrong with this poor lady? She turned to look at her brother. "Doesn't she have a man with her? Husband or father?"

He stood a few feet back, wringing his hands. Poor fellow. He looked so big and out of place in this little bedroom. "No one was helping her. I don't think so."

Boot thuds sounded in the main room, and they both looked toward the door. Ezra stepped inside and walked right up to the bed. Mara motioned toward the floor where the bloody mess still lay. "Watch where you step."

He shuffled around the bed, his eyes running over the woman's face. "What's wrong with her?"

Mara gave him a quick recap of the symptoms so far, ending with the reason she was still holding the damp rag against the woman's nose.

He bent closer, examining the red-rimmed eyes. He took the rag from Mara and studied the thin nose. Then he glanced up to meet Mara's gaze. "I almost forgot. I think you're wanted in the other room. I'll take a look here and see what I can find out. Zeche, can you stay in case I need something?"

Wanted in the other room? Ezra held her eyes for a moment longer, as if he were trying to prepare her for what was about to happen. Her stomach fluttered, but it was hard to say whether dread or excitement spurred the sensation.

Her brother dropped his focus to the woman on the bed and rested two fingers against her neck. Mara stood and steeled herself as she stepped out of the sleeping chamber.

The main room was quiet, so Mara moved to the wash basin to rinse her hands. Did he mean one of the other buildings? After using the dry towel, she turned toward the front door.

A whimper caught her attention from the corner. She turned and scanned the shadows, finally spotting a little blonde wisp of a girl curled up on the stone hearth. She couldn't be more than two or three years old. One fist settled in her mouth, and the other curled around a cloth doll. Her wide eyes radiated fear.

"Oh, hello." Mara kept her voice soft and musical, the same way she spoke to a new foal. She stepped toward the child, and then squatted low when she was a few feet away. "What's your name?"

The girl's lips thinned, as if trying to seal them closed so they didn't give her away.

Mara forced her facial muscles into a smile, hoping her eyes obeyed. "Did you ride on the stage coach?"

"Mama." The word was a whimper, barely discernable, but it pressed in Mara's chest. She fought the urge to pull the child into her arms.

"You came with your mama?" Mara looked back to the open doorway of her bedroom, but couldn't see anything other than the blank wall inside. A faint murmur of male voices drifted from the room, too soft to tell whether it was Zeche or Ezra speaking.

She turned back to the girl. "Your mama must be the pretty lady with lovely blonde hair like yours." She reached to stroke a lock that had fallen over one of the wide blue eyes. "She was feeling sick, so she's resting now, right in that room."

The girl stared at Mara, as if she was reading a deeper message inside each word. She no longer looked terrified though.

"Would you and your dolly like something to eat?" Mara stroked the yellow fabric that served as hair for the miniature figure.

The little girl bobbed her head twice.

"Good." Mara rose and slipped a hand over each of the child's little shoulders to guide her toward the table. "I'll get you a cup of milk to drink. Do you like potatoes?"

Another nod.

"And how about bread with butter?"

The little chin dipped once more, and a small light flickered in her eyes.

Mara poured a tin cup of milk and set it in front of the girl. Then she scooped a helping of meat and potatoes, and buttered a slice of sourdough bread. Too bad she didn't have anything sweet baked. She sprinkled a bit of ground cinnamon over the bread slice. That would have to do for now.

She set the plate and fork in front of the girl. The little waif had already finished the glass of milk. Mara refilled it, then settled into the chair beside her. The little angel crammed the bread into her mouth, chewing as quickly as she could.

"You don't have to hurry with your food. You have plenty of time and can have more if you'd like it."

Those big blue eyes cut sideways to look at Mara, but the girl held the bread at her mouth, biting, chewing, and swallowing as fast as her teeth would move.

Chapter Eighteen

Mara's attention jerked up when the cabin door opened, and Mr. Campbell stepped in. Finally, someone who could answer questions. He wiped his feet at the threshold, clutching his hat with both hands. His eyes found Mara and the little girl, and he stepped toward the table.

She stood and moved to load another plate from the food on the stove. "Please sit and eat, Mr. Campbell, while you tell me what's going on."

He obeyed, settling across from the child. "That looks good, Miss Katherine." The little girl ducked her head, but didn't stop stuffing potato slices in her mouth. How long had it been since she'd eaten a decent meal?

"Katherine." Mara spoke softly as she placed the plate in front of Mr. Campbell, then moved back to the chair beside the girl. "What a pretty name for a pretty girl."

She stroked Katherine's back as she leveled her gaze at Mr. Campbell. "What's happened?"

He met her eyes for a second while he scooped a bite into his mouth, then spoke around the food. "Mrs. Mavers looked squeamish for a few days, but I thought she was just tired out from the trip. Said they'd come all the way from New Orleans. Didn't realize she was so bad off until I heard her get sick a few miles back. Then I got here in a hurry."

Boots sounded, and Zeche stepped from the bedroom with Ezra behind him. Shadows hollowed the lines on her older brother's face, and Ezra's mouth formed a thin line. He clutched one of the thick medical books across his chest like a shield.

Neither man seemed eager to speak. The suspense had her shoulder muscles tied up in knots. "What do you think?"

Ezra blew out a breath. "I can't say for sure, but she seems to have some type of influenza, or maybe even yellow fever." He glanced at Campbell. "Do you know where she came from?"

"New Orleans she said."

Ezra nodded. "Probably Yellow Fever then. They had an outbreak a few years back."

"Is it catchin'?" The man eased back in his chair like he might jump up and run if he didn't like Ezra's answer.

"No, thank the Lord. Yellow fever's spread by insect bite. It's not contagious from person to person."

Mara eyed young Katherine. How much should they talk in front of her? The little one may not understand all their words, but their tone would surely frighten her.

Katherine looked up at her with those blue eyes that filled a third of her face. Mara slipped her arm around her shoulders and gave a little squeeze. But then she didn't let go. Katherine needed to know she had a friend in this new, scary place.

"Do you think she'll make it?" Mr. Campbell directed his question at Ezra.

Ezra's lips tightened. "Hard to say for sure, but she's not in good shape."

A sound drifted from the bedroom, and Ezra straightened as he listened. Mara didn't hear it again, but Ezra strode across the room and disappeared into the little chamber. He reappeared moments later. "Mara."

She met his troubled gaze.

"She's asking for her daughter…and for you."

Mara swallowed, then stood and scooped Katherine into her arms. This little mite couldn't weigh more than thirty pounds, but she snuggled into Mara's arms in a way that spread warmth through her chest. "We're going to go see your mama."

"Mama?" The little voice was full of innocence.

"Yes." Mara rested her cheek against the soft blonde hair as she stepped toward her bed chamber.

Inside the dim room, Mara stopped to let her eyes adjust. The bed swallowed Mrs. Mavers, even though it wasn't that large. She raised a weak hand when she saw her daughter.

"Katherine."

It was barely more than a whisper, but the little girl came to life, leaning toward her mother with arms outstretched. "Mama."

Mara held onto the girl as she stepped closer. There was no vomit to skirt this time. Ezra must have cleaned it up.

As she sat down on the edge of the bed, Katherine tried to catapult into her mother's arms. Mara did her best to break the force of the landing. Still, pain flashed across Mrs. Mavers' eyes. But then it changed to desperation, and moisture pooled in them as she clung to the little body in her arms.

Mara's own eyes burned, but she swallowed back the emotion.

Katherine wiggled until she was snuggled into her mother's side, one hand clutching Mrs. Mavers' dress, and the other wrapped around the doll with her fist tucked in her mouth. The woman's gaze lifted to meet Mara's. "Can you do something for me?" Her voice was still no more than a cracked whisper.

"Of course."

"I have no family. We were on our way to take a job in California. Until I got sick."

Mara touched her arm. "Please don't worry, Mrs. Mavers. You can stay here until you're well enough to finish your journey. I'd love to help with Katherine so you can rest."

If it was possible, the woman's eyes grew even sadder. "Call me Ruth. And what's your name?"

"Mara Reid. My brothers and I run this stage stop. I think you met my younger brother Ezra a moment ago."

"Mara." Ruth's voice gained strength. "I'm dying."

Mara shook her head as a weight pressed down on her lungs.

But Ruth continued, "I know I am, and there's no one to care for my little girl." Her hand caught Mara's arm. "Will you take her? And raise her as your own?"

Mara stared into the same wide blue eyes as Katherine's, although Ruth's were ringed in red. What was she asking? She wasn't talking about watching the girl for a few weeks or months. She meant for Mara to raise the child to a grown woman. Teach her right from wrong, and make decisions about her future. *God, is this Your will?*

Her eyes drifted to Katherine's sweet face. An angel, snuggled in the crook of her mother's arm. Her eyelids lowered to half-mast, and she looked like she hadn't a concern in the world.

Mara couldn't stop herself from brushing a few loose golden strands away from the child's forehead. It was silky, as soft as the down-like hair on a newborn foal. She longed to take the little one in her own arms, to shelter her from the coming pain.

She glanced back at Ruth, who watched her with an intense focus. Mara inhaled a deep breath. "All right."

The desperation eased in Ruth's eyes, but not the pain. "Thank you." She dipped her head to press a kiss on top of Katherine's head, and a tear roll down her cheek.

They stayed like that for several moments, and both mother and daughter seemed to be drifting into exhausted sleep. She should leave them alone. After all, their time together might be limited. But should she leave Katherine in case Ruth's condition worsened? What if she vomited again? Or passed out and Katherine rolled off the edge of the mattress?

So she sat there on the side of the bed. How would the rest of her life be different after the promise she just made? But she couldn't think about that now. Had to focus on caring for the two precious lives in front of her. In the quiet of the room, the loudest sound was Ruth's labored breathing. Her eyes closed, but the pucker of her brow revealed her sleep wasn't peaceful.

The sudden sound of Ruth's hacking cough sent Mara's heart into her throat. She rested a hand against her chest to still her pulse, and glanced at Katherine. The girl's eyes flew wide.

Ruth coughed again and groaned, rolling a little, as if to escape the pain.

Mara stood and stepped toward the door. "Let me bring in the rocking chair, and I'll sit in here with Katherine so you can both get some rest."

When she returned, she slipped her hands under the girl and lifted her to her chest. A sheen of sweat covered Ruth's face again. The fever must be rising.

She cradled Katherine's sleeping form as she stepped to the door and stuck her head around the frame. "Ezra?"

The three men sat around the table, heads down as they focused on something. Ezra looked up at her voice, then rose and strode to her.

"Mrs. Mavers' fever is rising again. Can you bring some wet cloths to help her?"

While Ezra complied, Mara sank into the rocking chair with Katherine, easing into the steady rhythm that always soothed. Her brother settled the cloths on Ruth's forehead and cheeks, then turned back to Mara and whispered, "I'll let them sleep, but call if you need me."

Mara nodded, and stroked Katherine's back while she rocked. This poor little girl. Soon, she might be *her* little girl. So many things she needed to think about now. Did Katherine have enough clothes? Where would she sleep? Mara's bed was just wide enough for one person to be comfortable. Maybe she could stitch two quilts together tomorrow and stuff it with hay so the girl could at least have a mattress. Then the men could build a bed when they had a chance.

She must have dozed, because Mara woke with a sharp crick in her neck. The room was silent, except for the soft, steady breathing of the girl in her arms. Mara looked down and couldn't help a soft smile.

Such a beautiful child. Delicate in a way Mara had never been, but brave, too. Some children might have pitched tantrums if they were hungry or separated from a parent. But Katherine had waited patiently and obeyed everything Mara asked of her.

A figure caught the corner of her vision, and she glanced up. She'd forgotten Ruth was still in her bed. She studied the woman's face. The cloth rested on her forehead where Ezra had left it. But her breathing wasn't raspy anymore. Mara's eyes drifted to her chest to watch the rise and fall. But nothing moved.

A boulder of dread dropped in Mara's stomach. *Oh, God, no!*

She struggled to her feet, trying not to jostle the sleeping child in her arms. When she got a closer look at Ruth's pale face, Mara spun and slipped out her bedroom door.

The main room was quiet, but a fire crackled in the hearth and Ezra sat in the wing-back chair. He looked up when she stepped closer.

"Ezra. Please check Ruth. I think she may have…passed." Mara hugged Katherine tighter.

He jumped up without a word, folded the book he'd been reading, and trudged into the room she'd vacated.

She sank into his chair as her legs gave out. This had been Pa's chair, and she let the familiar scent wrap itself around her as she looked down at the bundle in her arms. What were they going to do now?

A niggle of guilt slipped into her chest. She'd been bemoaning the change this would cause in her own life, but in the space of a moment, poor Katherine's whole world had changed. And one of the worst things was, Mara had no idea what her life had been before.

What was her favorite food? Did she like animals? Did she have any history of sickness? Oh, why hadn't she asked Ruth more questions when she had the chance?

And what was Katherine used to doing every day? Had her mother worked? If so, who had cared for the child? Ruth said she had no family left. Did that mean other family members had recently died? How much loss had this poor child already suffered?

The burning in Mara's chest intensified, climbing into her throat. Loss, she understood. First her mother, then Pa, and now the gaping hole from Josiah.

Mara snuggled Katherine's head under her chin, and allowed the tears to come. She sat there for long moments, warm salty drops streaming down her face. Crying for herself. Crying for Katherine.

At one point, Ezra walked through the room. Mara dropped her head. She had no desire to talk right now, with her heart so exposed and raw. But he strode past her, opened the front door, and closed it behind him.

She looked down at the sweet angel sleeping in her arms. She already loved this child, enough to bring on the tightness in her chest. She could be her mother. She could care for her, and teach her all the things she would need to learn as she grew. And how wonderful it would be to have someone to love. To connect with. To invest her time and energy into.

Mara allowed her head to sink against the back of the chair. It was dark outside the lone window in the room. Had the stage left already?

Oh, no. Her pulse sped up. The others didn't know about Ruth's last request to her. Even now, they might be working on some other plan for Katherine's care. She needed to talk with them.

But what to do with the bundle in her arms? Mara looked around the room. It was probably close enough to bedtime that the child would sleep through the night if given a comfortable place and the opportunity. Sleeping in her bed chamber wasn't an option, with Ruth's lifeless body still in there. And it would be too hard to climb the ladder to the loft with Katherine in her arms.

So she rose and shuffled the girl so she could hold her with one arm. With her other hand, she pulled several quilts from the trunk by the wall, then settled them on the floor in the only empty corner of the room. She hated to lay the child on the hard floor, but this was the best she could do for the moment. She dropped to her knees and rested the little figure on the blankets.

After she snuggled the last quilt around the sleeping form, she sat back on her heels. This corner was near enough to the fire the child shouldn't get cold. And when Mara finally had the chance to sleep herself, she would make a pallet beside the little girl.

Her little girl. She was a mother now. Katherine's face held such a serene expression, her little lips curving up slightly.

Mara's chest squeezed. She could sit here and watch her sleep for hours.

Chapter Nineteen

ara stepped outside into the quiet yard. A shaft of light filtered from the open barn door, and she headed in that direction. Inside, the three men stood in a circle around the kerosene lantern.

"She said she had a job in Sacramento." Mr. Campbell's baritone carried in the quiet. "I s'pose I can ask the sheriff there to advertise and see if he can find someone who knows them."

Mara stepped forward between her brothers and infused her words with a matter-of-fact tone. "I'm going to raise the child. Her mother asked me to, and I agreed."

The men all stared at her. Zeche's wary gaze looked her up and down, like he was debating whether she'd self-destruct or not. Ezra's brows scrunched into a thoughtful expression. Probably calculating the additional supplies they'd need, and where the extra bed would go. Decisions were pretty black and white to Ezra. Though he had a big heart when it came to people, he couldn't help seeing things in columns and rows and written lists.

"Are you sure you want to take that responsibility, Miss Reid?" The lines on Mr. Campbell's forehead deepened.

She nodded, confidence flooding her veins. "Yes. I'll make a mattress in my room for her to sleep, and I'll take full responsibility for her." She turned to her eldest brother. "And don't worry, Zeche. I won't neglect my other work."

He raised a single brow at her, a hint of exasperation in his face. "That wasn't what I was worried about." Then that stoic look took over his expression. "It's not a little thing, Mara. This would change your life. Most men don't want to marry into someone else's family." He regarded her. "Even if you've only adopted her."

Was his sole purpose in life to marry her off? Sometimes it seemed like Zeche took his responsibilities as man of the family a little too far.

"I think she should do it." Ezra's voice resonated around the group. Mara whirled to face him as he continued. "She promised the mother, and it doesn't sound like the child has any other good options. Except going to an orphanage, but that's not a good option. Mara's capable and has the time."

The deep grooves across Zeche's forehead gave evidence to his worry. Finally, he blew out a breath and looked at Mr. Campbell. "I guess we'll keep her for now, until we can get the details sorted out." He looked pointedly at

Mara. "No promises on a permanent commitment, but we'll see how things go."

That's what he thought. There was no way she'd give up her little girl.

Campbell nodded. "I better hit the trail then. You've taken all my passengers, but I still have a schedule to keep."

"I'll pack food for you to take," Mara offered.

"I'd be much obliged."

As she turned to head back toward the house, Ezra's voice trailed close to her ear. "Don't worry about checking Molly tonight, Mar. And if you need anything with the girl, you just let me know."

She paused long enough to send him a grateful smile. "Thanks." She'd forgotten all about the expectant mare. Right now, the little blonde-haired angel inside needed all the attention she had to give.

The next couple days were like Mara had slipped into someone else's life. She spent most of her time with Katherine. Playing games, telling stories, asking questions.

The girl stayed quiet at first, not speaking unless Mara asked a direct question, and even then she gave the shortest answer possible. Mara gathered that she was three years old, and her birthday was in "S'tember."

Katherine helped prepare meals and learned to set a plate, fork and cup at each chair around the table. The display was a bit haphazard, but the little cherub was proud of her accomplishment. And so was Mara.

She called Mara by name, but hadn't opened up to the others yet. Ezra could sometimes get a giggle when he tickled her or pretended to steal her nose, but she still didn't speak to either of the men.

On the morning of the third day, Mara took her out to the barn for the first time.

"You wanna see a baby horse?" She asked as she buttoned Katherine's faded blue coat to her neck.

The little girl nodded once, her big blue eyes solemn. Those little round cheeks were just right for kissing, and Mara couldn't help diving in for a quick peck. "Oh, you smell like lye soap and mint leaves," she teased, pulling back to look at the girl.

Katherine ducked her head, but her cheeks formed slight impressions where dimples would go. What Mara wouldn't give to see a full-fledged smile.

"Let's go then." She scooped her up and headed toward the door.

When they stepped into the barn, a soft nicker sounded from a stall mid-way down the aisle. Mara carried Katherine to the gate and lifted her higher so they could both peer over.

A wooly, black foal raised its little head and nickered again—a high, snuffly sound. Its nostrils opened wide, and its whole chest vibrated with the noise. Too precious for words.

"Hey there, little guy." She looked at Katherine. "Would you like to go in and pet him?"

Katherine's blue eyes were huge as she bobbed her head. Mara slipped into the stall, then stood the child on the straw-covered ground. "Let me hold him still, then you can touch him."

The colt was friendly enough. The boys must've been spending time with him. She'd planned to do it, but so much had changed with Katherine. Mara slipped a hand around the soft chest, and another behind its rump. She glanced back at her daughter. "Now walk up slowly, and let him sniff your hand."

Katherine did as she said, eyes focused on the little muzzle. Spellbound. The colt snuffled her fingers, then reached up to nuzzle the girl's shoulder.

Katherine giggled. A real laugh. The sound tinkled out like a joyful bell, echoing inside Mara's heart until she found herself laughing, too.

They spent a while working with the foal, stroking him and playing peek-a-boo as he hid behind his mama. A weight lifted from Mara's shoulders as she watched her daughter play with the horse.

Her daughter. Who would have dreamed it?

If only Josiah were here to share this new blessing.

Chapter Twenty

MARCH 24, 1865 ~ FOUR YEARS LATER
MISSION SAN JUAN CAPISTRANO, CALIFORNIA

Josiah stared up at the hundred-year-old mission bells as they sounded morning prayers. Their vibrant ringing was a call to action. Beside the bells, the mission wall rose into an arch with a cross mounted at the peak. A cross that had been a constant reminder to him of Whose mission he now carried out.

"You packed enough food to reach Mission San Fernando Rey, sì?" Father Domingo's strong Spanish accent pulled Josiah's attention from the mission wall.

He turned back to the little Mexican priest who'd played such a big part in his life these last nine months. "Sì, Father. I have enough food and water for a couple of days. I might push hard and make it to the second mission before I stop for the night."

Father Domingo's weathered brown hand reached up to clap Josiah's shoulder. His dark eyes squinted as his mouth formed a smile. "You are a fighter, Josiah English. Never forget your Father in heaven is fighting with you. Follow his signal."

Josiah propped his own hand on the priest's shoulder, so they stood in a sort of sideways embrace. "Gracias, Father. I'm trying. I thank him daily for you and your kindness."

"Pshaw. You have worked hard for the mission. It was in great disrepair when we came, but it is becoming a thing of beauty again. And for your part, God will bless you."

Josiah swallowed a lump in his throat. "He already has. But I pray He blesses me a little bit more."

Father Domingo's smile spread into a wider grin. "That I have faith in. And you must invite me to your ranch one day, so I might bounce your little ones on my old knees."

Heat burned Josiah's neck, but he tried to laugh it off with a chuckle. "I have lots to do before then."

Father Domingo raised his hand to Josiah's forehead. "God go with you, my son. May the Lord bless you and keep you. May He cause His spirit to shine upon you and be gracious to you. May He lift up His smile on you and give you peace."

The now familiar benediction washed over Josiah like a balm as he internalized each word. Bless him. Keep him. Smile on him. Peace. He'd found that peace here at the mission. But He desperately needed those other gifts as he traveled back to the Sweetwater River. And Mara.

She'd dogged his memory these last four years. At the beginning, guilt hounded him every time her image washed through his mind. But then a longing took over. To see her again. To help her understand why he'd left. To apologize.

But first he'd had to redeem himself. Earn enough money to start his ranch. To prove that he could be worthy of her. Prove himself a *suitable* husband.

It wasn't until he'd met Father Domingo on the road to the Mission that he began to comprehend his real worth. Josiah had been in need of a job, and the Father had been in need of a good worker. Together, with a haphazard group of priests and cowboys, they'd refilled the holes in the stone and brick walls, rebuilt the roof on the church, and repaired as many of the structures as possible.

But then came the sickness that not only consigned him to his mat on the stone floor, but nearly stripped his life from him. It had been then, in that lowest of lows—when he'd finally realized his lack of control. Not one of the hard situations in his life had been his to guide. Yet the God he'd always blamed for deserting him had really meant it all for his good.

The death of his parents. When the hotel closed, ending both his job and his home. Every time he'd slept on the roadside. Every hunger pain and bloodied nose he'd suffered as he fought to make a life for himself in those lean years. Even the Express closing. Each blow had carefully guided him to this place, molding him into someone God could use. His servant. No matter where the Lord landed him.

And just now, the peace easing his soul told him it was time to head home.

So with his Bible, food, and a few personal items packed in his saddle bags, he mounted Rose and reached down to pat her. "Thatta girl."

Rose stood quietly, but he knew the moment he dropped the reins and nudged her side, she'd stretch out into a ground-covering canter. Mara had done an extraordinary job training her, and a few more years had mellowed her into the best horse he'd ever ridden. She was not one he'd ever part with if he had a choice in the matter.

Looking back toward the mission wall, Josiah touched his forehead, chest, and then each shoulder in the sign of a cross. He raised his hand in farewell to Father Domingo as he signaled Rose into a trot.

Going home. His chest almost burst from the thought of it. With enough savings to buy a half dozen horses to start his breeding stock. A grin tipped his mouth. God was good. Of course, this time he'd spread that savings over many hiding spots around his person and saddle for the trip back to Wyoming Territory. He wouldn't be robbed of everything again if he could help it.

He'd follow the mission trail up the coast of California to Mission San Jose, then head east on the old Pony Express trail. After that, just one stop outside of Sacramento to pick-up the Arabian stallion he'd arranged to purchase, and a visit to the land office in the Wyoming Territory to stake his claim on the land for his ranch. In less than three weeks, he'd be home.

Should he go see Mara first? Or get started on his ranch and court her proper? He had to prove he was different now. That he was in this for the rest of his life.

Josiah relaxed into Rose's easy canter, pulling forth the memory of his land on the Sweetwater. It was just across the river from the Reids' property. One hundred sixty acres of pastureland, with a few buttes, and a solid mile of riverfront. Perfect.

So many memories filled his mind of traversing that exact property with Mara. Would they ride it again together? His gut tightened. Probably not. Most likely she married some Eastern gent. Maybe even with a child or two by now. The knot in his stomach twisted tighter until bile rose in his chest. It was too much to think of her having someone else's child.

But if she'd left the western country, could he get her address from Zeche or Ezra to write her a letter? Even if she had married and moved on, the need still burned inside him to explain why he'd been so stupid. To beg her forgiveness, even if he could never have a second chance.

Lord, I'd really love a second chance. Was that too much to ask? Maybe, but he'd been asking it every day for months. *Not my will, but Yours, Father.*

219

Josiah reined both horses down to a walk as they crested the rise. Acres of grassy land stretched out before them, a vibrant green from spring rains. The Sweetwater flowed on their right, and some kind of yellow, stemmy wildflower bloomed sporadically across the pasture. This was home.

He dismounted at the base of the rise, removed the saddle and bridle from Rose, then hobbled both his horses about twenty feet apart. His new two-year-old Arabian stallion was young and a little inexperienced in the ways of the female gender, which had made it easier to travel riding Rose and ponying the stallion. But Josiah had no doubt nature would kick in if he ever allowed the two horses free rein near each other.

He gave the stallion's glossy chestnut shoulder a final pat. "Enjoy the grass, boy." As he stepped back, he admired the long arched neck and petite dished face one more time. This fellow would throw gorgeous foals with any mare, but especially mixed with Rose's long legs and striking chestnut and white markings.

Josiah took his time walking across the field—maybe ten acres in size—and found the perfect spot for his house and barn. After eating a biscuit and jerky from his saddle bag, he gathered some larger rocks and staked out the corners of his house.

It would be a two-bedroom structure, with a decent sized great room and a kitchen big enough to move around in. And he would build a storeroom right off the kitchen for supplies. And eventually a root cellar for his garden produce.

Because he would have a great big garden. With enough vegetables to eat and can for the winter months. And maybe once he got things going, he'd order pipes to bring water into the house from the river. Some of the houses around Sacramento had water piped inside, and it made cooking worlds easier.

After the house was mapped out, he moved on to the barn, planning and marking until the pinks and purples of the western sun faded into twilight.

Tomorrow, the man he'd hired to help with the building would arrive. Abner was an average sized fellow, with a full beard, strong shoulders, and years of experience building houses. He seemed like a good chap, and came recommended by the store keeper Josiah had asked. Abner would bring with him a load of wood, shingles and tools, and the next step in this dream would commence.

Josiah eased himself onto the grass next to the Sweetwater, then laid back to look at the stars.

Thank you, Lord, for smiling on me.

"Look, Mama. There's the Indian's paintbrush."

Mara couldn't hold back a smile at Katherine's mispronunciation of the flower's name. Sure enough, cone-like spikes of vibrant red flowers rose up in a cluster from the green grass. "They're beautiful, honey."

"Can we pick them?" Katherine's blue eyes pleaded. At seven, her cheeks had lost their baby plumpness, and she'd grown into a lean, vibrant girl who loved everything outdoors.

"I guess so. Get down and let me hold Pepper while you gather them. Uncle Ezra will be back from checking the snares any minute now."

The three of them had ridden out together—Ezra, Mara, and Katherine—to check trap lines along the creek and river. But the recent rains and warmer weather had produced so many beautiful plants and baby animals, Ezra had ridden on to allow her and Katherine time to investigate the sights at their leisure.

"There. See, I picked four flowers." Katherine held up the bouquet for inspection. "One for you. One for Uncle Ezra. One for Uncle Ze. And one for me."

"They're perfect. Shall I hold them while you climb back on Pepper?"

Katherine's wiry form scrambled back up, and the old broodmare barely shifted at the change. Mara returned her daughter's triumphant smile as she handed the flowers back.

What would she have done without this angel in her life? Katherine fit so perfectly in their little family. She adored her uncles and they treated her like their patron saint. And, of course, no mother could love a daughter more than the love pumping through her veins now. And Katherine *was* her daughter in every way that mattered. Even legally, now that the adoption had gone through.

A noise sounded through the trees, and Ezra trotted into view on his gelding.

"Did you get anything, Uncle Ezra?"

"Sure did, squirt. This gray fox wasn't wily enough to outsmart our snares." He held up a bushy tale and wiggled his brows with a grin. After receiving the expected giggle from Katherine, he turned to Mara. "I need to check a couple more lines across the Sweetwater. You two comin' with me?"

Mara glanced at the sun, several hours past the center of the sky. "I think we better head back and start on the potatoes for dinner." She turned to her daughter. "You want to help me, honey?"

Katherine bobbed her head, her blonde braid bouncing with the motion.

Ezra raised a hand in farewell as he wheeled his horse and trotted away.

When Ezra neared the Sweetwater, a new thumping sound mixed with the rustle of the slow-moving water. The noise grew louder as his horse broke through the brush to the river's rocky bank. Across the water, a few horses grazed in the large pasture. Behind them, a structure rose from the grassy field. Beams formed the shape of an A-frame house, but wood only covered the sides about half way up. Two men could be seen in the distance, hammering at each end of a board.

A spark of excitement ignited in Ezra's chest and he nudged his gelding into the water. "Forget about the traps, boy. Let's go meet the new neighbors."

As he rode up the bank on the far side of the river, one of the horses in the little cluster snagged his attention. She looked awfully familiar. A paint, with chestnut and white marking splashed across her body.

He turned his attention toward the structure being built and studied the two men. Both looked oddly familiar, but it didn't seem like he'd seen them together. Maybe they'd come through on the stage.

The one facing him wore a full brown beard, and Ezra finally recognized him as a fellow he'd met in South Pass City. Adams…or Abner, maybe.

Ezra kept his horse to a walk as he approached. When he was about fifty feet away, the other fellow turned, and an odd feeling of familiarity washed through him. He blinked, and focused on the man. Could it be? Not possible.

He was about twenty feet away now, and jumped off his horse to move forward on foot. It wasn't until he stood five feet from the man that he finally believed his eyes. "Josiah?"

"Ezra." Josiah grinned. The look was a little sheepish, and the creases around his eyes dug in deeper than they had four years ago. But he was definitely the same Josiah.

Ezra strode forward to clap the man on the back. "Well it's about time you dragged your sorry hide back here." He stepped back to get a good look at the changes in this man who'd once planted himself as almost a part of their family. "Looks like you got old." Ezra gave him a light punch in the shoulder. Hard muscle met his fist.

Josiah grabbed his shoulder with feigned pain. "I'm not the only one." He turned to the other man, standing a few feet behind him. "Have you met Abner Michaels? Abner, this is my old friend Ezra Reid."

Ezra exchanged nods with the older man. "I've seen you around South Pass, I think." Then he turned back to Josiah. "So whose house is this?" He wasn't sure whether to hope it was Josiah come to stay, or pray he was just a hired hand passing through. What would even a short time in the territory do to Mara?

Josiah's smile eased, a sadness taking over his eyes. "It's mine. I hired Abner on to help get the house and barn up."

Ezra raised a brow. "You bought the land?"

"Staked a claim on it through the Homestead Act of '62."

Ezra released a low whistle. "Nice. Zeche's thought about doin' that, too." He looked around at the fertile pasture. "This is a good spot. What are you plannin' to raise?" He turned back to Josiah. Did the man still harbor the same dream he had four years ago?

The corners of Josiah's mouth tipped up. "Horses. See that Arabian stallion out there? I'm planning to cross him with Quarter Horse mares. In fact," Josiah leveled his gaze on Ezra, "I'd like to pick-up four or five more young mares if you have any good ones for sale."

Ezra nodded. "We've got quite a few two- and three-year-old mares. Talk to Zeche, I'm sure you can take your pick." He turned back to look at the house taking shape behind them, then raised his hat to scratch his head. "Still have a good bit of work to do here, don't ya? Zeche and I will come by tomorrow morning to help."

"I'd be obliged, but you don't have to. I'm sure you've got all the work you can handle on your own ranch, especially with foaling time coming."

"We'll be here. Just make sure you have enough coffee." He shot Josiah a half grin. "Never had coffee as good as you used to make it. Mara does better with her cookin' now, but she can still burn coffee with the best of 'em."

The strain around Josiah's eyes nudged Ezra's memory. He'd not meant to mention Mara unless Josiah asked. Oh well.

"How is...Mara?" Josiah said her name like it was painful in his mouth.

"She's fine. Her daughter keeps her pretty busy, but she still does her share of training." He pinched his mouth in a rueful smile. "Just not as many barn chores." The reminder of Mara sent a flash of awareness through his mind. "In fact,

I better head out now. She's probably got dinner ready and will have my head if I'm late."

He reached out to shake Josiah's hand. "Good to have you back, friend."

Josiah's lungs heaved like he'd been gut-kicked by a mule. Mara had a daughter? How could she?

He turned toward the house and stumbled through the open door frame. He'd told himself this was possible. Likely, even. But deep down he hadn't really believed she'd move on. Without him.

He sucked in one deep breath after another, replaying Ezra's words. *She's probably got dinner ready back at the ranch.* So Mara still lived at the Reids' ranch? The Rocky Ridge stage station? If she was married with children, wouldn't she and her husband have their own ranch? Maybe they had a separate house on the Reid property. If that were the case, it made sense she might still cook for her brothers, too.

The sound of hammering pounded through Josiah's awareness and he turned back toward the doorway. He had to get to work. His shoulders slumped but he was powerless to raise them.

It was finally real. He'd lost the woman he loved. And it was all his own doing.

God, I need Your strength now.

Chapter Twenty-One

"A certain Persian of dis—"

Mara almost smiled as Katherine wrinkled her brow to study the word. "Sound it out." She stopped stirring the buffalo stew to listen to her daughter.

"Dis-tinc-tion. A certain Persian of distinction had for years—" Katherine looked up from her McGuffey Reader as boots sounded on the steps outside. The door swung open to reveal Zechariah.

"Hi, button nose." He stepped inside and stopped to tweak Katherine's nose before turning to face Mara. "Smells good."

"Thanks. Ezra back yet?"

"He was unsaddling the gelding when I left the barn. Said to save him some food."

Mara dished bowls of stew for Katherine to place on the table while Zeche washed up. When she finally had them all seated at the table, Ezra thumped in.

"Sorry to be late, but you might think it worthwhile when you hear my news." He shot them a cocky grin as he strode to the wash basin.

"What news?" This from Zeche.

Ezra slid into his chair. "I'll tell you after the blessing."

A tickle of unease slid through Mara's midsection. She and Katherine had left him just an hour ago. What could have happened between then and now? Did he see an Indian war party? There were rumors of Cheyenne attacks on several forts in the Territories. Maybe the bands had moved in this direction.

She fought the urge to reach out and pull Katherine close while Zeche spoke the prayer. Instead, she added her own heartfelt appeal. *Lord, no matter what happens, please keep us in Your will. And give us wisdom.* She'd come so far in her faith over the last four years, since losing Josiah and gaining Katherine in her life. It was still a daily battle to be patient and trust in God's leading, but He had become her strength.

A nudge to her shoulder brought Mara's head up. She glanced over to find a corner of Zeche's mouth twitching, but he kept his eyes focused on Ezra. "So what's the news?"

How had she missed the end of the prayer? Tension settled into Mara's shoulders as she, too, focused on her younger brother.

"Well." Ezra drawled the word. He was eating up every minute of the spotlight. That couldn't mean the news was bad, right? She tried to loosen her drawn muscles, but her stomach still roiled.

"It seems we have a new neighbor across the Sweetwater," he continued. "He's building a house and barn in that big grassy area near the fork of Silver Creek."

Zeche laid his spoon on the table. "So close? Did you meet him?"

Ezra nodded. "I did. A workman from South Pass City is helping him build."

Zeche's brows lowered to form shadows over his eyes. "What sort of man is he? Could you tell?"

Ezra shot Mara a raised-eyebrow look. "Oh, I think he's a good sort. Just the kind of neighbor we need." A grin played at his mouth.

Oh, no. Was this another of her brothers' attempts to marry her off? They'd been scoping out every man within fifteen years of her age for a while now. She was twenty-four years old now—one would think they'd have given up and realized she didn't want a husband. There was no way she could love another man the way she'd loved Josiah. And there was no way she could endure the torment that came from losing that kind of love. She wouldn't go through it again.

Besides, it wasn't like she'd never have a family. She had Katherine. And this sweet little girl had brought a fullness to her life she hadn't known was missing.

"I'll have to go over and introduce myself." Zeche resuming his eating. "Mara, maybe you can pack a crate of food to welcome him."

"I told him you and I would be over first thing tomorrow to help with the house." Ezra glanced at Zeche as he spooned a mouthful of stew into his mouth.

Zeche nodded. "Did the man tell you his name?"

"Yep." Ezra swallowed a bite before continuing. "Josiah English."

Mara clutched the table. Josiah? The room went fuzzy. It couldn't be. She must have misheard. Josiah was their new neighbor? A buzzing radiated in her ears. She blinked. Hard.

A hand touched her arm. "Mama?" Something tugged at her sleeve.

Mara focused on breathing. In. Out. She blinked again, and the room came back into focus.

Another tug, and she looked down. Katherine's big blue eyes pooled in a worried expression. "Are you all right, mama?"

The hint of fear in that sweet, soft voice started an ache in Mara's chest. "Yes, honey. Mama's fine." She drew Katherine into her arms and relished the hug.

Zeche's eyes met hers. His gaze was penetrating, but she faced it squarely. No need to worry about her. She would not be hurt by Josiah again.

"Can you toss up another bundle of shakes when you get a chance?" Josiah swiped an arm across his forehead, then eyed his progress on this side of the gable roof. Almost a quarter of the way done. Looked like he was making good headway for a half day's work—until he compared it to Zechariah's progress on the other side of the ridge.

The man was well beyond the half-way mark. He rarely looked up, just fit each wood shingle into place, set the first nail, and in two blows had the nail head sunk deeply into the wood. Then he was onto the next one.

Zeche was good. But there was something about the stiffness in his shoulders that spoke of more than just efficiency. Or maybe it was the wary look he occasionally sent Josiah's way. And after each look, he only took one blow to sink the next nail deep.

"Bundle comin' up."

Josiah turned just in time to catch the bale of wood Abner tossed. Slipping the knife from the sheath at his waist, Josiah loosened the ties, picked up a shake, and settled back into position on the roof where he'd left off. Better get to work if he was going to finish before Zechariah.

He'd completed two more rows when Ezra's face appeared at the top of the ladder. "You still know how to cook, English? Didn't figure we'd go this hungry workin' on your house." A hint of a grin took the edge off his words, but the message still came through.

Josiah glanced up at the sky. The sun was just past the halfway mark, a good distance from when they'd begun working as it crested the eastern hills that morning. Laying down his hammer and nails, he shot Ezra an apologetic look.

"Didn't mean to starve you. I'll have lunch slapped together in two minutes."

The food he'd been cooking was a far cry from what he used to make at the Rocky Ridge stop. And couldn't even be called a meal compared to what he'd served at the hotel in Savannah. But that was another lifetime ago. And since he didn't have a stove yet, and very few food supplies, he and Abner had been living off dried beef, and anything that could be cooked in a pot over an open campfire.

Should he take time to build a fire now to heat up the stew from last night? He'd planned to serve it with the leftover cornbread. But that would take a good half hour to get the fire started and wait for the food to heat. A half hour he could be working.

At the bottom of the ladder, he turned to Ezra with raised brows. "How does cold beef stew and cornbread sound?"

Ezra nodded. "Better than goin' hungry."

Ten minutes later, the four men sat on logs around the cold ashes from last night's campfire. Josiah only owned two tin plates, so he and Ezra drank the stew from mugs. Not his best attempt at hospitality. It looked like a trip to the trading post in South Pass City would be in his near future.

The sun didn't burn as hot as it had the last couple days, and a soft breeze played through Josiah's hair as he ate. They settled into a comfortable silence, content to inhale the food that had been too long in coming.

Surprisingly, it was Zechariah that broke the silence. "Nice stallion you have there." They were the first words he'd spoken that day that weren't necessary to getting the job done.

Josiah gazed out at the shiny chestnut. "Thanks. I looked hard to find him. I call him Lo Bello—Spanish for beautiful. You're welcome to cross some mares with him if you like."

"Where'd you get him?"

"Just this side of Sacramento. A Spanish rancher there raises Arabians, along with his cattle. Gave me papers on this boy that trace his descendants back to the Godolphin Arabian." He waited for their admiring responses.

Nothing but blank looks. "The Godolphin was one of the three founding sires of the Thoroughbred breed."

Zechariah's eyes changed to understanding, and his head tipped in a slight nod. He placed his empty plate on the ground and picked a blade of grass, which he twirled between his thumb and fingers. "Hear Sacramento's turnin' out to be a nice place. Downright civilized now. I'm surprised you didn't set up a ranch right there."

Josiah eyed the man. Where was he going with that comment? Fishing for Josiah's intentions? If he wanted to know, he should just come out and ask. He picked up his own stem of grass and rested his arms on his bent knees.

"I've done a fair amount of moving around these last few years. Mostly California and the Utah Territory, but lots of places along the Oregon Trail, too. I haven't found any area

I like as much as this stretch along the Sweetwater. It's pretty here. Good grazing for the animals. Plenty of hunting still to put food on the table." He shot them an easygoing look. "And I like the neighbors."

Ezra had been quiet thus far, but spoke up now with none of the distrust in his brother's voice. "You'll make a good one, Josiah. And we'll be back to help out more the rest of the week." He shot a glance at his brother. "May just be one of us each day so we don't leave Mara and Katherine home alone for too long. What with all the Indian trouble lately."

Josiah didn't know what to question first. Mara? He wanted to ask everything there was to know about her. Katherine? How old was this daughter of Mara's? She had to be a baby still. He'd only been gone four years, and Mara hadn't had any other prospects when he left—that he knew of anyway. And where was Mara's husband? No one had mentioned him yet. Had he died? Was Mara a widow already? He was torn between horror and hope. And he should be ashamed for hoping.

And Indians? What kind of trouble? Was that how Mara's husband had died? Were Mara and the baby safe right now with no one there to protect them?

He glanced at Zechariah. "Do you need to go home now and check on them?" A large part of him craved the chance to do that himself, but that probably wasn't his best introduction.

The man shook his head. "She insisted we both come help." A muscle in his jaw worked.

Josiah summoned a breath and his fortitude. "Mara is…doing well then?" Hopefully they missed the crack in his voice.

"Stayin' busy." A grin quirked Ezra's mouth. "Between tending us menfolk and Katherine, she doesn't ride as much as she used to. Still handles a few horses, though."

That didn't really answer any of the questions racing through his mind. His fingers itched to shake the news out of Ezra. "How old is her daughter?" His voice was stronger this time.

Ezra's eyes twinkled. "Turned seven last September. And Mara's already teaching her how to train horses."

Seven? Josiah forced his mind to focus through the fog. How could that be? He'd only been gone four years. "What?" The word escaped before he could stop it.

Confusion wrinkled Ezra's forehead, and then his eyes widened and his brows shot up. "You don't know, do you? Sorry, Josiah. It never occurred to me you wouldn't have heard." He chuckled, leaning back against a large round stump behind him. "Katherine is Mara's adopted daughter."

Josiah's mind spun as Ezra unrolled the story of how the mother had died at their home—in Mara's bed, no less—and asked Mara to become the child's mother. Relief flooded his chest. She hadn't married. She hadn't moved on.

And then shame pushed the relief out. How could he be relieved Mara hadn't found happiness? What a selfish man he was. *I'm so sorry, Lord.*

Mara was special. No doubt about it. She deserved the very best of men. Anyone who would take in another woman's child and raise her as her own. Even adopt her so the child had a family in every sense of the word. His chest burned. He loved this woman more than he could possibly put into words. Would she ever give him the chance to prove that?

The men settled into quiet again, gazing across the pasture at the slow-moving Sweetwater River.

Finally, Abner clapped his hands on his knees and groaned as he rose. "Got to be getting' back to work. Just another hour or so an' we'll be done with the siding."

Ezra stood and stretched. "Guess that's my cue, too." The two seemed to have formed a pretty good team as they installed the long wood planks on the sides of the cabin.

Josiah prepared his tired muscles to stand, but Zechariah didn't move, just sat staring across the empty fire pit at Josiah. He sank back onto his stump. Did the man want to talk? His gaze was a gray storm cloud, penetrating through Josiah's protective layers.

Josiah met his eyes, opening himself to the scrutiny.

"What exactly are your intentions toward my sister?"

And there it was. The question he'd been waiting for. He shouldn't have worried whether Zechariah would shoot straight with him. The man was just fair enough not to ask the tough questions in front of an audience.

He kept his shoulders square, but relaxed his face into a friendly expression. "I plan to talk with your sister. Then I would very much like to court her. Prove to her I'm a different man now. A better man, with God's help. From there..." He raised his shoulders a half inch. "It's up to God. But I would love to spend the rest of my life with her."

He held Zechariah's gaze without a flinch. Let this man see how true his motives were. He was in it for life this time. Whatever it took.

Zechariah's face never shifted. Never softened. "Maybe you wanna come for supper tonight. Abner's welcome, too."

Josiah worked hard not to blink. Was that an invitation? The words were a stark contrast to the hard set of Zechariah's jaw. He forced his own mouth to curve into a friendly smile, and extended his hand. No matter the man's motives or intentions, he would take that invitation at face value.

He held out his hand for several moments before Zechariah reached to grip it. The shake was firm, but not fierce. His gaze never wavered from Josiah's, leaving the distinct impression that the assessment wasn't over.

"Don't mess up this time, English." Zechariah released his hand and turned toward the house, and the roof that awaited them.

Josiah stood for a long moment, adrenaline pumping through him. It may not have been a blessing exactly, but at least it didn't seem like Zeche would provide direct opposition. Maybe he'd even help with opportunity until Mara decided for herself?

God, please help me not mess this up. Because if God was for him, who could be against him, right?

Chapter Twenty-Two

"Mama, no!" Katherine's cry broke through Mara's thoughts just as a powerful jaw clamped hard on her shoulder.

"Ah!" She whirled, raising her elbow in a reflex against her attacker. Rico, their bay stallion reared backward in his stall, loosening his hold on her and flashing the whites of his eyes.

The mare on Mara's right jigged away from the shoulder-high wall of the stallion's stall, pulling the lead rope taught in her hands. Mara jumped forward, propelling them both away from the temperamental stallion's grasp. She'd forgotten Rico was in the barn today. That's what she got for not paying attention.

"Are you all right, mama?" The fear and worry in Katherine's voice squeezed Mara's chest. She turned back to where her daughter stood safely behind and far away from the stallion's stall.

"Yes, honey. I'm fine. He just nipped me, is all." Although it smarted something awful. But she resisted the urge to rub her shoulder where he'd sunk his teeth in. Instead, she reached her free hand toward her daughter. "Come on up and walk with me. Just stay far away from Rico when you go by his stall."

That advice was probably not necessary, because the girl already walked as close to the opposite wall as possible. Her daughter was gutsy in most situations with the horses, but a little healthy fear was good, too. At least enough to instill common sense and respect for the animals.

Her shoulder throbbed as they led the mare out to the pasture. The thump of hooves sounded to her right where Zeche worked one of the geldings in the corral. The short sprigs of grass in the fields were finally turning green now, but probably nothing compared to the virgin pastures Josiah had just purchased. Was Rose enjoying that tasty grass? Ezra had said he still kept the mare. But of course he did. No man in his right mind would give her up without a fight. Her chest yearned to see the horse again, but she wouldn't be pursuing that dream. She planned to stay as far away from Josiah as she could.

And how many other horses did he have grazing those verdant pastures with Rose? Her foot snagged a root, and Mara grabbed the mare's neck beside her. She barely managed to stay upright. She had to stop thinking about Josiah before she really injured herself.

241

But what would the men be working on now? Ezra had said he thought they might get the walls and roof finished today. Was it a small house then? A lone bachelor didn't need too much space.

And then an awful thought settled into Mara's brain. One that halted her body mid-step, her feet suddenly rooted to the ground. What if Josiah wasn't a bachelor? What if he was *married* now? The blood coursed from her head, leaving only a woozy feeling in its place. Surely her brothers would have told her.

"Mama?" Katherine stopped too, worry threading her voice. She tugged on Mara's hand.

But Mara couldn't pull herself from the questions spinning in her mind. Had Ezra said whether there was anyone else with Josiah? Only Abner, the hired hand, as far as she could remember. But maybe he'd left his wife at their previous home until he could get the house built here. He did have a history of leaving his women behind.

An overpowering rage started somewhere in her gut, and climbed up into her chest. If he'd brought his wife to live not two miles away from them, he was crueler than she'd ever thought. Her muscles tensed until it hurt to breathe.

But then a niggle of remorse started somewhere around her heart. Why was she bringing back the old pain? And she didn't even know for sure whether Josiah was married. *God, please take this from me. I'm sorry, I let my guard down against the bitterness.* She took a deep breath and exhaled. *I'm going to need Your strength a lot in the coming days.*

Another tug on her hand brought Mara's attention down.

"Mama, what are you doing?" Katherine's wide blue eyes examined her.

"Just praying, honey." Mara slipped her hand from Katherine's grasp and settled it around the girl's shoulders. "Come on, let's put this mare out, then we'll go start the biscuits. Did you finish writing out your sums while I worked the horses?"

"Yes, ma'am." Katherine held up her slate, covered with white scrawling numbers from one side to the other.

"Good job. What say we make a gooseberry pie with the last of the preserves?" She tweaked one of the girl's braids, forcing a smile for her daughter.

"Can I do the crust? Please?"

That excited face made her smile come a little easier. "That sounds like a great idea."

An hour later, they pulled the gooseberry pie from the oven. As Mara settled a pan of biscuits into the heat to cook, a blanket of longing settled over her. Being in the kitchen made her miss Josiah more than any other place. But she had to shake this off.

"I'll tell you what," she turned to Katherine, "while I start the meat boiling, you go pick out a book and we'll read until the men come in."

A delighted squeal greeted her words, and Katherine raced to the bookshelf in the bedroom they shared. Just being around this sweet girl of hers made things better.

A few minutes later, they were snuggled in the rocking chair by the hearth, reading the worn pages of *Aesop's Fables*. Katherine cuddled in Mara's lap, her hair smelling like the rose scented soap they both used.

"We'll read two stories, then the biscuits and meat should be done. All right, honey?"

Katherine bobbed her head, nestling deeper into Mara's arms. Mara started in on "The Tortoise and the Hare." It was one of the girl's favorites, and they'd read it enough she quoted some of the lines as Mara read them.

Just before Tortoise reached the finish line in the story, the sound of horses and male voices sounded from the yard.

Mara looked up and patted her daughter's leg. "Sounds like your uncles are back. We'd better get up and start on the gravy. Can you please set the table for me?"

They started to work as the deep timbre of voices calling to each other continued out in the yard.

Mara tested the beef in the boiling pot. Tender enough. After pulling the empty skillet to the hot part of the stove, she scooped the meat from the water and sliced it into flat chunks, then settled them in the hot cast iron pan. While that fried, she opened the oven to look at the biscuits. They were just turning golden. Perfect. The aroma was enough to start her stomach growling as she pulled the pan from the oven and turned to place it on the work counter.

The cabin door opened then, and voices spilled into the room. She needed to speed things up a bit, or the boys would be waiting. And hungry men didn't wait well when they smelled food cooking. At least not her brothers.

Mara turned back to the skillet and flipped the meat strips over so they could crisp on the other side. Now for the gravy. She reached for the flour from the shelf, then scooped a cup of milk from the pail on the counter, careful to dip under the layer of cream on top.

She turned back to the meat, ready to scoop it out of the pan and onto a plate. She glanced toward the men to tell them she was almost ready—

And froze.

Her whole world narrowed down to one single person. Josiah.

He stood watching her, hands in his pockets and a look on his face as earnest as a young preacher.

He took a step forward. "Hello, Mara."

Her blood pumped hard through her chest, speeding until it raced in her ears. He was here.

Josiah was here.

She'd dreamed of this moment. Literally. Had very vivid dreams of seeing him again. He would come back for her, and she would throw herself into his arms. Then he would kiss her until all the pain was gone.

But looking at him now, standing as he had so many times before. It was too much like the past. Too much like her memories. The ones that brought so much pain as she'd relived them after his parting.

Now his shoulders were a little broader, tapering to a trim waist. Ropy muscles bulked his forearms. And those blue eyes. They forged so deep inside her, tinged with a sadness that burned the back of her eyes. Emotion pressed down on her chest, making it hard to breathe.

She forced herself to turn back to the work counter, putting her back to them all. She picked up the tin of flour. What had she been doing with this? Gravy. She squeezed her eyes closed. She had to regain some focus. But all she saw with her eyes shut was Josiah's image burned into her memory. That would never do. She popped them open again.

She forced herself through the last few steps to finish the meal. The meat had seared a little too much on one side, and the gravy was probably a lumpy mess. She couldn't bring herself to care, though. He was here. The shock of it had stolen all sense from her.

With the meat and gravy both ready in serving tins, Mara faced the work counter and inhaled a deep breath. *Lord, please give me strength. Your strength. Fill my mind with Your thoughts. And help me to be strong.*

With another deep breath, and a plate in each hand, Mara turned to face the men.

"Your Uncle Ezra says you're going to be a fine horse trainer one day." Josiah loved the pink that spread across the little girl's cheeks as she ducked her head.

"Yes, sir."

She was as adorable as they came. With her blonde braids, clear blue eyes, and deep dimples. A heartbreaker. Even at the age of seven.

He couldn't help a glimpse at Mara. She was capable of stealing hearts, too. Even more beautiful than he remembered. Her wide eyes were the same shape as Katherine's, except their color was a deep caramel brown. He knew it from memory, even though she wouldn't look in his direction.

Her focus shifted between her own plate and Katherine's as she helped her daughter cut the meat, then resumed her eating.

What was she thinking? She hadn't said a word to him yet, not even in greeting. Was she that angry? But her eyes didn't snap fire at him. She just...ignored him. Like he wasn't there.

Lord, I'm sorry I brought so much pain to her life. Thank You for Your forgiveness, but show me how to make this right.

"So you worked on the telegraph line, too?"

Josiah turned to face Ezra, bringing his thoughts back to the conversation. "Signed on with the Overland Telegraph Company in Genoa, then worked all the way through to Salt Lake City."

"We have a telegraph here now." Ezra grinned, nodding toward a small table in the front corner of the cabin. A machine sat atop it, with wires running from the wall.

"Nice. Sure makes communication easier." He'd come to grips with his dislike for the whole system.

"Yep. It's much easier to change our supply order now, and to sell the horses, too."

Supplies. Yes. "Speaking of ordering things, could I order a stove through your supplier? There's only so much you can cook over an open camp fire." He offered a wry grin to soften his words, then turned to Mara. "This meal is great. Better than I've had in many weeks."

She didn't look at him. Not even a flush to her cheeks to show she'd heard the compliment. Was he invisible?

"Sure, of course." Ezra kept on with the conversation, as if he hadn't noticed the lack of response from his sister. "Make a list of things you need before you leave tonight, and I'll send the request."

Josiah nodded. "I'd be obliged." Then he turned to the cute blonde pixie who sat across from him. "So how about you, miss Katie. Are you a good cook like your mama?"

She ducked her chin. "Yes, sir." Adorable.

"Has she taught you how to make cinnamon crisps yet?"

Her eyes lit like a summer sunrise. "Yes, but we haven't made them in a long, long time." She drew out the last "long" as if it'd been decades. Then she turned pleading eyes to Mara. "Mama, can we make cinnamon crisps tonight? Please?"

"We already made pie for tonight, honey." Mara's voice held an undertone of steel, but she didn't spare him a glance.

He ignored the barb. "I'll tell you what, Katie-girl. Pie's just about my favorite dessert in the world, so why don't you and I plan to make cinnamon crisps another time. Have you ever cut them out to look like people?"

Katie stared at him, her face a picture of fascination. "No, just circles an' squares an' triangles."

"Well, we'll have to make sure we cut some into little girls with cute blonde braids like yours."

She crinkled her nose, and if he'd been close enough, he would have tweaked it.

"Eat your food now, Katherine." Mara's voice put a decided end to that vein of conversation.

Had that command been for him, as well? Josiah speared a bite of meat and raised it to his mouth.

After another moment, Zeche spoke. "Might take you up on the use of your stallion. He'd add some height to that new broodmare we got, maybe throw a prettier head than she has, too." He looked to Josiah. "I'd be happy to trade breedings with our Rico for any of your mares."

Here was his chance. "Actually, I don't have my broodmares yet. I was hoping to buy some three-year-olds from you, if you have any for sale."

A motion caught the corner of his vision, and he turned to look at Mara. Her back was stiff as an oak board, her shoulders squared, and her eyes shooting daggers at him. What had he done now?

His mind ran back through the words he'd just said. He'd offered to let them use his stallion. He'd said he wanted to buy some of their mares ready to sell. That should all be good news. Right? Did she think he was trying to barter breedings for horses? He'd planned to pay cash for every animal. Should he say that? *Lord, please give me wisdom here.*

"Sure." Zeche pushed his empty plate away and leaned back in his chair. "We have a good crop of mares ready this year." He nodded toward the plate Josiah had scraped clean. "If you're done, we can look at them now."

Josiah dared a glance at Mara before responding. She'd dropped her focus back to her lap. "Thanks."

Zeche scooted his chair back, which commenced a chorus of scraping as they all stood. They moved as a herd toward the front door, but Mara separated from the group, carrying a stack of dirty dishes toward the work counter.

Josiah paused. If he went outside now, he would miss his chance to speak with her. But even now, Zeche was out the door, and expected Josiah to be on his heels. Could he come back in to talk to Mara after they looked at the horses?

"Katherine."

His thoughts were interrupted by Mara's voice.

The little blonde pixie halted at the door and turned to Mara. "Yes, ma'am?"

"Can you please stay and help me clean the dishes tonight?"

Disappointed confusion clouded the girl's face. "But I always help Uncle Ze in the barn after dinner."

"I need you in the kitchen tonight." Mara's voice was all strained tension.

Katie's shoulders sagged as she turned back toward her mother.

Mara still didn't spare him a glance, but spun back to drop her load of dishes into the wash bucket.

Josiah moved through the open doorway and closed it behind him. It may be a warm spring outside, but the atmosphere was cold as a mountain winter inside that cabin.

Chapter Twenty-Three

*T*he next day, Josiah eased Rose down to a walk as the Rocky Ridge station came into view. The butterflies in his stomach did another flip at the familiar sight.

It had been dark when Zeche and Ezra showed him the five mares for sale last night, so they'd suggested he come back during daylight hours.

So here he was again. And this time he had to talk to Mara. His nerves were wound tighter than a horse jumping through a ring of fire.

As he neared the station yard, Rose released a loud whinny, and two answering neighs drifted from the direction of the barn. Did she remember her old home? The only movement visible came from the riding pen with the high fences. Two figures rode there—one the elegant outline of the strong feminine figure he'd dreamed about for years.

And beside her rode a smaller profile—one more girlish and carefree than Mara's upright posture. That little girl was as cute as the day was long. Not hard to see why she was wrapped around Mara's heart so tight.

He tied Rose in front of the barn, then went to stand at the rail to watch the women ride, taking up his old spot. Seeing Mara ride was like watching an eagle fly. Her movements were elegant. Effortless. Majestic.

It was easy to tell when she first caught sight of him. She rode next to Katherine, giving instructions on something. Her voice was so soft he could only make out every other word. Something to do with asking the horse to lower its head.

When her gaze connected with his, she froze. Her words stopped mid-sentence, and at least two full seconds passed before her back stiffened, and she turned her face away.

She spoke to her daughter again, picking up where she'd left off with her instructions. Was it his imagination or did her voice shake a bit? They were too far away to tell for sure.

The pair rode for a quarter hour longer before coming to the center of the arena to dismount. Katherine climbed down without any assistance, even though she was just a little wisp of a girl and had several feet to drop to the ground.

Josiah met them at the gate and fell into step beside Katie. Maybe she would be a good buffer between him and Mara's stony gaze.

"Why did you watch me ride, Mr. English?" Katie's question held all the forthrightness and innocence of youth.

"Well, Miss Katie. Your uncles have told me what a good rider you are, but I have to say I didn't really believe them. But now I see you're even better than they said. I can tell your mama's teaching you everything she knows." He curled his hand to keep from tweaking her cute little button nose.

The girl beamed, but a quick glance at Mara showed no break in her rock façade.

So he focused his attention on the female in the group that seemed to appreciate his conversation. "What's your horse's name?"

"Pepper. She's going to have a baby in three months."

He raised his brows. "Really? And do you take care of her?"

Katie's chin bobbed. "Yes, sir. She's my special horse."

They reached the barn then, and Josiah held the door as the two horses and their handlers moved through. He followed Katie until she stopped Pepper in front of the post where a halter hung. After the girl unfastened the girth that strapped the saddle around the horse, he lifted the heavy leather from the mare's back.

"Where does this one go?"

"I'll show you." She skipped over to the wall and touched an empty rail. "Right here."

As soon as he'd settled the saddle on the wood and draped the damp saddle blanket on top to air out, Katie grabbed his hand and pulled.

"Do you want to see where Pepper's baby is now?"

It had been a long time since he'd been around a child, and never one as charismatic as her. He couldn't stop the smile pulling his face as he followed her back to her horse. She showed him the mare's swollen abdomen, and helped him rub his hand over the protrusion.

"Mr. English, my brother is in the house if you'd like to speak with him." Mara's cold tone intruded on their fun, and sent a fresh pang through his chest.

"Actually, I'd like to talk with you first." He almost added *if you don't mind,* but stopped himself. No sense giving her the option of backing out of this conversation. From the solid set of her jaw, she would most likely refuse anyway, and he'd have to do some begging. Whatever it took.

Something flashed in her eyes—something like wariness—and then a veil slipped over them. If only he could read her thoughts. Know what she felt about him now. It seemed anger was a part of it, but could there be any softer emotions left?

Without another look at him, she turned to her daughter. "Katherine, please go put Pepper in the pasture, then ask Uncle Ezra to help you with your sums."

"Yes, ma'am. Mr. English, are you coming inside, too?"

"I'll be there in a few minutes, Katie-girl."

Her face radiated a sunny smile as she led the quiet mare outside.

Josiah and Mara both watched her go until the barn door closed behind her, then Mara pivoted to face him.

"Speak."

He swallowed a knot in his throat and studied her eyes. Implacable. *Lord, please give me the words.*

"Mara, I'm sorry for leaving like I did. For hurting you." He watched her face, but she avoided his gaze. Just kept her focus on some point past his head. He forced himself to keep talking. "I know I messed up. I was confused—about a lot of things. But that's no excuse. I was stupid."

His voice grew stronger now. "It took God a while to get my attention. It wasn't until I started working at the mission with Father Domingo, that I realized I don't have to control every part of my life." He forced a chuckle. "It wasn't ever in my control to begin with. He's been guiding everything—the good and what I thought was bad. I just didn't see it."

He took a small step forward, and she didn't move. "I get that now, Mara. I've worked hard the last four years, and God's blessed me with enough to start a small ranch. Nothing fancy. Not very big. But it'll be the start of this next phase of God's plan. And the best part is, I don't have to do it alone." His voice almost cracked on those last words as he poured all the hidden parts of his soul to her. The important things God had taught him, mostly the hard way. He wanted her to know it. To see him as he was now. As he would be when God finished with him.

He stopped to watch her face. The expression hadn't changed, but a rim of red circled her eyes. What did that mean? Should he ask his next question? He had to chance it. Had to be honest with her.

"Mara, I know I was pretty heartless when I left. But do you think you could ever forgive me?" He held his breath, studying her.

She stood quiet. Didn't respond, just kept staring into the distance. Seconds passed, maybe even minutes. Had she heard him? Maybe he'd hurt her so much she completely blocked out his words. Or was she so angry, she couldn't respond? Had he said something terribly wrong? Each moment that passed tightened the knot in his stomach. He should say something more.

But as he searched his mind for something that might help, Mara turned to look at him. For a moment, it seemed like she was seeing him for the first time.

"I don't know." Her voice was barely more than a whisper, and filled with a sadness that squeezed his chest.

Her shoulders rose and fell, as if she were taking a deep breath. Then she met his gaze, looking squarely in his eyes. "I forgive you, but that doesn't take away the pain."

For a single moment, the mask disappeared from her expression, and the hurt that showed through her eyes twisted his heart. He had to fight to keep from pulling her into his arms. But he couldn't rush this. Couldn't mess up this time.

"Mara, I'll do whatever it takes to prove—"

"I need to get inside," she interrupted his words. And just like that, the façade was back in place over her features. She turned, untied her horse, and strode out of the barn, half-dragging the animal behind her.

There was nothing to do but stand and watch, a raw ache filling him. Would he be able to heal the hurt he'd caused? Not by himself.

Josiah placed the nail and swung the hammer hard. The crack of metal on metal resounded through the meadow. The nail head seated into the wood in two blows. He'd driven so many nails over the last few weeks, the pounding still echoed through his head during quiet moments.

As he paused his hammer to place another nail, the echo of Abner's blows from the roof of the barn drifted down to him. They had the structure of the house pretty much finished, thanks to the Reid men who'd been coming to help for half days at a time. Now they were making good progress on the barn.

Another week or so, as long as the weather held, and they'd have everything done that required Abner's help. He'd miss the man's presence, even though he rarely spoke unless questioned. He'd become a comrade. Put as much sweat into these buildings as Josiah had.

Before hoisting the next board into place, Josiah glanced up at the sun's position. Still mid-afternoon. This evening he'd take the final payment to Zechariah and pick-up the five mares he'd purchased. Which meant he'd see Mara.

He hadn't been back over since their conversation in the Reid's barn last week. It seemed like a good idea to give her some space. A little bit of time to get used to the idea of him being around again. But the image of her pain-filled face haunted him. How could he have been such a heartless cad?

Conviction washed over him, and Josiah sank to his knees right there beside the half-finished barn wall. *Oh, Lord. I have a better idea of what I've done now. Please, Father, forgive me. Help me make it right.* He stayed in that position, his heart lifting its own plea. And then the peace was there, before he even realized. Like a balm over his heart. *Thank you. Show me how to make it right.* He raised his head to look at the clear blue sky. *And, Lord, if it's not too much to ask. Could you show me how to win her love again?*

A smile touched his mouth. He was asking for the impossible, but God could do anything, right?

He finally rose to his feet, picked up the board he'd been holding, and positioned it against the wood posts of the barn wall. What could he do to show Mara he cared? That he was different now.

She'd always been so sweet with the special things she'd done for him, back in those days he rode for the Express. She'd have a warm meal ready when he woke up after an all-night ride. Packed special things in his food bundle when he left on an Express run. Could he do something like that for her now?

He thought through his meager supplies. He only had the bare necessities, although Abner had ridden to South Pass

City a couple days ago and brought back more food stuffs. But he still didn't have a stove, and the campfire wasn't a place to make sumptuous delicacies to win the heart of a fair maiden.

Unless... His mind ran through his supplies. Yes. There should be enough of what he needed.

Excitement coursed through Josiah's veins as he hammered the last two nails, then put his tools away. Time to start the fire and get the Dutch oven heating. He was making peach cobbler.

Chapter Twenty-Four

"Y ou want me to take yer horse to the barn?"

Josiah shot a glance around the empty yard of the Rocky Ridge station before turning to answer Abner. "Thanks. I'd appreciate that."

Near the cabin door, he eased off his mare, careful not to jostle the pot tied to the back of his saddle. An unconventional saddle pack for sure.

A motion behind the barn caught his eye. Mara's brothers walked from the structure into the pasture where an array of horses grazed. No sign of Mara or Katie, though. Did that mean they were in the barn or the house?

He handed Rose's reins to Abner, then untied the heavy Dutch oven from his saddle and lifted it down. When the man rode on with both horses, no barrier remained between Josiah and the house. He inhaled a deep breath and let it out, releasing a few butterflies with the spent air. Then he stepped forward.

Just a few moments after he knocked on the door, it swung open several inches to reveal half of Mara's face. The look in her eyes changed from caution to wariness when she saw him, but she opened the door wider. Her form filled the opening, not giving him room to enter. "The boys are out with the horses."

He only smiled, holding out the pot like the gift of the Magi. "I brought something for you. Thought you might like a sweet."

She studied his offering, not making a move to take it. Her forehead pinched, but she just stood there.

"Do you want me to set it in the kitchen? It's kind of heavy."

She raised a brow then, but spun and swept the door wide.

He let out a breath as he strode forward. At least she'd let him inside. The salty aroma of fried meat cloaked him as he entered and thunked the heavy iron pot on the work table. "Something smells good in here." With a glance at the covered frying pan sizzling on the stove, he turned back to Mara. "Is that fried potatoes and buffalo meat?"

"Beef." She pushed past him on her way to the stove, and raised the lid to stir the mixture in the pan. A loud sizzle filled the air, crescendoing when she poured in a bit of water from a mug.

"Smells wonderful."

"Zeche will probably want you to stay for dinner." Her back was toward him, shoulders as stiff as her voice.

He curled his fists to keep from settling his hands on those shoulders and rubbing the starch out of them. How long had it been since he'd taken this woman in his arms? But now wasn't the time. He turned away and stepped out of the kitchen, stopping to stand in front of the table.

A noise sounded outside the door. Before he could turn, it flew open, admitting a whirlwind of blonde hair and green skirts. "Mr. English!" Katie slid to a stop in front of him, and dropped her chin, suddenly shy.

"There she is." He dropped down to sit on his heels and reached to chuck the girl's chin. "How's our Katie today?"

She gave him a smile bright enough to cure influenza. "Mr. English, did you come to make cinnamon crisps with us?"

Warmth wrapped his chest. "Since I call you Katie, why don't you call me Josiah? Deal?"

She giggled. "You're the only one that calls me Katie."

"Really?" He stole a glance at Mara, who was watching from the kitchen. Her face wasn't quite as stony, but her eyes gave no hint of her thoughts. Turning back to Katie, he asked, "What do other people call you?"

"Katherine. 'Cept Mama sometimes. When she's mad, she calls me Katherine Anne Reid."

He bit back a grin. "Well, Katherine Anne Reid. Do you mind if I call you Katie?"

She locked her hands behind her waist and twisted back and forth. "Nope. I like it."

Josiah's smile wouldn't stay locked inside anymore. "All right then, Miss Katie." His lower legs began to throb, so he stood. "I don't think we'll need to make cinnamon crisps tonight, because I brought you and your mama something special."

"What is it?" Katie hopped and pressed her hands together.

"Something sweet for the sweetest girls I know. Peach cobbler." He pointed to the counter.

The girl squealed and ran to the pot on the work counter. "Mama, can we eat it now?"

"After dinner, honey. Please go tell your uncles the food will be ready in a quarter hour."

"I can tell them," Josiah intervened. "I need to settle up with Zeche on the horses I've purchased, then we'll be off. Abner's along to help me get the new horses back across the river."

Mara's back visibly stiffened at his words. Her eyes narrowed, and she spun away from him.

Her response wasn't what he'd expected at all. Surely she wasn't upset he was leaving. Did it have something to do with the horses? He looked at Mara's rigid back, then at Katie peering under the lid of the Dutch oven at the peach cobbler.

"All right, then. I'll see you both later."

"Wait, Mr.—I mean, Josiah. I'll come with you."

"I need you to stay in here, Katherine." Mara's voice held an edge that weighed down Josiah's heart.

Katie must have picked up on the brook-no-arguments tone, for she only protruded her lower lip and dropped her gaze to the floor. How could Mara possibly say no to that cherub face?

"Next time, Katie-girl." He tapped her nose, then turned and headed for the door. Between Mara's glares and Katie's sad face, it was time for him to head out.

Ezra met him halfway across the yard with a handshake and a hearty backslap. "Good to see you, English." Definitely a warmer welcome than the man's sister had given.

"Thanks. Zeche in the barn? I've brought the final payment, and we need to get these girls home."

The corners of his mouth fell. "No hurry. Why don't you and Abner stay for dinner?"

Josiah glanced up at the sky that already showed pink to the west. "I'd like to get them settled before it gets too dark."

"All right." He turned to walk with Josiah to the barn.

Now was his chance to ask. "Ezra. Is there…uh…any reason Mara might not want me to buy these horses? That you know of?" Other than the fact she hated to be near him. But no need to bring that up.

The younger man rubbed the back of his neck as his steps slowed to a stroll. "It might have something to do with Zeche selling that mare to you all those years ago."

"Rose?" A knot started to form in his gut.

"Yep. She got pretty upset about the whole thing. Even swooned right there in the kitchen."

Weight squeezed Josiah's chest. Pain for what Mara had gone through—what he'd put her through—gripped him again. He'd been so caught up in his own struggles back then, he hadn't even thought about breaking the news to her gently. In fact, he should have asked her if she would approve him purchasing the mare. That was obvious now.

Josiah scrubbed a hand over his face. He had more apologizing to do.

Two days later, Josiah rode toward the Rocky Ridge station on Willow, one of the three-year-old mares he'd just purchased from the Reids. Rose trotted along on a rope beside him as he whistled a tune. No rhythm he could name, just a happy melody. Maybe it was the call of a nightingale or some other cheery bird.

As he neared the yard, two figures came into view, sitting against the side of the house where the sun shone brightest. The cheery blue of Katie's dress stood out against the brown wall of the cabin as she snuggled into Mara's side.

When he was about twenty feet away, he reined in Willow and slid to the ground. He barely had time to turn and brace himself before Katie catapulted into his arms.

"Josiah!"

He picked her up in a bear hug, relishing the sweet scent of roses in her feather-soft hair. "Katie-girl," he said in a hoarse whisper. His throat burned, but it didn't matter. This sweet bundle of innocence had worked her way into his heart faster than leaven in biscuit dough.

She leaned back in his arms and planted her hands on either side of his face. "Did you come to make cinnamon crisps?"

A chuckle escaped him. "Not just yet, Katie-girl." He glanced toward Mara. "I came to ask you and your mama a question."

"What?" Her eyes rounded even more than usual.

"Well, my question for you, Katie Anne..." he tapped her nose with his finger, "...is whether you've ever been on a ride along the river?"

Her eyes lit. "Yep. Mama took me all the time last summer, but then it got really cold. So what's your question for Mama?"

"Well." Josiah kept Katie in his arms as he strode toward the side of the house where Mara sat holding a book. He eased down to a sitting position, about three feet from her. She inched in the other direction, but not too far.

He ignored her movement, keeping his focus on Katie. "I actually need a little help from your mama. See, I have this great horse named Rose." He pointed to the mare standing calmly in the sunshine, eyes at half-mast and one foot cocked while she napped. "She's normally a really good girl. But every now and then, she does things that I know she knows better. So what I'm thinkin' is, she needs a good trainer to remind her what's right and wrong. Now, Katie, do you know who I think is the best trainer around?"

The little angel gave a sneaky smile. "Uncle Ze?" Too cute.

"Nope."

"Mama."

He tapped her nose again. "Right." Then he turned to Mara, changing his tone to be soft and serious. "What do you think, Mara? Would you be willing to go for a ride and see if you can work the kinks out of Rose?"

He didn't breathe as he studied her face, waiting for a response. This approach could go either way. Either it'd soften her up or she'd resent his asking. *Lord, you know my heart.*

Her shoulders weren't quite as stiff as the last few times he'd seen her. But it was several moments before she answered in a quiet voice. "I could ride her in the pen here."

Katie piped up. "But, Mama, we want to go for a ride by the river. Please." How could Mara even think about resisting the puppy-dog pleading that covered her angelic face?

"I guess so. But just a short one."

Josiah didn't try to hold back his grin. Apparently, Mara couldn't resist her daughter either.

Mara settled into Rose's easy rhythm as they rode along the Sweetwater. Oh how she'd missed this horse. The mare had filled out over the last four years, making her a wider seat, but she still had the same smooth stride and quick response that had made her a dream to train.

Katherine rode beside her on Pepper, keeping up a steady chatter with Josiah, whose horse ambled on the girl's other side. Those two had bonded quicker and stronger than Mara expected. Why hadn't she seen that coming? She should have put forth a lot more effort to keep her daughter away from him. The last thing she wanted was the child's innocent young heart to be hurt when Josiah left again.

Of course, he said he wouldn't. That he'd learned to find his worth in God. And he did seem…different. More mature, perhaps. Wiser? Yes. More stable? Maybe. He was building a house and barn just across the river. But could she trust him? *Lord, please show me the right thing. Show me Your will.*

"Mama, can we trot now?" Katherine's voice pulled Mara from the prayer.

She looked at them both—Katherine's eager face, and the pull of a smile tipping the corner of Josiah's mouth. The flips in her stomach forced her to look away. No matter how well her memory documented that smile, the force of it always caught her off guard.

"Can we?" Katherine's pleading again.

"I guess. Just make sure you stay between us. And keep your hands on the saddle so you don't jerk Pepper's mouth when she bounces you."

"Yes, ma'am."

Mara gave Rose the lightest squeeze with her heels, and the mare shifted into a light, easy jog. Oh, how she'd missed this weightless motion. Katherine's giggles beside her escalated as she bounced along to Pepper's jolting trot. The old broodmare was kind and gentle, but not exactly a dream ride. Not like Rose. Way too soon, they pulled back to a walk.

"That was fun, Josiah." Katherine giggled again, and his hearty chuckle joined hers. Mara bit her lip to hold in her own grin.

"Sure was, Katie-girl. You picked a good spot to trot. I remember one other time your mama and I had to ride fast through there. We'd just seen an Indian war party, and had to high-tail it back to warn your uncles. Your mama wouldn't let us just trot, though, we had to run flat out the whole way."

Katherine's eyes rounded. "You ran from an Indian war party?"

"Yep, but we were movin' so fast they never caught us."

"I see Indians all the time, but they're not the fighting kind. They're the kind that bring us food and buffalo hides. And one time they brought me a doll."

From her rambling, it sounded like Katherine had completely opened up to Josiah. But how could she not, when he had such an honest magnetism about him? It was hard to fight her own attraction, especially when they were out doing

270

what she loved so much. Where she had so many special memories with him.

But she had to fight it. Maybe they should go back now. Except she hadn't done what she'd agreed to on this ride. The whole reason for coming was to work out whatever bad habits Rose had picked up. Not that she'd found anything so far.

The next time Katherine stopped chattering long enough to draw breath, Mara broke into the conversation. "So what's Rose doing wrong?"

Josiah's forehead creased and his mouth formed a thin line. "She's, um… She's kind of gotten hard in the mouth at times. She won't always turn or stop when I first ask her to."

Mara raised her brows at him. Rose was the most responsive horse she'd ridden in years. "You two keep walking while I work with her for a minute."

She turned Rose away from the other two animals and put her through her paces. Several turns, trot, canter, back to a stop, back up. The mare did it all flawlessly, almost as if she could read Mara's mind.

Finally, she rode back to where Josiah and Katherine stood watching. "I can't find anything wrong with her. She's responsive to everything I ask. Just make sure you're using your legs and seat to direct her, too. When you turn, give her a little squeeze with your outside leg so she'll move away from the pressure. Kind of like you're closing a gate there, so she has to go the other way." Mara gave an exaggerated demonstration, pushing her left leg against the horse's side, and lifting her right leg so there was a gap between her heel and the animal. Rose obediently turned right.

"And when you ask her to slow, lean back in your seat a little. She'll feel your movement and respond before you make any change with the reins." She glanced at Josiah to make sure he was following her words.

But he wasn't watching her demonstrations. His eyes were glued to her face, and the look in those blue-gray depths stole her breath. It was love. The same thing she'd felt for him all these years. Even when she'd been so angry or tried to forget him, the love had always been there.

Mara bit her lip and looked away. She couldn't open herself to this man again. This was dangerous.

Chapter Twenty-Five

wo weeks later, Josiah savored creamy shepherd's pie as he sat at the Reids' table, surrounded by the family. These people were as much his kin as anyone he'd known since his parents died—a lifetime ago.

Katie sat across from him, chattering about the foal born that morning. That girl was the cutest little magpie when she got going. And what a special gift for him that she'd accepted him without reserve, despite her mama's aloof attitude. But even Mara's coolness had warmed some over the last couple weeks. At least she would talk in normal conversation when he was around. Although she didn't actually speak to him unless he asked her a direct question. Still, her eyes didn't shoot darts at him when he entered the room. Maybe the walls around her heart had thinned. *Thank you, Lord.*

"Did you know Mama let me rub the foal with a rag to help dry her?" Katie's words pulled him back to the conversation. "I had to be really quiet so Sarah didn't get upset."

"That's pretty special. Is Sarah the foal's mama?" He shot a knowing glance to Mara. Sarah was the mare he'd ridden when he was recovering from his accident, all those years ago. Did she remember it?

When his gaze found Mara, she watched him. Not with pursed lips like usual, but not with a smile, either. Her wide brown eyes used to be so easy to read. Not anymore. What was going through her mind now?

"Yes, Sarah's a good mama. Do you want to go see them?" Katie dropped her fork on the plate with a clatter and gripped the table like she would bolt for the door the moment he gave the word.

Josiah chuckled. "Right after dinner. I can't pass up your mama's good cookin'."

With a resigned sigh, Katie picked up her fork and speared a slice of potato. Josiah took another bite of pie to keep from grinning.

"Speaking of cooking." Ezra spoke up. "Your stove should be on the next supply load that comes through here. About a week if they don't run into trouble with the Indians."

Josiah studied the man's face. "That's good. Has there been trouble in this area?"

"They raided Camp Rankin again, about two hundred miles from here. And some of the other stage stops have been harassed on and off. Enough to keep us all on edge."

"Are there still friendly bands in the area?" He'd never forget that day he walked out the front door and found a swarm of Indians roaming the yard. What an exotic land this place had seemed back then.

"Most of them moved further west. Every now and then a small party will come through, but most of what we see these days aren't the friendly type. So far, we've left them alone and they stay away from us."

"Just make sure you keep a rifle with you all the time." Zechariah's warning was almost a growl.

Ezra shot a meaningful look at his older brother. Zechariah raised his brows, and the younger man nodded. Some kind of secret code?

Zechariah turned back to Josiah. "If you're ever here during an Indian attack, we plan to hide in that old dry well behind the storage building. There's a rope inside to get to the bottom. Women and children first, of course." He looked pointedly in the direction of Mara's daughter.

"Of course." As if that were ever in question.

Katie fidgeted until the meal was finally over. The moment Mara excused her, the little girl jumped from her chair and ran around to his side of the table. She grabbed his hand and pulled, using all her little bit of body weight. "Come on, Josiah."

"Hang on there, Katie-girl." He turned to Mara, who had begun stacking dirty plates on the table. With his free hand, he reached to touch her shoulder. "Mara."

She spun around, her wide eyes meeting his. "Yes?"

They were mere feet apart, the closest they'd been in a long time. His hands itched to pull her nearer, but Katie's firm grip on him kept him focused on his question.

"Will you come with us to the barn? Leave these dishes and I'll do them after we see the foal." He gave her a lopsided grin. "Katie can help me."

The faintest hint of a smile touched her face, sending his heart thumping like a runaway horse. For a long moment, it looked like she would say no. Finally, her quiet voice broke her stillness. "All right."

On their way to the barn, Katie clutched both of their hands, practically dragging them. "Wait til you see how long her whiskers are, Josiah. And her mane is sooooo soft." She dragged out the "so" and ended with a dramatic sigh.

He sent Mara a raised eyebrow glance. She met his look with one side of her mouth quirked. A rush of love for both of these females washed through him. He would be happy anywhere, doing anything, as long as they could be a family. Soon. Lord willing.

"You have to be quiet when we're inside." Katie's voice dropped to a stage whisper, filled with all the melodrama of a theatre star.

"Yes, ma'am." Josiah gave a solemn nod as he held the barn door for the ladies to enter.

The little paint foal was a cutie, to be sure. And he could gladly watch Katie giggle all night as she played with it. He scratched and petted the filly when she instructed, and laughed when the little thing snuffled her ear. Mara eyed them from the stall door, her presence drawing him like a magnet. He stepped back to join her and leaned against the wall with little more than a foot of space between them.

"She's cute." Mara said, almost too softly to hear. Was she talking about the girl or the horse?

"They both are." More than he could put into words.

At last, she pushed off from the wall. "Say goodnight to the horses, Katherine. Time to ready for bed."

"But, Mama, can I stay up late since Josiah's here?"

Josiah spoke up. "It's my bedtime, too, Katie-girl. How about if I walk you inside?"

Her shoulders slumped, but she turned toward the stall door and trudged through it.

When they stepped back in the house, Ezra was already settled into the chair by the fireplace.

"Say goodnight to Uncle Ezra and Josiah." Mara pointed her daughter in the direction of her uncle.

While Katie obeyed, Josiah spoke in a low voice to Mara. "Would you have time for a walk after she's tucked in?"

He held his breath as she gazed at him with questions in her eyes. "I…" She was about to refuse, he could see it in her face. But then her gaze changed. "I guess so."

He released his pent-up breath. She'd actually agreed. His heart picked up speed, soaring like an eagle flying high over the Sweetwater Valley.

After Katie wrapped her soft arms around his neck and planted a peck on his cheek, the females disappeared into the bedroom, leaving him with warmth flooding his chest. He turned to the table that still held dirty dishes, and whistled as he carried stacks to the wash bucket.

He had the little corner clean by the time Mara stepped from the bedroom and closed the door softly behind her. After hanging the frying pan on the hook in the wall, he wiped his hands on a towel and ambled toward her.

She reached for her cloak hanging on the peg by the door. "We'll be outside for a minute, Ezra."

"All right." Her brother never raised his head from the book in his lap.

Mara reached for the latch, and Josiah grabbed the door over her head to open it for her. She strode through the opening, and once down the steps, he had to lengthen his stride to catch up with her. Was she trying to outrun him? She moved in the direction of the pasture behind the barn. As they neared the fence, her steps slowed, but she didn't speak.

He should start the conversation, but with what? Small talk about how pretty the stars were? Or jump right in and tell her he loved her more than he'd ever thought possible? Maybe it was a little too soon to mention that.

But before he could put words together, Mara broke the silence. "Stars are pretty tonight." She must have read his mind.

"Yep. Seems like they're brightest this time of year. The spring, I mean. Even more than when we used to stand here and look at them in the winter sky." He couldn't stop his eyes from drifting to her face.

A faint smile touched her lips. Was she thinking about what they used to do under those winter stars? Even now, his mouth held the memory of those few kisses. But better not to dwell on that.

"I was wondering." His boot toed the dirt. "Would you and Katie like to come over and see my ranch soon? I'd like to show you Lo Bello, my stallion." He stopped to gauge her expression. Would the invitation scare her off?

Her face was unreadable, especially with uneven shadows of night, and he fought the urge to speak again. He had to wait until she was ready to talk.

"Katie's been wanting to see your new house." Her tone was almost wistful. Or maybe that was his imagination.

He scuffed the ground again. "The house is, uh, a little bare still. But the barn and pastures are coming along." Meaning the house had walls and a floor, but nothing else. No inside doors, not even a counter in the kitchen. Just one chair he'd nailed together and a very rough version of a kitchen table. After the shell of the house was finished, he'd been completely focused on completing the barn and fences so he didn't have to hobble his new horses in the yard all the time.

She eyed him, her head tilted a little. "Is there something we can bring to help?"

"Um. I don't know. I haven't spent much time inside. Mostly focused on fences so I can get the animals settled."

"All right." Her voice was hesitant. "I guess I'll see what I can do when we come. Would you…like Zeche or Ezra to come help with the fences?"

Was she afraid to be alone with him? But yes, now that he thought about it, it would be better if one of her brothers came as chaperone. They might be out in the middle of the wild western territories, but he would do nothing to compromise Mara—not even her reputation.

"If either of them would like to, I'd be pleased for the help."

"Tomorrow then?" She turned to gaze at him in the moonlight.

"Tomorrow." Satisfaction coursed through his veins.

The barn door creaked behind them, and they both turned. Zechariah, stepped from the building carrying a bucket. Probably the milk.

He halted when he spotted them. "Mara?" His voice held an undertone of question. Could he not see them well enough in the darkness to tell them apart from Indians? Or was he asking Mara if she was comfortable out here alone with Josiah?

"Hi, Zeche. We were just coming in."

Disappointment pricked Josiah's chest. But at least they'd had a few minutes together. Just getting her to agree to walk with him was a blessing. And he'd savor every opportunity as a gift.

Turning, he touched Mara's elbow. "I'll see you inside before I head home."

Mara soaked in the sight before her as her horse picked its way across the Sweetwater River. Josiah had chosen the perfect place to build his ranch. The house and barn sat near the middle of the meadow. Close enough to the river so it wouldn't be hard to carry water, but not so close he'd need to worry about flooding. This large pasture would be plenty for the horses he'd keep close to the house. And she knew from memory that miles of additional grassland lay just beyond that patch of trees. It was ideal. Beautiful.

"Look, there's Josiah." Katherine gave her mare several strong kicks, but with Katherine's slight frame and Pepper's laid back ways, they only served to push the mare into a faster walk.

"Josiah!" Katherine yelled and waved wildly.

He held up a wooden rail near the end of the fence line, but Katherine's shout brought his head up. He dropped the log and strode toward them.

As he came closer, the grin that covered his face sent Mara's stomach into flips. She couldn't let him affect her like this. Even though she'd decided to allow herself to enjoy this day. A holiday from chores and schooling and training horses. A chance to study this new Josiah. Here in surroundings where he would be at ease, she could take his measure. Decide whether he could really be trusted. But she couldn't let her heart be swayed by a mere smile.

"I didn't expect y'all so early."

They barely reined the horses to a stop in front of him when Katie slid from her mare and leapt into his arms.

"There's my Katie-girl." He swung her up and turned to Mara and Zeche. "Would you like to see the place? We can put your horses in the barn or hobble them out in the pasture. Whichever you prefer."

Zeche dismounted and reached for Katie's reins where they still rested on Pepper's neck. "I'll settle the horses. I've already seen the set-up a few times." His mouth twisted in the hint of a rueful grin.

Josiah raised a brow. "Put your own blood and sweat into it, huh?"

"Yup."

As Zeche led the three animals toward the barn, Josiah turned the force of his gaze on her. A twinkle flickered in his eyes. "What do you think, should we start with the horses?"

Katherine bounced in his arms. "Yes!"

He extended his free elbow in Mara's direction. Should she take it? She hadn't expected a guided tour on his arm, like a lady of leisure touring a country estate. It'd been so long since she'd lived near a town, and never in a big city like

Josiah had. Were there certain rules to walking on a man's arm?

Nibbling her lip, she risked a glance at his face. His eyes shone a warm blue, with soft lines crinkling the edges. Something about them infused her with just enough courage to step forward and slip her hand in the crook of his elbow.

Strong muscles flexed under her fingers as they walked. She had to resist the urge to step nearer. She was close enough now that his scent surrounded her—filling her senses with wood and nature and the strength of him.

Chapter Twenty-Six

$\mathcal{A}$ s they walked and Josiah spoke about the land, his plans for the pasture, and his hopes for the breeding stock he'd purchased from Zeche, Mara couldn't focus on the words. Couldn't pull herself away from the heady feeling that came from being so close to him. Even the sight of the gorgeous Arabian stallion didn't completely pull her out of the dream. And what had Josiah named him? Lo Bello? Fit his elegant profile perfectly.

The barn was well planned, with a clean layout and a few advantages their own barn didn't have, like a window in the front of the loft and a pulley system to raise loads of hay. His voice resonated with pride as he talked through the things he had yet to build.

He'd set Katherine down when they first entered the building, and she ran from stall to stall, exploring and giggling. "You need a kitty cat, Josiah. Like our Pussy."

"You think so?" His tone was unconvinced, but he didn't shoot the idea down right away.

"I know. You can have one of her kittens next time."

He looked to Mara, brows raised. She still clung to his arm, and the warmth of his breath flowed around her as he faced her. Heat climbed her neck, but she had no power to stop it.

Instead, she responded to the question in his gaze. "Pussy does seem to be in the family way. And we're always happy to give them to eager homes."

"Maybe I need a kitten then." His voice drawled with amusement.

At the end of the barn a horse nickered. A familiar sound that pulled at Mara's senses like an old memory. She knew the low tones of that call.

Releasing Josiah's arm, she stepped forward, her heart pounding. As she neared the last stall, a horse head bobbed over the half-wall. Chestnut with splashes of white, and the nostrils flared in another nicker.

"Rose." Mara unhooked the door and stepped inside, running her hands over the horse's neck as she breathed in that familiar warm, spicy scent. "Hey, girl."

The mare draped her head of Mara's shoulder, snuffling her back in an embrace. Moisture stung the backs of Mara's eyes. Oh, she'd missed this horse.

She let herself stay there for several moments, pulling away only when Rose shifted her weight and snuffled again.

Mara sniffed as she stepped back and stroked that glossy neck. "It's good to see you, too."

"Is that Rose, mama?" Katherine's voice pulled Mara back to reality, and she sniffed again to clear away the emotions.

"Yes, honey."

While her daughter finger-combed Rose's forelock and chattered to the horse, Mara slipped out of the stall, putting distance between them. It wouldn't do to get attached again. Rose was Josiah's horse now.

Turning, she noticed him watching her. But the shadows from the dim interior covered his face, and she couldn't read his thoughts. The last thing she wanted was to make him think she'd been pining for the mare. At least it looked like he'd taken good care of her.

She stepped toward the open barn door, avoiding Josiah's gaze as she passed him. "Come, Katherine. Let's go see the house."

When they stepped back into the yard, Josiah stopped and looked around, settling his focus on Zeche. "It looks like your brother's already working on the fence. I should go help him."

She glanced toward the fresh wood siding of the house. "Aren't you forgetting the inside?"

His face pinched. "There's not much to see in there. Yet."

Was he embarrassed about his home? Mara raised her skirt and stepped close enough to grab his arm, then headed toward the door. "Then tell me what you have planned."

Katherine joined in the apparent fun, grabbing his other hand to pull. "Come on, Josiah. Tell us what you have planned."

He allowed himself to be dragged until they reached the front door. Then he stopped and disconnected his arms from their grasp. With a flourish, he pushed the door open, then folded into a deep bow. "M'ladies."

Katherine giggled, and Mara found her own mouth curving. He was so strong and rugged, the courtly bow looked a bit out of place.

They stepped into the room, Josiah close enough behind her she could feel his presence. "And this, m'ladies, is my humble abode. Its furnishings are meager for such grand ladies as yourselves."

Mara held in a gasp as her eyes adjusted to the dim lighting—or lack thereof. The room was barren. In fact, it gave a whole new meaning to *sparsely furnished*. A single slat-back wood chair sat next to a rough wood table. By the fireplace, a black pot perched on a wooden crate. And that was it. No other chairs, no shelves. No trunks or pegs on the wall. Not even a mantle over the fireplace.

"I, um, know it looks rough." His voice was close to her ear, and held almost a hoarse quality.

She turned to study his face. He was watching her, and their gazes locked. "Don't be ashamed of it, Josiah. It's a beautiful house." She forced her mouth into a soft smile. "It just needs a few things to make it feel homey."

His Adam's apple bobbed. He was too close. But she couldn't pull herself away. Held there by a force unseen, but still very real.

A tug on Mara's skirt tore her gaze away from Josiah. She looked down into Katherine's round, blue eyes.

"Mama, I like this house even better than ours. It has *two* bedrooms." Her little voice was so full of awe.

"That's great, honey." She scanned the rafters of the spacious room. "Josiah built a very nice house, didn't he?"

Another tug on her skirt. "Mama, can I go see what Uncle Ze is doing?"

"I guess so. Why don't you take him a drink of water?"

"Here, Katie-girl." Josiah strode to the box next to the fireplace. "I have a clean canteen I just filled."

"Thanks, Josiah." Katherine grabbed the thermos and darted out the open front door. "Uncle Ze!" Her voice drifted back to them as she ran.

As the echo of her call quieted, a stillness blanketed the cabin. She and Josiah were alone. Very alone. Mara wiped her clammy hands on her skirt, and walked further into the room. It held three windows—two flanking the front door, and another in the side wall. She stepped toward that end of the room.

"That's where the kitchen will be." Josiah's voice followed her as she stopped in front of the window. It was real glass, not easy to come by in this territory where everything had to be carted in over bumpy trails. The view through that glass was superb, displaying part of the river and part of the verdant tree line. That was probably a deer trail from the woods to the water.

"I have a storeroom through there." He pointed to a door near the window. "With an opening to the outside. And eventually I'll dig a root cellar underneath. There are two bedrooms in the back and a loft overhead."

She turned to face him. "It's nice, Josiah. The whole ranch is beautiful. You've done a fine job." Unwelcome moisture stung the backs of her eyes.

He stepped forward and reached out, as if he would pull her into his arms. But Mara spun back to the window. She was getting too close. Why had she thought she could come here...with him?

A small figure appeared through the glass, in the distance by the river. Katherine looked to be refilling the canteen.

"She's a remarkable little girl." Josiah's baritone drifted from not far behind her.

Mara swallowed. "She's special. I don't know what I would have done without her—" Her voice caught, but she forced herself to continue. "—all these years."

"She's blessed to have you as her mother."

If only he knew how she messed up all the time. Lost her temper or her patience almost daily. There were so many days she worried she wasn't teaching Katherine the right things, or that she would miss a terribly important step in this parenting process.

"Mara, there's, ah… There's something I've been meaning to tell you."

Her shoulders tensed. She couldn't take another emotional blow. Not from Josiah.

He continued. "I'm sorry I bought Rose the way I did. I thought I was doing a good thing at the time. I mean, I knew your brother planned to sell her. But looking back, I was selfish. I should have talked with you about it."

Mara couldn't help but turn slightly so she could watch him at the edge of her vision.

Josiah's gaze was on the floor. He raked a hand through the loose brown waves of his hair. "I'm sorry. I'd like to give her back to you."

Give her back? He was offering to give Rose back to her? Mara turned to face the window again so he couldn't see the emotion coursing through her. Rose—her friend and dearest companion all those years ago. But could she take the animal away from Josiah? He'd paid a fair price for her.

An image flashed through her mind of him riding the mare. He looked so good on her. Of course, his broad muscled shoulders would take her breath away on any horse. But this man and animal seem to have bonded. And his riding skills were as natural as breathing now.

She turned back to study him. His expression held sincerity, but faint lines had formed around his eyes. She examined their blue depths. Sincere, yes, but there was a sadness there. This was a sacrifice for him. How could it not be? And yet, he was offering. For her.

"No, Josiah. You keep her. She's right for you." More resolve sounded in her voice than she felt. Good.

A lump bobbed in his throat. "Are you sure?" His voice cracked on the last word. Was he so relieved?

She nodded.

His mouth tipped the smallest bit. "You'll have to ride her for me every so often, to keep her straight."

Mara allowed a small smile to touch her face. "All right."

Josiah's gaze found hers again and held there. Intensity radiated from his eyes.

Her breath caught as pressure tightened around her throat. He was too close. She wasn't ready for this. Wasn't ready to let this man into her heart. *Oh, God. What do I do?* She took a step back, her body bumping into the hard window behind her. She was trapped here, unless she darted around him toward the door. But did she want to run?

Josiah didn't move forward. Didn't close the distance.

"Mara." His voice was soft. Gentle. The intensity in his gaze still held her, but it didn't push. "I'm sorry for all the ways I've hurt you. With God as my strength, I plan to make it up to you every day for the rest of my life." His mouth curved into a sad smile. "I'm not perfect, but I promise I'll try not to bring you pain again. You may not believe me now, but I'll show you."

The flurry of emotions whirling through Mara left her chest aching. Could she believe him? Trust him? *Lord, give me Your wisdom.*

His face softened into an easy smile. He turned and offered his elbow. "Shall we see if Katie and Zeche need help?"

Mara inhaled a deep breath, then released it, some of her fear leaving with the spent air. A portion of peace crept in to fill the empty place. Could Josiah be God's answer for her? She'd have to give that question more prayer. But for now, she straightened her shoulders and stepped forward to take his arm.

Katherine's giggles drifted to Mara as she unpinned a pair of work pants from the clothes line. Josiah's deep chuckle mixed with the girl's tinkling laughter where they sat in the grass next to a smattering of wildflowers. Mara's eyes drifted to the pair in time to see her daughter settle a wreath of the flowers in a crown on Josiah's head. He raised his chin like an emperor, then rose to his knees and bowed low before Katherine. Another round of giggles ensued.

Mara couldn't help but grin herself as she turned back to the line and reached for one of Ezra's shirts. Those two were inseparable these days, any time Josiah was around. And when he wasn't there, Katherine talked about him constantly, chattering on about the fish Josiah caught, or the deer that grazed in his yard every morning.

Of course, he was around quite a bit. He'd come for supper four nights in just the last week. Now that his stove had arrived, he always brought some kind of special treat— yeast rolls, a pie, or cinnamon buns. One time he'd even brought a pound cake with sweet cream covering it. Oh, that had been so good. And he always insisted on cleaning the dishes after the meal, usually letting Katherine help him if she was done with her school work and chores for the day. And that, of course, made her eager to finish early, in case Josiah came.

A honking noise drifted across the yard, and Mara spun to locate the source. Josiah sat on the ground with his hands cupped around his mouth, Katherine watching him intently. The honking sounded again. Then he reached forward to pluck a blade of grass, and helped Katherine fit it into her own hands. Mara smiled. He was teaching her to make a duck call.

She turned back to the clothes and her thoughts. As good as Josiah was for Katie, she felt bad about him coming over so much, and doing so much work when he came. He had his own ranch to run, and every moment he spent at the Rocky Ridge was time he should be making progress at his place. There was still so much to do there—building fences, planting hay, and who knew what else. He'd started from scratch, after all. And on top of everything, one of the mares he'd bought from them was due to foal any day. He said she looked like she had about another week. That meant his nights would be long, too, keeping an eye on the mare in case she needed help during the birthing.

He was a different man from the Josiah who'd lived at their home station four years ago. Still had the grin that sent butterflies through her stomach, but more mature now. Thoughtful. A bit more careworn maybe, but he seemed to have a wisdom about him. He said he would prove his dependability now. She hadn't believed him at first. But every action seemed to verify his words. It was getting harder and harder not to trust him.

Reaching for the last shirt from the clothes line, Mara glanced back at the pair across the yard in time to see Josiah whisper something into Katherine's ear. She giggled and whispered back. He rose and reached to help her up, holding one hand behind his back as he did so.

Mara couldn't tear her gaze from the two of them as they advanced toward her, suspicious grins spilling over their faces. What were they up to now? Katherine stopped about ten feet away, but Josiah kept coming.

When he stood right in front of her, he brought his hand around to reveal a beautiful wreath of wildflowers. She drank in the vivid colors of Snowberries and Buttercups and Forget-me-nots. The aroma of the blooms wafted to her. Mara reached a hand to touch one of the soft purple flowers. "It's beautiful." Her gaze came up to meet Josiah's.

His mouth pulled in that half grin, but lit his eyes like a boy on Christmas morning. "Katie helped me make it."

How could she resist that boyish pride? Mara reached for the circle of flowers, but he pulled them back.

"Let me." Josiah stepped forward and raised the crown to place it on her head. He was so close now, breathing was almost impossible.

Her eyes found his again, and almost drowned in their liquid blue-gray depths. "Thank you." Her mouth mumbled the words before her mind could process them.

His hands drifted down to her shoulders, then slid to her elbows. Everywhere his fingers touched left her nerves tingling. But she couldn't look away from those eyes. A slight pressure on her arms pulled her closer. Was he going to kiss her? Her gaze drifted down to his mouth. Did she want him to kiss her? Maybe.

And then his hands grasped hers, and he raised one of her palms to his lips. The moment his mouth touched her soft flesh, goose bumps surged up her arm. She almost stepped forward to start the kiss herself, but his eyes caught her attention first. They held a deep twinkle. *Later,* they seemed to say.

He turned her hand over and laid another gentle kiss on the top of her fingers, then turned and walked toward the house. "C'mon, Katie. What do you say we make those cinnamon crisps now?"

Chapter Twenty-Seven

With a leather pad protecting his hands, Josiah pulled the sizzling shepherd's pie from his new oven. He carried it directly to the table, settling it in the middle. He should probably drape a cloth over it to keep the heat in until the girls arrived. Now that the foal was finally born, he'd had a good excuse to invite them for dinner.

After lowering the cherry cobbler into the oven to cook, he closed the iron door and peered out the window again. Two figures rode horseback through the creek. A light blue dress graced the taller womanly form, and the young girl on the chestnut horse beside her wore pale yellow. They were both pretty as a field of buttercups. A familiar yearning took over his chest. *How much longer, Lord? Sorry for being impatient, but it seems crazy to love them so much and not be able to call them my own.*

With any luck, he'd have a chance to be alone with Mara long enough for a kiss. He'd wanted to so badly the other day when he gave her the flower crown. But he couldn't do it in front of Katie. Not the first time. Not until Mara was his wife. Then he'd kiss her in front of the whole world if they wanted to watch.

After a glance around the table to make sure all was ready, he strode through the front door to meet them in the yard. Katie kicked her horse into a trot the minute she saw him, then pulled her to a stop in the yard.

"There's my Katie." He held Pepper's reins while the girl slid off, then opened his arms for the usual bear hug. As she threw her hands around him, he soaked up the sweet, little-girl smell. Mara reined her horse in next to Pepper, and he released Katie to help her mother.

He patted the gray gelding who fidgeted as Mara dismounted. "Who's this guy?"

Mara raised an eyebrow in a wry look. "A two-year-old trial."

He bit back a grin. "Let me get them settled in the paddock."

Mara blew out a breath. "Thanks. And then we should probably look at the foal if you want any peace at dinner."

Katie grabbed his hand. "Yes. Can we see the baby?"

He fought the urge to ruffle her hair. "Well, of course. We have our priorities. You help me take the saddle off your horse, Katie-girl. And then we'll go see that filly. I need you to pick a good name for her."

The girl's eyes rounded, and she hopped once, clapping her hands. "Yes."

After settling the saddle horses in the corral, they crept into the barn. At the sight of him, the day old filly released a high-pitched nicker.

"Hey there, girl." He opened the door to the stall and slipped in. "Let me catch the feisty thing, then you can both come in and pet her."

He eased up next to the mare, then slid a hand over the filly who hovered at her mama's side. "There now, girlie. You're getting used to this aren't you?" The little one's ears twitched as he crooned, and he slipped one hand around her chest and the other behind her rump. He guided the tiny body closer to the stall door so they would have room to move around away from the mare. "Come on in."

"Oohhh…" Katie breathed as she crept inside. "Look at her little head."

The black filly did indeed have a petite head, even though she wasn't sired by his Arabian.

"I think we should name her Arabelle, like my dolly Ezra got me. Cause she has a pretty head, too."

Josiah couldn't help a chuckle. "Arabelle she is, then." He stepped back to allow room for Mara to pet the feather-soft coat.

After Mara found the filly's tickle spot on her neck and scratched a moment, her gaze lifted to his. A soft smile touched her face. "She's beautiful. You should be so proud."

Oh, he was. So proud and so full of love, his chest was bursting.

Katherine kept the conversation lively at dinner, telling him about how Uncle Ze was going to let her train a foal all by herself this summer. She talked about the baby chicks that had just hatched, and offered to give half of them to Josiah if he wanted.

He looked to Mara as he tried to find the right words to dash her hopes. "That's awfully nice of you, Katie. I bet your mama's going to need those chicks, though. But maybe I can plan to buy some from the next batch. By then, I should have my own chicken pen ready."

Mara spoke up, raising her face to look at him. "I think Katie had a good idea. You'll need some chickens, and this batch will give you a little start. We can keep them until you have your pen ready. No rush. They'll need to wait until they're big enough to stay warm without the hen, anyway."

His heart surged. He could get used to loving this woman, especially the way she looked at him now. And that cute blush that crept into her cheeks made her even more beautiful.

After they'd eaten their fill of dinner and cherry cobbler, Josiah stretched out in his chair at the table. What could he do to make this evening last longer? He glanced at Mara's empty tin mug. "More coffee?"

She rose before he could stop her. "I'll get it."

Josiah almost stood to take the pot from her, but she made quick work of pouring. So he eased back in his chair.

Yes, he'd love to spend the rest of his life getting used to this. A family dinner at home. *His* family. In *his* home. *In Your timing, Lord. Help me to wait for Your timing.*

"Josiah, can I go out and see Arabelle again? I promise I won't go in the stall." Katie gave him one of those puppy-dog looks that he could never deny.

But this didn't sound like his decision. "That's up to your mama, Katie-girl."

"Please, Mama." She turned that same look on Mara.

Fine lines appeared between Mara's brows. "I don't know, honey. I guess it's all right with me, but I'm not sure Josiah will want you near the foal without him."

Then the little angel turned back to him and he lost all power. He put on his mock stern face. "Just make sure you don't go in any of the stalls."

Katie rushed around the table and threw her arms around his neck. "Thank you, Josiah. I love you so much."

Moisture stung his eyes and the back of his throat. He clutched her little frame for dear life. "I love you too, Katie-girl." He didn't care that his voice cracked.

After a moment, she pulled away and turned to dash out the door.

"Don't stay long," Mara called, just before it banged shut.

As the wood reverberated from the force, Mara turned an embarrassed smile to him. "Sorry. She gets excited."

Josiah blinked back moisture and offered a wobbly grin. "I'm glad she's so happy."

Mara began stacking dishes on the table and Josiah stood to help. He should tell her to stop. To sit and enjoy herself while he cleaned up. But working together seemed right.

While she washed the dishes in the bucket on the low counter he'd built for that purpose, he stood beside her with a clean rag and dried each piece before placing it in the proper place on the shelf. His new tin ware was still shiny and uniform.

As she handed him the last pan, Mara reached for the sides of the bucket that contained now-dirty water. He laid a hand on her arm. "Let me get that."

She didn't answer, but stepped aside.

He listened for Katie as he dumped the water outside in the dusky light. No little girl noises, but the normal evening sounds echoed amongst the cricket chirps and the flowing of the river. All seemed well.

When he stepped back inside, Mara gazed out the kitchen window. She glanced back at him with a soft smile, then turned to the glass again. "The river's so peaceful. I could stand here and watch it for hours."

The image she made was too beautiful for words, with her long hair hanging down her back, tied only in a pale blue ribbon to match her dress. Dare he touch her? Would she welcome him? The last thing he wanted was to ruin the moment.

But an unseen force pulled him forward. Josiah stepped up behind Mara, and rested his hands on her shoulders. They both faced the window, but he couldn't think about anything except the woman so near. He expected to feel her muscles tense beneath his touch. But instead, she leaned back ever so slightly until she rested against his chest.

Thank you, Lord. Josiah slipped an arm around her waist and pulled her to him, resting his chin on the softness of her hair. He breathed in the familiar scent of roses.

After a few moments, she exhaled a sigh, her body so close it melded into his.

Oh, Lord. You've blessed me indeed. Josiah didn't speak, just enjoyed the feel of this woman in his arms. She surely felt the gallop of his heart. But he had no secrets from her. And he certainly wasn't going to deny his love.

After a while, Mara spoke. "Thanks for spending so much time with Katherine. It's been good for her." Her voice was wistful, and just the sound of it formed a knot in his throat.

"I'm glad I have the chance. She's special." He released a soft chuckle. "There's no way I could fight off her charms." He pressed a soft kiss on Mara's hair. "I think I've come to love her as much as I love you."

She shifted in his arms, and Josiah loosened his grip as she half-turned to look at him. Her eyes were round, luminous. The look tightened his chest. They showed fear. Vulnerability.

"Josiah." Her voice was barely louder than a whisper. "I'm not sure I'm ready."

His heart ached. From the nearness of her. From the fear she still held. The fear *he* had planted there. What could he do to show her it would be all right? That she didn't have to be afraid of him hurting her again?

Before his mind realized what he was doing, he lowered his mouth to hers. Oh, sweetness. She was everything he'd dreamed of. But he had to keep the kiss gentle. Just a soft touch. A simple effort to remove her fear.

Way too soon, he forced himself to pull back. He found her gaze again and searched. Her eyes were a liquid amber now. So beautiful.

He planted a kiss at the top of her forehead, then pulled her to his chest again. "Take all the time you need. I'm not going anywhere."

Josiah whistled as his mare stepped out of the river on the side opposite his ranch. He shouldn't be going to the Reids' in the middle of the day. But he wasn't very productive around his place with his mind so distracted by Mara. She needed to hurry up and marry him so he could get something accomplished around the ranch.

His mouth found the tune again as the mare followed the path over a low hill. This was one of the three-year-olds he'd bought from Zeche. She had good manners. He just had to be clearer with his signals than with Rose.

As they crested the hill, a wide ribbon of smoke caught Josiah's attention to his left. It wasn't from the direction of the Rocky Ridge Station, but he couldn't see the origin over the trees. Maybe once he rounded the bend ahead.

It might have been his gut overreacting, but something didn't feel right. As he continued riding, the air took on the scent of smoke and goose bumps rose on Josiah's upper arms. Was the grass on fire? Surely not with the wet spring they were having.

When the trees thinned, an odd sight appeared about three hundred feet ahead. Teepees. He had to blink before his mind believed it. Josiah reined in his horse. They were still protected by some tree cover, but he didn't dare move closer. From what he could tell, the Indian camp was settled in between two buttes, so no one would see it unless they came in from the side he was on.

He leaned forward to peer around a tree. There were ten teepees that he could see, but most likely more hidden. Should he make a run for it to the Reids'? If he left the trail, he could probably get there without the Indians in the camp seeing him. Were there others moving around the area, though? An arrow of fear shot down his back. If he ran into a war party, they would likely murder him on the spot. Or maybe just torture him. Was that something to hope for?

God, show me which way to go. Protect me. And please, Lord. Keep Mara and her family safe. Urgency tightened his chest. He had to get there to warn them.

He reined his mare to the right, off the trail and into the thicker trees. Leaning low to avoid branches, he urged the horse around stumps and finally out into the meadow that bordered the Rocky Ridge station.

The buildings looked undisturbed in the distance. A figure trotted on horseback in the corral behind the barn. All good signs. The Indians must not have been here yet.

He kicked his mare hard and she lunged into a canter. It was bouncy enough to send his teeth into his throat, but he hung on and urged her faster.

Zechariah met him in the courtyard. "What's wrong?"

"Indians," Josiah gasped. "A camp full." He struggled to catch enough breath to speak through his parched throat. "Between the twin buttes."

Zeche grabbed Josiah's arm and nearly jerked him off the horse. "Get inside and tell Mara to pack supplies. Then get the girls in the well. Ezra and I'll let the horses out and meet you there."

No need to tell him twice. Josiah sprinted toward the cabin and jerked the door open. He paused for his eyes to adjust to the darkness.

A gasp pulled his attention to the right.

"Josiah!"

He caught a glimpse of Katie's blonde braids just before she threw herself against him. He clutched her, but his eyes searched for Mara, finally finding her next to the work counter. "Mara."

"Yes?" Her gaze took on a glimmer of fear, probably picking up on his tone.

"Indians. There's a camp not half a mile from here." He swung Katie into his arms and strode toward the kitchen as he spoke. "Need supplies, then get to the old well. Food, water, blankets, lanterns, and oil. And anything else you can think of."

Her face blanched as she nodded, then spun to the row of crates that held food stuffs. His fingers itched to comfort her, but now wasn't the time. Later.

He lowered Katie to her feet, then turned her shoulders in the direction of the bedroom. "Katie-girl, I have a special job for you. Can you find four blankets and put them in a stack right here?"

She nodded and scampered into the back room.

He reached for the two lanterns hanging on the wall near the front door. They should probably take one more, in case they were down there for a while. How big was the well, exactly? Better to have too many supplies than not enough. He scanned the room. There, by the ladder to the loft. A tin of oil, a box of matches, and another lantern on a shelf. He grouped them all by the door, then moved to the kitchen to help Mara.

"I hope this is enough food." She handed him a large cloth bundle. "I'll fill the canteens."

He deposited the food bundle next to the lanterns, then took a canteen from Mara and dipped it into the fresh water bucket next to the two she held.

Her gaze raised to meet his, fear clouding her amber eyes. "How long do you think we'll be down there?"

"I don't know." *God, place a fence of protection around us.*

"Here's the blankets, Josiah. Do you need anything else?" Katie's voice was muffled by the stack of quilts she carried.

He capped the canteen, and turned back to survey the collection by the door. "I think that's enough. Let's get out there."

He stepped out the door first, then scanned the yard and the tree line around them. All seemed quiet. Too quiet?

"Come on." He beckoned to Katie and Mara, and they strode out into the unknown.

<h1>Chapter Twenty-Eight</h1>

osiah, Mara, and Katie all carried full loads as they rounded the corner of the cabin and finally stopped at a square of wood almost covered by the thick grass around it.

Josiah dropped the lanterns and blankets on the ground and sank to his knees to raise the wood. A dark hole gaped up at him, with a dank, earthy smell wafting up to his nose. The opening couldn't be more than four or five feet across. Would they all fit down there?

He fumbled through the supplies on the ground and found the matches. After lighting the lantern wick, he turned the flame to a low height to conserve oil. When he lowered it into the hole a few feet, the dirt walls illuminated, showing a rope hanging from the edge. *Thank you, Lord.*

But was the rope strong enough to hold them? It looked to be tied to a spike in the ground, and the braided leather cords seemed to be fairly new. Maybe Zechariah installed it for this purpose when Indian attacks became a concern. He could only hope. And pray.

To make sure the ground below was dry, he grabbed a small rock from the ground and dropped it down the hole. A quiet *thunk* sounded when it landed. No splash. There was dirt in at least that one spot.

Josiah reached for the rope. They had to get down quickly. Did he dare let Mara go first? He gave the cord a hard jerk. He'd have to.

Turning to face her, he allowed his eyes to drink her in. Stray hairs framed that beautiful face, accentuating her wide brown eyes. Those eyes were windows to her soul, showing her apprehension...but also trust. That trust he'd been praying to see for months now. Josiah's heart tightened. *Lord, please don't let me fail her.*

He touched her arm. "Do you think you can go down first? I'll need to help Katie down."

Mara's chin dipped firmly. "Fine."

She reached for the rope and Josiah helped her position her knees at the edge of the hole, but misgivings welled in his chest. What was he doing letting Mara take the first plunge? He had no idea what was at the bottom, other than one small piece of ground. "Maybe I should go first."

She stopped adjusting her skirts and looked up at him. Her face revealed a calm determination, and she laid a hand on his arm. "It's all right, Josiah. I can do this."

Oh, his chest ached. He swallowed past the lump in his throat, then set his jaw. He'd have to put her in God's hands. "All right."

She looked at her daughter, who kneeled behind Josiah. "You do exactly as Josiah says. All right, honey?"

"I will."

Without another word or glance, Mara slipped her arm through the lantern handle, gripped the leather rope, and lowered herself down.

Josiah held the top of the rope secure, and didn't breathe for the eternity it took her to reach the bottom. But he did pray. Just three words, over and over. *Father, protect her.*

His chest was close to bursting by the time Mara's lantern stopped descending.

"I'm here. The bottom's dry."

Thank you. And then to Mara he called, "I'm gonna drop the blankets down."

"Go ahead."

Each quilt fluttered into the hole, and he could see Mara better now as she stood in the little circle of light. She must be at least thirty feet below the surface. Somehow, they would all need to eventually get back out of that hole. But that would be a blessed problem to have.

He turned back to Katie. "All right, Katie-girl. How would you like to ride down on my back?" They would need to get the rest of the supplies down, but the men could help him with that once he was at the bottom.

And where were the men? He looked around. Ezra jogged toward them, another rope in his arms.

With Ezra at the top of the well opening, and Katie's arms wrapped tightly around his neck, Josiah lowered them down the rope. He leveraged his feet against the side of the wall as they descended, his muscles straining as the depth seemed to stretch farther and farther. "Keep your legs tight around my waist, Katie-girl." The little limbs tightened around his midsection, easing his worries a tiny bit.

When his feet landed on solid ground, he almost kept going to his knees. Only propping himself against the dirt wall kept him upright as Mara lifted her daughter from his back. He pushed against the side to turn and wrap them both in his arms, protection welling up in his chest. *Please, God. Keep my girls safe.* Mara snuggled into him, and Josiah inhaled the faint scent of roses and loam.

"I'm dropping down the food bundle, English." Zechariah's voice sounded from above.

Josiah pushed Mara and Katie back away from him. "Stay against this wall until we get all the supplies down."

Mara nodded, but there wasn't much room to stand back in this tiny dirt hole.

Josiah squinted up to the opening where light flooded in. "All right."

The huge bundle of food stuffs blocked the light for a moment, and Josiah positioned himself underneath. He caught it squarely, but almost tumbled backward with the force of it. Dropping the bag next to Mara, he called, "What's next?"

One after another, the men tossed down the supplies they'd grabbed from the barn, along with a few personal items. No telling what the Indians would take if they showed up at the house, or how long they would be there.

Ezra fastened a second rope above and dropped the end down, then lowered himself. Zeche was the last to come, and stopped to settle the wood covering over the well opening before he descended.

Mara had arranged the supplies in a stack and spread a blanket over them, so two people could sit on top like a bench. She eased down on the floor though, and snuggled Katherine on her lap.

Josiah sank down beside them. "You don't want to sit on the blanket?" He kept his voice soft, the sound almost intimate as the dirt walls absorbed the noise.

She turned those wide eyes to him. "We're comfortable here."

How was it that no matter what disaster happened around them, one look through those windows to her soul could warm his insides? Josiah slipped Mara's hand into his own, and threaded his fingers through hers. The warm touch of her skin, the way she curled her fingers securely around his, she calmed his nerves like nothing else could.

He turned to look at the men. Ezra perched on the stacked supplies and Zechariah leaned against the wall between his siblings. The fit was tight, but at least they were safe. Lord willing. "What'd you do with the horses?"

Zeche's mouth pinched in a grim line. "Let 'em out."

Josiah's mouth pressed in the same expression. Would they be able to find all the stock once this trouble was over? How much money and hard work would be lost in this skirmish? But maybe by releasing the horses, they would save more than if the Indians got their hands on them.

"How many Indians did you say you saw in the woods, Zeche?" Ezra regarded his brother.

"It was hard to tell. Mostly looked like shadows moving through the trees. Just saw one on horseback clear enough to know he was Cheyenne." He turned to Josiah. "We would have been fish bait if you hadn't come to warn us."

A knot tangled in his gut. He hadn't realized Indians were spotted within sight of this place. "Do you think they saw us hide?"

Zeche squinted. "Don't think so. They were in the trees on the other side of the barn, so they wouldn't be able to see this spot from there. As long as they don't have men by the creek."

"What do you think they have planned?" Josiah's voice rumbled in the small space.

Zeche exhaled a long breath. "I would imagine they'll take whatever they can get. Supplies, for sure. We're not up there to be murdered, but I'm sure that was part of their plan."

A sharp inhale came from Josiah's left. He turned to see Mara's face so pale it almost glowed in the lamplight. He gave her hand a gentle squeeze, but it trembled inside his own. So he unthreaded his fingers and slipped his arm behind her back. She snuggled into the crook of his shoulder, fitting so perfectly. His lips found her soft hair and planted a kiss. "We can only pray, love." He whispered the words for her ears only.

"Josiah?" Katie's small voice pierced the silence.

"Yes, Katie-girl?" He spoke in a hushed tone, grazing her soft cheek with a finger from his free hand.

"Will you tell me a story?" She turned those blue puppy-dog eyes on him.

"Hmmm… What kind of story?"

"From when you used to live here and ride the horses."

Ah, his favorite memories. "All right." He paused for dramatic effect, scrunching his forehead as if he were thinking deeply. "Once upon a time, there was a young knight who lived in a very cold land, where snow covered everything. He lived in the castle, near the princess and her family, and the knight had to travel a long distance to slay the dragons."

Katie sat enraptured as he told the story of the Princess and her brother, the Prince, rescuing the Knight from certain death in the icy mountains. Every so often he snuck a glance at Mara and found her watching him with a warm look in her eyes. Looking every bit the princess she was.

Just when he got to the part about the Knight helping the Princess with her chores, a low rumble sounded. It was almost as if the ground around them shook. Bits of dirt began to rain from overhead.

A high-pitched cry sounded from the opening above, muffled by the wooden covering. An army of screams and cries and yells permeated their hideaway, sending Josiah's pulse into a gallop.

Katie whimpered, and Mara snuggled the child's head to her chest. Josiah pulled them tighter into the circle of his arms and prayed like he'd never prayed before.

Make them blind to the covering over this well. Send an army of angels to fight this enemy.

The commotion overhead seemed to last forever. At one point, it grew in volume, if that were possible.

And then a series of mighty bangs sounded. The ground shook again and more dirt rained down from above.

Screams pierced the air. The booms didn't stop—just continued in rapid succession for at least a minute. Was this the end? Had the apocalypse begun, and the earth was being destroyed? *Oh, God.*

And then with no warning—silence.

The booms stopped. The shaking of the ground slowed until all was still. No screams. Nothing.

Josiah turned to the other men, the apprehension on their faces matching what thumbed in his own chest. What was happening up there?

A whimper sounded from Katie, but Mara shushed her with a soft whisper, rocking gently within Josiah's arms.

After a few moments, a new sound worked its way into Josiah's awareness. A popping noise. The pops were random, and accompanied by a low hum. What in the world? Fear gripped his chest, even as his eyes met Zechariah's. It was plain from his expression, he heard it to.

Josiah threw his gaze up toward the sky, hoping Zeche caught his message that he would go up and check. The other man gave a slight shake of his head, and glanced at Mara and Katherine. He mouthed the word *Stay.*

Josiah frowned, but gave a quick nod. The hum grew louder. If Zeche was going up, he needed to move quickly.

"I'm going up to check on things." Zechariah spoke in a loud whisper as he turned his back to them, grabbing the new rope Ezra had tied at the top. He tested it, then reached as high as he could and lifted himself up, one handhold at a time. The muscles in the man's arms and neck flexed and bulged as he moved, evident in the dim light even through his shirt. Josiah swallowed. If there was ever a fight in the area, he wanted Zechariah Reid on his side.

When Zeche reached the top of the hole, he eased the covering to the side and raised his head above the ground. The moment daylight shone into the opening, the hum became a low roar, and the popping sound became easily identifiable.

Fire.

If the noise wasn't clear enough, the acrid smell wafting down into their hiding place was a sure giveaway.

Mara's body tensed under Josiah's arms, but she didn't speak. He stroked her forearm with his thumb as they waited for a report from Zechariah.

The man finally looked down at them. With the sun behind him, his face was completely shadowed. "The whole place is going up in flames. I'm gonna climb out and see if they're gone."

"Be careful." Mara's words were almost swallowed in the roar from overhead.

Zechariah wriggled over the edge and into the smoky air above.

"Is Uncle Ze gonna be all right?" Katie's voice came out in a loud whisper.

"I hope so, honey," Mara answered. "We should pray for God to keep him safe."

"Dear, God." Katie bowed her head to rest on her pressed hands. "Please keep Uncle Ze safe, and don't let him be burned up."

Tears stung Josiah's eyes as goose bumps pricked his arms. Katie and her pure faith were right on target. *Lord, answer this little one's prayer.*

It was an eternity of prayers and pounding hearts, but Zechariah finally appeared at the top of the well opening. "It looks like they've left, but the buildings are all ashes."

Josiah hesitated before asking questions. The last thing he wanted to do was alarm Katie. But he had to make sure things were safe before he let Mara and Katie come up. "Do you think they're watching from the trees?"

"I don't see anything moving. Can't say for sure unless I ride out there, though."

"I'm coming up." He had to get a look at things himself before he'd take a chance with the girls. He planted a kiss in Mara's hair before loosening his hold on them. His hands didn't want to untangle themselves, but he pulled free and pushed to his feet. Gathering his strength, he gripped the rope Zechariah had used. *Lord, I'm not asking for the same show of strength Zeche had. Just help me not to fall and make a fool of myself with this thing.*

Through sheer determination, he made it to the top. Although he was out of breath, and possibly missing some of the tooth powder he'd ground off by clenching his jaw with the effort. The air outside was gray and smoky, and didn't do anything to help his lung capacity. The first deep breath left him coughing, but he struggled to his feet and stood next to Zechariah.

It took a long moment to absorb the destruction around them. The barn was a flaming skeleton, with timbers dangling from the few rafters still in place amidst the flames. They would likely fall at any moment. The old bunkhouse still glowed too, although it was reduced to only the floor and a foot or two of walls. Where the storage building once stood, now lay only a few smoldering boards. The house on the end of the half circle was in much the same condition as the bunkhouse. Still on fire, but utterly destroyed. Josiah had to force himself to swallow past the lump clogging his throat.

"I'm thinkin' those loudest booms were the ammunition exploding in the storage building." Zechariah's voice rumbled, despite the background noise of the crackling fire.

Josiah looked at the smoking wood in front of them again. "Likely so." Then he eyed the distance between the burning house and the dry well opening, a new fear creeping in. "Do you think there's any chance of fire getting down in the well shaft?"

Zechariah examined the same distance. "We better get them out, just in case."

Zeche tied a series of knots in the rope to help with climbing, and Josiah leaned over the edge to help pull each person up. Mara came first, followed by Ezra carrying Katie.

Mara struggled to her feet outside the well, and stepped out of the way so Ezra could come up while she absorbed the images around them.

Desolation.

Everything they had. Gone. A whole lifetime. Dissolved to ashes.

She scanned the pastures as far as she could see. A few forms grazed in the distance to the right, a sight that brought a burning sensation to prick the backs of her eyes. They had at least a few horses left. Maybe the others had gone that direction, too.

An arm slipped around her waist and pulled her close. Josiah. What would she have done without him beside her through this ordeal? She looked over at him, trying to force a cheerful look onto her face. Katherine sat perched in his other arm, both small hands clutching his neck.

His eyes searched hers, overflowing with concern and love. She'd been a fool to shut him out. A fool to live in fear that she might get hurt again. Who knew what tomorrow would bring? Or if they would even have a tomorrow? Only God knew, and He'd sent Josiah back to her.

Chapter Twenty-Nine

osiah forced his eyes open in the darkness. Where was he? An earthy odor permeated the air, along with a hint of fresh pine. Ah, yes. His barn.

He stretched, squeezing his eyes shut against the ache in every muscle. They'd put in long hours at the Rocky Ridge over the past few days, clearing debris and cutting logs for the new house. His arms hadn't stopped throbbing since the fire.

He had a house full of sleeping guests, with Mara and Katie sleeping in the master chamber, and Ezra stretched out in the extra bedroom. Zechariah had been bunking with Ezra, but he left for town the day before to pick-up supplies. If all went well, he'd be back that afternoon.

Josiah could have bedded down on the floor in the main room, but it didn't feel right to sleep in the house with Mara there. Not yet, anyway.

A smile tugged his mouth. She'd been a different person since the fire. Not depressed or teary-eyed like he would have expected. But open and fervent. Like she was determined to live each day to the full.

They hadn't had a spare moment alone together. But one day soon, he'd be asking her to marry him. If nothing else good came from the fire, it had convinced him that each day was precious. And he wanted to spend every single one of them with this woman.

Tossing aside the blanket, he rose to his feet and ran a hand through his hair. He'd washed in the river the night before, but a shave would be a good idea this morning. But first coffee. And breakfast for everyone.

A low nicker pierced the air as Josiah stepped out of the barn and strode toward the house. His muscles tensed at the sound, his eyes scanning the tree line around the house. The Indians that had camped across the river left right after the burning of the Rocky Ridge Station, but it was always possible another war or hunting party moved into the area.

As his eyes searched the fence near the source of the sound, Rose's stocky form appeared in the dusky light. She released another soft nicker, ears pricked at him as if she expected him to produce breakfast.

Josiah's shoulders sagged. Not Indians. A bird twittered in the trees, and another returned the message. All normal morning sounds.

He stepped toward the fence and patted Rose's neck. She responded by snuffling his hand, searching for oats or apples.

"I'll feed you in a bit, but you've gotta stay quiet, girl." He spoke in a whisper. Dawn barely lit the eastern horizon, but maybe he still had time to get breakfast started before everyone arose.

The hinges on the front door creaked when he opened it. That needed to be oiled soon, maybe after breakfast. A rich aroma filled his nostrils, followed by a yeasty scent. He stopped for a second and closed his eyes to savor the fragrance. Just for a moment, he was back in his old kitchen in Savannah. Surrounded by ingredients and cooking utensils that would have delighted a Parisian chef.

He pulled his eyes open and took in the stunning sight before him. Mara stood at the cook stove, watching him with a soft smile on her lips. Her long hair hung loose around her shoulders, shimmering in the light from the lantern.

"Good morning." Her voice came softly, like the first few rays of the morning sun.

His body pulled him forward before his mind could object. In four steps he strode up behind her and slipped his arms around her waist. His mouth found her neck, and he breathed her in, then placed a single kiss there. "Good morning."

Mara didn't seem eager to move. Didn't try to squirm out of his hold. Instead she settled her hands over his, as if to keep him there. Ah, this woman.

After a moment she reached forward to pick up a wooden spoon and turned the eggs in the pan in front of her.

Josiah inhaled again, taking his time to draw in the aroma of Mara's rosy scent mixed with the smells of cooking breakfast. "I like coming in to find you in my kitchen."

She didn't answer, but finished fluffing the eggs, then placed the spoon on the counter. In a smooth motion, she turned in Josiah's hold so she was facing him, then raised her arms to hook them around his neck.

His heartbeat exploded in his chest, emotion and desire churning inside him. He lowered his forehead to rest on hers, forcing his lungs to breathe. Was it too soon to ask? Maybe, but love for this woman might just kill him if he waited much longer.

He swallowed to cool the desert in his throat, then opened his mouth to speak. "Mara. I know I should wait to ask. You deserve so much better, but I...I can't wait. Would you marry me? You and Katie?" Oh, he'd made a mess of that. But it was out, and now he couldn't breathe as he waited for her reaction. He raised his head a few inches so he could watch her face.

Moisture pooled in her amber eyes, and his stomach climbed into his throat. But then her beautiful lips formed a smile that lit her eyes and every part of her face. "Yes, Josiah English. I would love to marry you."

It took a full moment, but finally the impact of her words sank into his dense brain. Yes. She said yes. He swooped in to seal the agreement with a kiss, but a hand on his chest stopped him.

Mara's smile had cocked sideways a bit. "But I can only speak for myself. You'll have to ask Katie for her answer."

He couldn't stop a victory whoop as he scooped Mara up and spun her around. When her feet landed back on the floor, she leaned heavily on him. She was shaking. Was she scared? *Oh, Lord. Don't let her regret the decision already.*

Josiah scanned her eyes for remorse. But there was none he could see. Only...love. Was that really love? There was no holding back his kiss this time. Josiah lowered his mouth slowly, savoring every millisecond he held this remarkable woman.

But he'd no more than gotten started when something tugged the back of his shirt. What now? It couldn't be Mara, her hands were tight around his neck, pulling him closer...closer. The tug came again. He almost groaned as he forced himself to break the kiss and turn around.

A little button-nosed cherub stared up at him with sleep-rumpled blonde hair. "Josiah, what was that noise?"

Heat climbed up his neck as he realized what Katie had just witnessed. He released Mara, sliding his thumb over the top of her hand as he did, then reached to grab Katie and swing her up into his arms.

"The best thing ever, Katie-girl. Your mama just told me something that made me happier than a horse penned in a field of clover. And now I have a question for you." He tapped the end of her nose.

She wrinkled it like she smelled cooked cabbage. "What?"

"How would you like it if you and your mama came to live with me? Forever and always. And I could be your new Papa?" Asking that last question squeezed his chest almost as much as asking Mara had. What if she didn't want that?

But Katie's face bloomed into a smile that lit up the room. "Really?"

He grinned. "Only if you want to."

She threw her arms around his neck and squealed. "Yeah!"

Josiah wrapped both arms tight around her and inhaled a shaky breath. Mara shifted behind him, and he turned to include her in the embrace.

Blessings beyond what he deserved.

Josiah pulled Mara closer on the bench of his half-finished front porch, as she snuggled into the crook of his arm. As soon as they had the barn and storage building completed at the Rocky Ridge station, he'd finish the roof and railing for this porch. But for now, the porch floor he'd built was enough to enjoy the vivid pinks and purples of the sun setting over the Sweetwater River.

And he would enjoy every moment of this last evening with Mara and Katie. When the Reids all moved back to the new Rocky Ridge Station tomorrow, this place would be so lonely. How much longer until he heard back about when the minister would come to wed them? He'd sent a telegram to Father Domingo at the mission, too, but it was most likely impossible for the Father to come so far just for this ceremony.

"Penny for your thoughts?"

He glanced down to find Mara's deep amber eyes watching him. His thumb stroked her cheek while he gathered his thoughts into words. "Oh, just thinking how I'm going to miss my girls when you leave me tomorrow. And then I was counting the days until you'll come back."

The gold flecks in her eyes shone and she snuggled deeper into his side. "And how many days did you count?"

He gave her a lopsided grin as his chest thumped. "Soon."

Mara turned her face back to the river, which was a good thing, because he needed to bring his heart rate back down.

"I had the funniest notion when I was reading scripture this morning." Her voice was soft, whimsical.

"Really?" His thumb ran over her cheek again, enjoying the smoothness there.

"Yes. I was reading the story of Jesus' birth, in Matthew. It struck me that their little family was a bit like ours will be. You know—Mary, Joseph, and Jesus? Not that Katherine's as special as Jesus was. But…God put their family together. He hand-selected each of them. Just like He hand-selected me for Katherine, and you for us both."

She turned those amber eyes on him again, and Josiah's chest did another little flip. Not because of her beauty this time, but because of her wisdom. He swallowed past the lump in his throat. "You're more like the first Mary than you even know." And then a slow smile tugged his face.

She raised a brow at him. "What?"

"I was just thinking that Father Domingo used to say Catholics consider the Virgin Mary to be the patron saint for cooks."

She chuckled, a clear musical sound. "I like it."

He tightened both hands around her. "I suppose soon I'll have my own Saint Mary."

She laced her fingers through his. "Soon."

"Until then, maybe we should rename the Rocky Ridge Station in honor of its resident patron saint. We'll call it Saint Mary's Station."

She turned to him, brow raised again. "You think so?"

His gaze roamed from her mouth back to her eyes. "I think it fits."

Epilogue

osiah tugged on the sleeve of his nicest navy cotton shirt and shifted under the warmth of the sun. Why had they picked a spot out in the open, where there weren't any shade trees? And not a breeze around.

A hand gripped his shoulder, and he turned to face Father Domingo. The man's kind eyes were outlined by a myriad of lines displaying his years of wisdom. "God is with you, my son. What God joins together, He will bless."

The air left Josiah's lungs in a rush, releasing the tension in his muscles with it. "Yes." His eyes drifted around the yard again.

This really was the perfect day, with sunshine sparkling on the Sweetwater River behind him. Father Domingo stood to his right and Ezra on his left. Across the distance between them and his cabin, the grass shone a vibrant green, and a handful of horses grazed near the river.

Yes, God had blessed them with a beautiful day for a wedding.

Josiah's eyes found their way back to the front door of his cabin. What was taking so long in there?

"I guess I shouldn't have told her to do whatever it took to make herself pretty," Ezra drawled from beside him.

Josiah spun to face the man, and not even the quirk of Ezra's mouth calmed his ire. "Your sister could come out in a buffalo hide and she'd still be the prettiest woman west of the Mississippi. East of it, too."

Ezra winked, but Josiah was spared his response because of a motion from the house. The front door opened, and out slipped Katie. She could have passed for a fairy, with her pale blue dress floating around her, and her blonde braids wrapping her head like a halo. And the bouquet of purple Indian Paintbrush she held added the perfect touch. The cutest little pixie he'd ever laid eyes on.

The doorway widened again, this time pulling all the way open. Zechariah Reid stood in the opening, his broad shoulders filling the frame. He turned slightly, and stepped aside to reveal the most beautiful image Josiah'd ever seen.

Mara was radiant. Her soft blue gown matched Katie's, but the look was stunning on his bride. *His bride.* Emotion swelled in his chest, and clogged his throat. He'd never felt so vividly alive before this moment. Her eyes found his and never wavered, even across the expanse of grass between them.

She tucked her right hand into her brother's arm, and her left held Katie's as they proceeded down the stairs and toward the river. Toward him.

When they were mere feet away, the threesome stopped. Josiah's gaze flickered to a beaming Katie, and he shot her a wink. Her smile smothered her face, wrapping from ear to ear.

"Here you go."

Josiah turned to face Zeche. The man's eyes were piercing—almost wary. As though he wasn't sure whether he should really trust Josiah. And he didn't extend Mara's arm to give her over. Zeche's protective instincts had always showed strongly, and now how hard must it be to turn over responsibility for his little sister to another man? Josiah's chest tightened at the thought doing such a thing with Katie.

He willed the man to see his sincerity in his eyes. He would cherish and protect Mara no matter what it took. At last, Zeche turned to his sister and gave her a soft look, stepped back to offer her hand to Josiah.

Josiah swallowed as he accepted that hand and looked into Mara's face. It was impossible to describe the impact she had on his chest. On his ability to breathe. But her beauty was so much more than her wide brown eyes and full lips, and the curves perfectly accentuated by her dress. It was the depth of her heart that showed through every action. It was the love that glittered in her gaze.

As he took both her hands in his, he had to stop himself from pulling her tight into his arms. They turned together to face Father Domingo, and he forced himself to focus on the ceremony.

When the time came to speak his vows, he swallowed down the lump in his throat. As God was his witness, he would do everything within his power to love and honor this woman with every last breath in his body.

Mara's voice was clear and sweet as she promised to do the same.

And then the priest rested a hand on each of their heads and bowed his own. "May God, the eternal Father, keep you of one heart in love for one another, that the peace of Christ may dwell in you and abide always in your home."

Josiah moistened his parched mouth, then spoke his "Amen" with the others before Father Domingo continued.

"May you be blessed in your children, have solace in your friends and enjoy true peace with everyone."

Your children. Yep.

"May you be witnesses in the world to God's charity, so that the afflicted and needy who have known your kindness may one day receive you thankfully into the eternal dwelling of God."

"Amen." The entire group spoke the word together.

Father Domingo removed his hands from their heads, and Josiah lifted his gaze. The priest watched him with a bit of a twinkle in his dark eyes. "Josiah English, you may kiss your bride."

Josiah turned back to Mara, and the love shining there stole his breath. His bride.

He took a step forward and pulled her tight against him. Everything around them faded as he lowered his mouth to hers. Her lips were pure sweetness, more than ever before. He infused every ounce of love he could into the kiss.

God had blessed him beyond what he'd ever imagined.

Did you enjoy this book? I hope so!

Would you take a quick minute to leave a review?
http://www.amazon.com/dp/B01LXP8PNL

It doesn't have to be long. Just a sentence or two telling
what you liked about the story!

~ ~ ~

To receive a FREE short story and get updates when
new Misty M. Beller books release, click here:
http://eepurl.com/bXmHwb

Historical Note

This has been a special book for me, and one I wrote early in my writing career. I'm excited to finally be able share it with you!

Something I dearly love about writing historical fiction is all the amazing stories I find about events in the past. The Rocky Ridge Pony Express and Stage Station was a real place, situated on the edge of the lovely Sweetwater River.

I tried to stay as true as possible to dates around the Pony Express, telegraph, and stage timelines, including the very real Indian attack on May 27, 1865, when 150 Cheyenne and Arapaho Indians burned the station and cut 400 yards of telegraph wire. The station attendants really did hide in the dry well. When the ammunition in the buildings exploded, the Indians fled. The station was rebuilt and named "St. Mary's Station." You probably thought I fabricated the whole event, but it really happened!

Josiah and Mara will always hold a special place in my heart. Thanks for taking them into yours, as well!

Love and blessings,

Misty

About the Author

Misty M. Beller writes Christian historical romance and is the author of the bestselling Mountain Dreams Series and the Texas Rancher Trilogy.

She was raised on a farm in South Carolina, so her Southern roots run deep. Growing up, her family was close, and they continue to keep that priority today. Her husband and daughters now add another dimension to her life, keeping her both grounded and crazy.

God has placed a desire in Misty's heart to combine her love for Christian fiction and the simpler ranch life, writing historical novels that display God's abundant love through the twists and turns in the lives of her characters.

Writing is a dream come true for Misty. Her family—both immediate and extended—is the foundation that holds her secure in that dream.

Sign up for e-mail updates when future books are available!
www.MistyMBeller.com

Don't miss book 2 in the

Sweetwater River Tales

Coming soon!

Also look for
Misty M. Beller's
Mountain Dreams Series:

Book 1

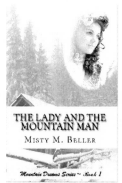

Amazon.com/dp/B00MQB7F4U

Book 2

Amazon.com/dp/B00T8XN9Q2

Book 3

Amazon.com/dp/B00WH8RBPA

Book 4

Amazon.com/dp/B011GC7VHA

Book 5

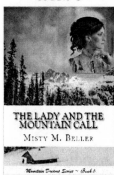

Amazon.com/dp/B01A7ONF1O

Also look for:

Misty M. Beller's

Texas Rancher Trilogy:

Book 1

Amazon.com/dp/B01064BQCU

Book 2

Amazon.com/dp/B010EN1YSO

Book 3

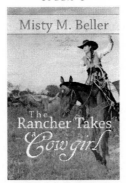

Amazon.com/dp/B0186HDTN8

CPSIA information can be obtained
at www.ICGtesting.com
Printed in the USA
LVOW12s1548191017
553030LV00001B/296/P